The SAFFRON EATERS

N. R. Phillips

DEVON BOOKS

First published in Great Britain in 1987 by Devon Books

ISBN: 0 86114-820-7

British Library Cataloguing-in-Publication Data

Phillips, N R
    The saffron eaters.
    I. Title
    823'.914(F)   PR6Ø66.H48/

Printed and bound in Great Britain by A. Wheaton & Co. Ltd

DEVON BOOKS

Official Publisher to Devon County Council
An imprint of Wheaton Publishers Ltd, a member of Pergamon/BPCC Publishing Corporation PLC

Wheaton Publishers Ltd
Hennock Road, Marsh Barton, Exeter, Devon EX2 8RP
Tel: 0392 74121; Telex 42794 (WHEATN G)

SALES
Direct sales enquiries to Devon Books at the address above.
Trade sales to: Town & Country Books, P.O. Box 31, Newton Abbot, Devon TQ12 5AQ. Tel: 080 47 2690

PUBLISHER'S NOTE
This novel is a work of fiction. Names, characters, places and incidents are the product of the author's imagination, or are used fictitiously, and any resemblance to actual persons living or dead, events or locales, is entirely coincidental.

This book is dedicated to the likes of High George and Tommy Blue, Old Robbie and his maid, Sarah. To Silas Rouncefield, Martha Polglaze, Mary Trenowden, Quizzy Maggie and Steve Trevorrow, all of whom are fictitious, though I have borrowed a nickname here and there. They represent the last of the Cornish, who are following their beautiful language into oblivion.

Chapter One

We are still friends, Steve and I, we still tell the old yarns whenever nostalgia overwhelms us or a few pints loosen our tongues. Cleo is rarely mentioned, and then only when her name is brought into the conversation by one of the others, for the memories are too painful for all of us. Uncle Joe might ask what news of her, or John Ashton refer to her in some supercilious remark which invariably fails to conceal his prurient curiosity, but Steve inevitably changes the subject to more felicitous memories.

When I last returned, some digression in conversation diverted the recollections to our childhood and the war. Uncle Joe was there, the one who cannot read or write and is the least affected by outside influences, and, I suspect, with fear of the talk becoming maudlin, he said, 'Remember Maggie's 'at, can 'ee?'

This is Uncle Joe's yarn. It could have been Tim Penberthy's yarn, but he is no good at yarns, or jokes. Or Freddie Curnow's yarn, but Freddie has become a man of collateral and dignity. Or John Ashton's yarn, but he has a yarn of his own, such as it is. Steve has always been more of a listener than a teller, and a twinkle came into his dark eyes as he glanced at me and prepared to hear Joe's yarn for the umpteenth time, for the thing had been his idea in the first place.

You might say that the yarn could equally have been mine, for I was present that spring evening when the war was almost over and they were walking along the beach and the wind was in the east.

They saw the biggest frenchie ever. It was floating in the sea, undulating with the waves like a Great Dead Ling. Yes. I confess to being there, with Steve, Tim, John Ashton and Uncle Joe, who was a little younger than the rest of us boys.

'What's that?' Joe asked. We told him. 'Get on,' he said, 'Nobody has a tuss as big as that.'

They fished it out with a stick and laid it on the sand, standing in

1

reverence before the great condom before taking it to a tidal pool in the rocks and floating it in the clear salt water.

'Must have been made for a bleddy elephant,' said Tim.

'See the bleddy g'eat ring on 'n,' said Steve.

'Pr'aps ours will be as big as that,' said Uncle Joe wistfully, yet with an awesome dread in his voice, 'one day.'

'Some hopes,' said Tom.

'Look at this,' said Steve.

He lifted it from the water, full and bouncing, stretching the rubber until it nearly burst. He dipped it and filled it again until it was an enormous transparent balloon, too heavy to be held by the ring alone. They began giggling. Quietly, then hysterically, as Steve bounced it up and down, resting the weight on a cupped palm to prevent an explosion. He put it back in the pool to allow the water to take the weight, then he tied the neck in a knot.

'Let's . . .' he said. But laughter and streaming tears prevented speech. 'Let's take it up to the top of the station steps, and . . . and . . .' He fell to his knees in mirth, with the others falling about him in anticipation of his idea. '. . . and drop it on somebody's head.'

He hid it under his coat, fearful lest it burst as they climbed the long flight of granite steps, and he be soaked to the skin around his belly. The others gave him a few pushes and shoves, but the great wobbly thing held until they reached the top and peered through the railings at the pedestrians far below.

An unsuspecting courting couple, walking arm in arm, were seconds away from the deluge, but Steve backed out. He was speechless with laughing, kept shaking his head to say he couldn't do it.

'Give it to me,' said Tim, and Steve rolled the undulating white sausage onto Tim's outstretched hands.

Miss Margaret Pender had spent most of the day at home, peeping through her curtains to see Who was Who and What was What in the street where she lived, downalong. She had called in to see Tommy Blue's wife so that Tommy Blue's wife could see her new hat, and to see what news of Tommy who was on his way home after being sunk by a submarine, a U-boat. Now she was having a bit of a round, to show off her new hat before going home to listen in to the wireless.

'It's Quizzy Maggie!' Steve said. 'She's my auntie. She'll do.'

Tim leaned out through the railings as Maggie came into the target area below his outstretched arms.

'She's not really my auntie,' Steve said, as the silent laughter died away and they peered through the railings at the approaching figure, alone in the street below.

Tim allowed time for Maggie to take two more steps before bombs away, he allowed for a little drifting in the remaining breeze, and let it roll off his fingers.

They thought he had misjudged, let fly prematurely, and that the missile would land at her feet, explode on the ground and drench her shoes and shower spray up her skirt.

The enormous bloated condom hit Maggie so square on the top of her head that not a drop touched her coat. There was a momentary ring of spray around her as, with a dull explosion, the frenchie shoved her hat down over her eyes and Maggie was temporarily blinded. She thought she had been killed by the last bomb of the war, dropped by some renegade German pilot operating from an aircraft carrier or from some uncharted island in the Western Approaches. She let out a fearful shriek and stood, transfixed in fright. The wide-brimmed hat held a ring of bright water with the shattered rubber floating dejectedly in it like a stranded fish, gasping for breath through its circular mouth.

The boys gazed down in silence at their awful crime, admiration for Tim's skill as a bomb-aimer tempered by the sight of the havoc and ruin that had been Maggie's hat. They withdrew their heads from the railings, out of the victim's sight, lest she recover her wits and turn skywards to curse the enemy. They knew not whether to laugh or cry and alternated between the two, brushing tears from their eyes on sleeves of coats.

'What a shot,' said Tim at last. 'What a bleddy *shot*,' and peered furtively again through the railings at the scene below.

Maggie was holding the catastrophe that had been her hat in both hands, looking at the swirling thing slopping around in the brim. Her flicking tongue licked salt water from her lips as she contemplated the devastated floral bouquet, and her senses slowly returned. Recognition came in a split second of revulsion and disgust and she withdrew both hands from her hat in a reflex of aversion, as though she had touched Sin. Momentarily the hat stayed suspended in the air and then fell squarely to the ground, its parasite still swirling in the clear salt water.

'Agh!' she said, clenching her fists. 'Agh!' Shrieking louder and louder, 'AAAAAgh!' and she kicked the hat along the ground. Lifting her skirts with one hand she kicked it again, and again and again, running at the hat with her skirts held high, while the boys watched spellbound from above. 'My 'at,' Maggie shrieked, aiming another vicious kick. 'My 'at. My 'at!'

'She's gone nuts,' Steve said quietly. 'Bleddy nuts.' They withdrew from the scene and walked slowly up the road from the station steps in silence.

Maggie never found out who did it. In all the years since then no

3

one ever told her. The girls got to know about it; Mary Trenowden and Martha Polglaze called them 'dirty muck' and tried to keep a straight face. Iris Pollard nearly wet herself with laughing even though she was so young. Robbie Stevens' maid was too young to be told and in any case she was too religious. They all were, all that family, especially Robbie. I remember when Steve came home from the army and went to Chapel with his mother on the first Sunday and Robbie tried to get him to teach in Sunday School.

'Glad to see 'ee home,' Robbie said.

'Glad to be home,' said Steve. 'Two years away is long enough for me.' He was laughing, but the old man said, 'You're very wise, my son. Stay here where you d' belong.' Steve couldn't even remember what Robbie's maid was called, for during his two years away he had forgotten much, and she had changed from a school-kid he barely remembered to a lovely girl with dark, shy eyes which were on him whenever he looked at her. She was small still, but with a neat figure under her long coat, and her hair was brown with a few even waves flowing from under her Sunday hat. Her hands were kept demurely before her, clutching her Bible and hymn-book, and Steve noticed a nervous movement of fingers in her grey gloves.

Others came to talk to him, to welcome him home, while his mother talked to Robbie about the Chapel and Robbie's wife who was sick. Martha Polglaze was there with Mary Trenowden, and they spoke to Steve as they passed. 'Hello, Steve,' and giggled silently to each other as they walked up Fore Street.

'We d' want a good man for the Sunday School,' Robbie said. 'I edn able to do it now. Sarah here d' take the little cheldern, but we d' want somebody for the older ones.'

Sarah. Of course! Her name was Sarah. 'I don't think I could do that, Mr Stevens,' Steve said. 'I'm no good with cheldern.' He saw the grey-gloved fingers tapping on the Bible as Sarah looked at the backs of Martha Polglaze and Mary Trenowden receding past the Digey Corner. 'Though I would't mind helping out now and then.'

'Well, that's all right,' Robbie said, 'I knaw you're going to be a busy man.' And to Steve's mother, 'We're going to have a round, down along the front. If you've a mind to, come too.'

Steve's mother was glad of the invitation as she required an excuse for parading her son, who had now grown into a dark smiling man, towering above her as her husband had. Steve had his father's dark, good looks and mischievous brown eyes. She was proud of Steve for his father's sake, and for her own sake, for all the work in bringing him up alone; alone, and in such dismal, terrifying times when he might have been so easily led to Sin and the Devil.

She had prayed her thanks in Chapel, and now felt justified in showing him off to the town, and Steve acquiesced for he was proud of his mother too. As they walked along Smeaton's Pier, picking their way through the drying nets and mooring ropes radiating from the granite bollards, Steve stopped to look at the boats lying in neat rows around the curve of the harbour. Sarah stopped with him as the two parents walked on down to the yellow-painted cast-iron lighthouse at the end of the Quay.

'What will you do now, Steven?' Only his mother called him Steven.

'Finish my time with the carpentry. That's what mawther d' want. But I would like t' go fishin'. That's what I want.'

'There edn no fish.'

'No.' He looked along the lines of gigs and punts and the long-liners, lying in their tiers, eyeing them up, judging their merits, and their cost. 'I've two more years to serve of my time. Not much chance of going fishing before then.'

'You could go with Faether.'

'I want my own boat!' Sarah was too young to understand the way a man felt about these things. She had never been away, never left the town and her parents. She had not seen the world as he had. She was still very young, he decided.

Steve went to Chapel now and then with his mother and, once in a while, helped Sarah in Sunday School with the older children. He found some of their more pertinent questions impossible to answer, unlike Robbie to whom everything was clear and definite if only people could see it, with the help of the Bible. It was all there in the book. But Steve could not find it. So he went less and less to Chapel, and more to the pubs and dances on Saturday nights, while on Sundays he went off alone to walk on the moors or along the cliffs where they had learned the paths as boys.

The girls saw that he was home, and that the army had changed him. They saw how quiet he had become, and how mature. They talked about him among themselves as if he was a stranger.

'I see Steve is home.'

'Steve who?'

'Steve Trevorrow. You know, used to be in our class. He's been away in the forces. Been out abroad. Saw him in Chapel with his mawther, talking to that Sarah Stevens. He said "Hello" to me. He's gone better looking.' Giggling.

'My dear Mary! You're man-mad. In any case, I 'spect he's got a girl away somewhere. Besides, you know what these men are in the forces, you know what it's like out abroad. Nawthen but brothels and whores and that. I don't want no man who's be'n out there. You don't know what they've be'n up to.'

'Freddie's been away. You don't mind Freddie.'

'Freddie didn't go abroad.'

'Well, they've all been away somewhere. I only said he was home.'

'I suppose he'll be going to the dance on Saturday. I'll have a good look at him, see if he's changed.'

'See if he's . . . experienced!'

And Steve served his time as a carpenter that he might have a trade to fall back on, and saved his money to buy a boat. He grew a beard when there were none in the town, and some of the smart alecs called him Saint Steven behind his back in anticipation of a new nickname in the town, but it didn't stick. And when the time came round for the Easter services, two years after he came home from abroad, and the Chapel was decorated with spring flowers, he saw Sarah up to the pool, on Good Friday. Everybody went up to the pool on Good Friday to sail their boats or to watch other people sailing boats. Sarah was alone, watching the men and boys playing with their model boats, and was dressed in the clothes she had worn to Chapel that morning, a new spring outfit worn for the first time. Martha was up there, with Freddie Curnow. Mary Trenowden, with a group of friends. Everybody was there. They always were.

Mary laughed at Steve's wet feet, calling him a 'great cuddle', told him he ought to grow up. Told him also that she would be at the dance on Saturday night, up to the Palais de Dance, where Hepworth's studio is. 'I'll see 'ee there,' he said. There was no commitment in that.

Sam Pascoe was at the pool, the one who has the taxis now, who had been in Steve's class at school. The illiterate Uncle Joe. Tim, home from college. Me! I was there. 'Home again, Shimshai?' they said. 'You students have a damn good life, looks to me.' But they were men, and I still a boy.

Came time to go downalong, and Steve and I caught up with Sarah, walking down the Stennack. You had to be careful what you said to Sarah, her family being so religious. I tended to avoid them.

'Nice bit of weather,' Steve said.

'Lovely,' said Sarah.

'How's your faether? How's Robbie?'

'Grand, thank you.'

Once you start talking to people like that, just in passing, as you might say, then you can't just walk on and leave them behind. You have to be civil to people.

'Father was saying, only the other day, that he hadn't seen you for a while. Wondered what you are doing.'

6

'I've gone on my own,' Steve said, 'now that I've finished my time. I have plenty of work. I've been busy.'

Sarah had very expressive features. She didn't smile to be pleasant or polite, but when she did smile it was all in her eyes, the small mouth puckering briefly, mischievously, as if her smile was telling secrets.

'Father will be retiring soon,' she said.

'Is Robbie that age? He don't look it.' He changed the model yacht from one arm to the other, to ease the weight of the leaded brass keel. 'He made this boat for me, you know.'

'I know.' Like a zephyr, or one of those flukey breezes which drop down over the bay from Carrack Gladden, when the wind is to the south-west, the smile was in her eyes and gone, almost before he saw it. She must be, what, twenty? Robbie and his Missus must have been getting on a bit when they had Sarah. The only one.

'How's your mawther?' he asked.

'Not so good. She doesn't get out much.'

He noticed that her speech had changed, that she was using better English. He had noticed that about Sarah before. Her accent was as broad as his, but her English was better. She didn't say 'she don't', 'we d' go', things like that. Steve reckoned she read a lot, as he did.

'I'll drop in and see them some time.'

'You are welcome. Any time. You know that.' This time the smile stayed a while. And he smiled back at her. She was a dear little maid, really. 'How is your mother?' she asked.

'Not so well, lately. The doctor said she ought to rest more, take things a bit easy. You can seen her doing that!'

'Give my regards,' Sarah said. And Steve let her go ahead, up on the grass verge there above the Ivory Works, to let a car go by. She was a trim little thing, small but well made, with a fine waist and shapely calves below her long new coat. She was not wearing a hat, and her wavy hair fell over her collar in tidy curves of shining brown. He came up to her side again, when the cars had passed, and said, 'Going to the dance tomorrow, are you?'

'Father doesn't like me going to dances. Not by myself.'

'I'll take 'ee. If you'd like to go.'

'Will 'ee?' her pleasure was spontaneous, and her smile radiant and open. She forgot to say 'Will you' instead of 'Will 'ee'. Steve felt as if he had offered her a gurrie-full* of diamonds.

'Can 'ee dance? ' he asked, laughing.

'Yes, I can dance! We belonged to dance at the socials. You know that.' Then, turning away, her smile gone, 'You're having me on.'

*Gurrie: wooden box with handles for carrying fish.

7

'No, I'm not. Tell Robbie I'll come for you at nine o'clock. Better not have any drink, I suppose.'

'Father doesn't like strong drink,' she said firmly. And then, lest we thought she was apologizing for Robbie's beliefs, 'And neither do I.'

He told his mother he was taking Sarah Stevens to the dance.

'I thought you were taking Mary Trenowden,' she said. 'I thought you were supposed to be going with her.'

'I'm not *going with* her,' Steve said. "Not like *that*. I can take who I like.'

'Well,' she said, 'I suppose you know what you're doin',' adding her greatest compliment to any prospective daughter-in-law: 'Mary is a good hard-working girl. She d' come from a good hard-working family.'

'And so do Sarah.'

"Es, that's true. But they're very narrow-minded, that family.'

'They've been very good to you, over the years.'

' 'Es, that's true.'

'Robbie was like a father to me.'

'That's true,' yet adding, 'but Mary's a good hard-working girl.'

Steve said no more, and called for Sarah as promised. Robbie asked him in, and they sat in the front room while Sarah went to put on her coat.

'Will 'ee have a dish of tay?' Robbie said. No one had called for his daughter before, and he was happy that the first one should be Steve, but he didn't quite know what to say in these new circumstances.

'No thanks,' Steve said, sitting on the edge of the chair, unable to relax for the first time in Robbie's company. 'Not just now.'

There was an awkward silence between them, and Steve said, 'How's Mrs Stevens? I haven't seen her for a brea while.'

'She's gone to bed. She d' go to bed early.'

'Oh.'

Sarah came in, smiling happily, and Steve stood up, anxious to go. She wore no make-up, for her father disapproved of his daughter looking like a painted Jezebel, but she had a good natural colour in her face, and Steve could see that she had taken a lot of trouble with her hair. Robbie came to the door to see them out, and stood watching them from the top of the flight of granite steps as they made their way off to the dance.

She gave him a smile of delight at the prospect of an evening's enjoyment, and Steve wondered if he should take her arm, but decided against it in case she thought him forward. He paid for her to go in, something he avoided with the other girls, seeing them inside after he had been for a drink with the boys. Not that he was miserly, just that if you didn't take them in there was no commitment. You could dance with anybody, take home whoever you fancied. This time he would be taking Sarah home.

She danced quite well, but there was always a little restraint, she wouldn't let herself go, abandon herself to his guidance and the slight pressure from his arms and hips. One or two others asked her to dance and she was pleased, but asked Steve if he minded, for he was the one who had brought her, and when the interval came and they went to the refreshment bar she was flushed and excited, talking to the other girls while Steve queued for tea and sandwiches.

Steve thought he'd better ask Mary to dance, as he'd said that he would see her there, but she approached him in the queue and said, 'I like your new girlfriend,' with a smirk of disapproval. So Steve thought, To hell with her, and when Sarah was dancing with Uncle Joe, Steve asked Iris Pollard to dance the tango.

'She's a good dancer,' Sarah said, revealing that she had been watching Steve while dancing with Joe.

'She d'go dancin' a lot. Every Saturday,' Steve said. He didn't say that Iris Pollard could dance the tango with him and make him feel so bloody randy that he felt he would go crazy if he didn't find out what it was like to screw somebody before long. She was common.

The dance became crowded when the pubs chucked out, with a crowd of men standing by the door and encroaching on to the floor, so that the dancing space became smaller. Steve could see that Sarah didn't like the crush, or the leers of the drunks who were swaying on the edge of the crowd. They were continually bumping into other couples, and being bumped, as the music became smoochy and low when the Blue Rhythmics played a slow foxtrot and the lights were dimmed. Then they played a waltz and the couples clung to each other, drowsily circling the floor, and Steve was continually saying 'Sorry. Sorry,' as they were knocked aside by dancers who neither knew nor cared where they were going.

'I think I'll sit down for a while,' Sarah said.

'O.K. We can go, if you like.' It was eleven o'clock. The dance finished at half past.

'There is so much smoke in here,' she said.

'Well, let's go then.'

He stood in the foyer, waiting for her to get her coat. Iris came out and gave him a look of conspiracy. There was only one thing she would leave a dance early for, and assumed that Steve was after it too, thought she didn't think he would get very far with a Chapel Virgin. 'She won't be a Chapel Virgin tomorrow,' she said in Steve's ear as she passed, 'knowing you.'

'Your turn next week,' he said.

'If you like!' she looked at him full in the eyes. It was an invitation, an offer, and Steve felt the blood flow into him as she flounced away up the stairs.

Sarah came out from the ladies' cloakroom and they left.

'Had a nice time?' he asked.

'Lovely, thank you,' she said.

They walked down over the hill at the back of Faull's that was, and there by the police station he was about to go on through Will's Lane towards High Street and her home, when she said, 'I don't have to be home before quarter to twelve.'

What could he do with her? He was in half a mind to take her home and go back to see Iris. He felt like a Chapel Virgin himself.

'We can have a stroll along the Quay, if you like. For a breath of fresh air.'

'Yes. All right,' she said.

They walked side by side down Lifeboat Hill and along the deserted harbour front, where the wet sand reflected lights from the houses in shimmering colours in the black night. The surf at the harbour mouth shone white in the starlight, and the breaking waves spread mirrors on the sand.

'It's a lovely night,' she said.

'Yes.'

'I haven't been out this late for years, especially on my own.' They walked close to the railings, and were pushed together when passing between them and the promenade seat bolted to the ground. She didn't move away when they passed the seat and had more room, and he wondered if he should put his arm around her. Mary liked him to put his arm around her, though she shrugged him off when they met anyone that they knew. 'We don't want people talking,' she had said. He kept his hands in his pockets. Somebody might come along, and Sarah might not like it.

They walked in silence down past the lodge and the lifeboat slip, past the Fisherman's Co-op, through Quay Street and on down over Smeaton's Pier, Sarah looking at him occasionally and smiling.

'You ought to go dancing more often,' he said.

'Perhaps I will.'

'Wouldn't Robbie mind?'

'Depends who I'm with.'

On down over the Quay, past the punts, laid up for the winter, their keels in the air and gunnels supported by big wooden wedges to stop the timbers sagging. Past the old granite lighthouse with its iron balustrade, and the barometer kept in a box inside the iron door, and the piles of nets lying like hills of black cobweb between the bollards. At the end of the Quay they stopped, to look at the starlight sparkling in the breaking surf, and then Steve said, 'We'd better not be long,' thinking of the long, sensuous legs of Iris slipping between his thighs as they tangoed round the Palais de Dance. *'Your turn next week'*, and she thought he meant it, because he had been abroad and was experienced.

'No,' Sarah said, 'I'd better not be late,' and they began strolling back.

When they reached the lighthouse again, Steve said, 'I'll just have a look at the glass a minute,' and went between the stern of Taffy's punt and the lighthouse to check the barometer.

'I didn't know there was a barometer in here,' she said, and came past the punt to have a look.

'In here,' he said, opening the case, and she came close to him, peering through the shadows of the great squat granite lighthouse, and he slipped his arm around her waist as she came so close that he felt her hair brush his cheek. She turned and placed her head against his chest, saying nothing, while he kissed her hair. Then she said, lapsing back into the dialect of their youth and speaking slowly, in a whisper, 'How did you ask me to go to the dance?'

'Because I wanted to.'

'You belong to take Mary Trenowden. How did 'ee take me?'

'Because I wanted to, I tell 'ee.'

She caught him by the elbows, her hands clasping and releasing as she spoke quietly into his lapels.

'You've never took me to a dance, or brung me home before.'

'You don't go to dances.'

'I do sometimes. You never paid no account to me, before.'

'Well, I am now.'

'Yes, but how? Why, I mean?'

'Because I like 'ee. That's how.

'You think you can take anybody home, don't 'ee? Anybody you fancy.'

'No.'

'I don't leave any old Tom, Dick and Harry take me home, you know.'

Chapel Virgins rarely went out without their parents, or to dances or to the pictures or anywhere, unless with a crowd. You're all right with a crowd! But . . .

'Tim Penberthy took 'ee home. A couple of times.

'Well? What if he did?'

'Nawthen. Nothing.'

'I never left'n kiss me nor nawthen.' She rubbed her cheek gently against his lapel and her hair smelled sweet. 'I never left'n kiss me.'

'I never said you did.'

'Well, I don't belong to leave anybody kiss me.' And she was inviting him, pleading with him, to kiss her, with her head buried in his lapels to hide the desire that she knew was in her eyes.

Then her hands left his elbows and rested briefly on his hips before slipping slowly around his waist and he could not prevent his hardness from pressing into her, while her breasts felt even firmer against him as she pushed him gently against the granite quoins of the lighthouse door. She allowed him to fumble with the buttons of her coat and slip his arms around her to feel the shape of her back through the thin material of her dancing dress. She lifted her head and kissed him on the lips, putting both arms around his neck, trembling with passion as she pressed herself on to him, and refused to let him go until he was out of breath and his knee felt weak between her thighs, and he was wet and knew that she was wet and he dare not touch her with his hands until she finally broke away and rubbed her face against his chest, making strange little noises which he had never heard from a woman before. He kissed her once more, there in the lighthouse door, behind the upturned stern of Taffy's punt, holding her head in his hands, knowing that they must go home to Robbie.

'Come on,' he whispered, 'I'll take 'ee home.'

They said nothing more as they walked on upalong to her house, walking apart, not touching or looking at each other, until they reached her door and Robbie was there, waiting, and he did not kiss her again.

Robbie said, 'Goodnight, my son.'

'Goodnight, Mr Stevens. Goodnight, Sarah.'

The next time he saw her in Chapel, on Easter Sunday, she blushed scarlet into her hymn-book and was gone before he came out into the wet, slow drizzle in Fore Street.

He married Mary, in the end. She was always there, and he took her to dances and saw her in Chapel on those special occasions when he went with his mother. Easter and Christmas, mainly to hear the singing. Sarah Stevens was there every Sunday, with her father, who always came and spoke to Steve, saying how nice it was to see him there, in the house of God. She rarely spoke to Steve, except to pass the time of day, though she no longer blushed every time she saw him, and became more and more demure, more prim and proper.

A few took her out, for a walk after Chapel or occasionally to dances, but it became known that she was a cold-blooded prude who kissed like a wooden doll and wouldn't allow a feel or a squeeze because it was a sin before you were married. Once, before he was married, when Robbie was laid up with a cold and couldn't come to

Chapel, Steve saw her walking alone along the path to Clodgy when he was returning from one of his walks along the cliff. It was a summer evening and he had stopped by the coastguard's hut to watch the sunset. You won't see the hut there now; it's been taken away. He saw her coming while she was still a long way off, almost as far as Carthew, and he sat where she could see him, beside the path, so that she could turn back and avoid him if she wished. As she came nearer he saw her hesitate, as if to turn about, for she had obviously seen him, but she came on up the path to where he sat smoking a cigarette.

'Hello, Sarah.'

'Hello, Steven.' He expected her to walk on, instead of which she stood beside him.

'I haven't seen 'ee lately. Didn't expect to see you out here,' he said, searching her face for one of those expressive smiles, but the face remained impassive.

'I haven't been out much,' she said, 'Mother has been poorly.'

'How's Robbie?'

'He's laid up with a cold. He hasn't been to Chapel.'

Briefly she allowed her face to reveal that she was irked by this continual conversation of old people and sickness and stated, to change the subject, 'I came out to watch the sunset.'

'That's what I'm doing,' he said, looking up at her standing beside him in her prim Sunday best. 'Have a sit down.'

She came to sit beside him on the flat granite rock, there beside the sea at Clodgy, and brushed the granite clear of lichen before she sat.

'Hang on a minute,' he said and unstrapped the flap of his canvas pack. 'I've a towel in here, you can sit on that.' He spread it on the rock and she sat beside him, drawing her frock around her knees as she sat, to cover her legs.

'Been swimming?' she asked, in surprise.

'Yes,' he said, and folded the pack to hide the fact that there was nothing more in it but a book and a guernsey and a thermos flask. No swimming-trunks. The last of the sun was still warm on their faces, and over to the west the sky was lit in yellows and greens with scarlet linings to the streaks of cloud.

'I haven't been swimming for years,' she said. She hadn't been swimming since she was about fifteen and Robbie had disapproved of her developing body being seen in a clinging swimming costume. 'I used to like swimming,' and as an afterthought, 'years ago.'

'We all did,' he said.

'Mary is a good swimmer,' she said, with a quick questioning glance at him.

'She went yesterday,' he told her, and questioned her in turn, but she revealed nothing. 'All the crowd went. Out Porthmeor,' and to force her to disclose herself more fully, added, 'You ought to come with us, all the crowd d' go, every Saturday.'

'I'm working on Saturdays,' she said, thereby declaring that she would not go at all, for it was forbidden on the Sabbath. He thought of her pushing herself on to him in the doorway of the lighthouse, the hard breasts against his chest, said nothing, and looked to the westward at the setting sun dipping onto the fire-flecked sea. The sky changed from yellow, through orange, to black and scarlet, and the disc slid beneath the horizon before they spoke again.

'Did you see the green light?' Sarah said.

'What green light?'

Sarah waited several seconds before saying, 'The after-image.'

'No.' He had no idea what she was talking about, and they were silent again while the light of the summer's day followed the sun to the west and the twilight crept over them from the east, across the bay behind them.

'I've never been any further,' Sarah said, looking down the line of darkening cliffs. 'I don't know the way.' She was speaking quietly, dreamily, in her best English. 'I should be afraid of falling, if I went any further.'

'You can't fall,' Steve told her, 'if you keep to the path.'

'No, I suppose.'

He wondered whether to try and kiss her, and turned his head to look at her, only to find that she was already looking full at him, and there was something so superior, so mature, in her look, that he felt nervous and afraid of her reaction should he touch her. Yet, as he looked, a great blush spread across her cheeks, and she smiled before turning again to the sea, unashamed, or unaware, of the flush of colour. Or perhaps she thought, in the fading light, that her blushes could not be seen.

'I suppose you know the way,' she said, and hugged her knees, 'very well, if you've been on the path before.'

'Yes, I come out here a lot, especially in the summer.'

Abruptly she stood up. 'It's gone cold,' she said. 'I'd better be walking back.' She waited while he put the towel back in his pack, watching him intently, before they began the slow descent from the headland along the path to the town. She said nothing, and Steve felt embarrassed at the silence between them, at the loss of communication, and could think of nothing to restart their conversation.

By the time they reached Carthew, the darkness was almost upon them, and the lights from the town and the lighthouse across the bay were beginning to show as yellow dots on the blackness of encroaching night. When they had climbed the final rise, where the path ascends again and passes between two boulders of blue elvan stone protruding like sentinels astride the track, Sarah stopped as if to rest, or see the view, and said to him, 'That night,' and he stopped beside her, thinking how small she was. 'That night, when we went to the dance.'

'Yes.'

'I don't belong to be like that.'

He was going to say 'Like what?' to force her into detail, but said instead only, 'I know.'

'I mean,' she went on, 'not with anybody.'

What a fuss, Steve thought, over a kiss. And so long ago, when he was also like a Chapel Virgin and had not known the thrill of it either. Before he had Iris, before asking home so many others, before so far with Mary.

'It was only a kiss,' he said, indifferently, without looking at her.

He was unaware of the pain that for a fleeting second racked her eyes, or of the look of understanding, compassion, that followed.

'I just don't want you to think,' she said, 'that I'm . . . common.' Steve then, in turn, was thankful for the night, for he felt himself blushing at her use of the word, even in the negative sense, of herself.

'I don't think you're common, Sarah,' he assured her hastily, and was relieved that he had not attempted to kiss her again out on Clodgy Point, for she would have rebuffed him, humiliated him with righteous virtue for his sinful lusts. 'I think,' he said, 'that you are a very respectable girl.' How could the daughter of Robbie Stevens be anything else?

They walked back to town, employing the noncommittal talk of trivialities to guide their relationship from the brink of inextricable embarrassment, back to the level of friendship again.

They climbed the hill to Ayr, with the sound of surf breaking on Porthmeor behind them, and Steve turned off upalong, though this had not been his intention. He decided to go home by a detour, down Bullan's Lane, rather than risk being seen by Robbie as he walked with his daughter. He made some excuse about calling to see Sam, who lived in the council houses, for Robbie would surely believe there was 'something in it' should they be seen together too frequently, which, for Robbie, would be about twice.

Sarah went down to minister to her mother, make a glass of hot lemon and honey for her father, and go early to bed. She could read nothing on Sundays but the Bible. There were no newspapers, and no radio permitted on the Sabbath. Robbie asked why she was so late, where had she been, and Sarah almost rebuked him for being overanxious and restrictive in his concern for her, to remind him that she was a grown woman and that men of her own age had been away in the forces. She was going to remind him, as she had so often almost done in the past year, that her mother was married at eighteen, and that Robbie was a man away to sea at sixteen. But she restrained herself, thinking again of the peculiarity of that early marriage and the long years before she had been born to bless it. She knew as little of her parents as they did of her.

She told him that she had been to Carthew, which, in passing, she had, and what a red sky there had been, foretelling a fine day tomorrow. She told him she had seen Steve Trevorrow out there. There were always a few people walking as far as Carthew on a summer evening, but Clodgy was too far for most and, as like as not, one or two would be alone there.

When Steve reached home he went straight up to his bedroom and took a pair of swimming-trunks from the chest of drawers and shoved them into his pack with the towel. Time and again he forgot to take them. His mother sang out as he went upstairs, 'That you, Steve?'

'No,' he said, completing the ritual, 'it's me.' He came down for his belated tea, which he ate to the usual barrage of questions, allowing them to drift unheeded through his mind and answering them only when compelled; he knew his mother was unaware of asking most of them. 'Where've you been? Who with? Do you know the time?'

'Been out the cliffs,' he said. 'Walked to Zennor and back,' and he told her, for she was sure to hear it from someone else, as sure as God made little apples, that he had walked from Clodgy with Sarah Stevens. 'I saw Sarah Stevens. We stopped to watch the sunset.'

'Braem late sunset tonight,' she said, making him smile. 'You must have gone courtin'.'

Steve was reconciled to being, in his mother's eyes, always a boy, though sometimes he reminded her of his age. 'I'm twenty-one, Ma.' he told her once when she had scolded him for coming in late and smelling of drink. 'I've been two years in the damned army. I'm not a boy any longer.' But she heard nothing but the 'damned'. 'There's no need for language.'

'I'm not gone courtin' Sarah Stevens,' he said. 'I didn't know she would be out there. She's a nice girl. Nawthen wrong with her, but just because I took her to a dance, *once*, you'd think I'd dammee . . .' he stopped, and decided that he might as well tell her. 'I'm going to marry Mary Trenowden.'

I was away at the time of the wedding, so was spared the suffering of that joyful occasion, but Steve had told me of it all. Tears all round from the women, of course.

'Women are hard, Boy,' he said, 'to be able to cry like that,' and in saying it revealed a greater understanding of human nature than I had credited him with. I saw, for a moment, a Steven Trevorrow who was not to be seen again until Cleo came into his life, so long after, and our friendship had matured sufficiently for him to tell me of his love.

The flags were up for Steve's wedding on all four lodges and most of the boats, for Steve belonged, as all his family belonged. And Mary's family belonged too, for they were fishing people more than Steve's. Some of the boats flew no flags, but there's always somebody not speaking to somebody in a town like this. It was a good match. Everybody said so.

Steve had done well to choose Mary. Yet, on reflection, it had not been quite like that. There had been no conscious decision that here, above all others, was the one girl that he could never live without. Just the one that he could life *with*, for he loved her more than any other.

Steve's mother did not cry at the wedding for her life's work was fulfilled on that sunny morning, and she knew that the gezzahs* in her belly were soon to devour her remaining strength. She had no more time for crying, and strength only to last long enough to see her two grandchildren, born in the first years of Steve's and Mary's marriage. She was buried among the graves of our forebears up to Barnoon, overlooking the sea where her other Steven had waited restlessly since that night when the fires of hell had erupted with the torpedo in the bowels of his ship.

Peter Tregenza was the undertaker, another one who had been in Steve's class at school. He was preparing to screw down the lid when Steve went to the cupboard under the stairs and brought forth a dusty old bottle of cheap white wine which he wiped clean, wrapped in a teacloth, and placed in the coffin beside her.

'She saved it for him. For Father. For when he came home. He was posted as 'Missing'. She saved it all this time.'

Sure enough, it was Peter who nearly cried.

*Gezzahs: Spider crabs.

Chapter Two

In returning annually to my roots, back through the sappy years of many-branching adolescence, I am able to draw succour from my native earth. The Cornish nourishment has the peculiar quality of restricting growth. Development is slow, sturdy, with no etiolated stems spreading beyond themselves to bear sickly fruit and die. The growth is rather like that of the wild woodbine which here grows precariously among the bouldered slopes of the granite hills, and whenever any shoot becomes too bold, too adventurous, it is seized upon by many others for support, dragged back into the bush and restrained, to flower in unison with the rest.

Whenever I find myself growing away, beyond my beginnings, there comes a need to bow my head, come down, and stabilize my rambling identity in the tangled fragrance of Cornwall, in case the slender vine which feeds me breaks and leaves me withering in the English air.

Sadly, the honeysuckle, which scents the days of summer, is a blossom that I rarely see, for I avoid my land in the time of its blooming, and make most of my visits in what has become known as the 'off season'. For many years I did not return at all, for I thought I had no real ties here any more, and after my college days I made the mistake of believing that I no longer had anything in common with my former friends. These pretentious notions were strangled to death, by knots formed in childhood, when I returned after my first long absence.

I was sitting alone in the pub one day, scrutinizing faces to see if I remembered them, when who should walk in but Uncle Joe, of all people. Joe couldn't read or write, I remembered that, and I had grown so arrogant as to confuse this and his broad accent with stupidity, forgetting the hours we played together as equals on the beach and in the knickers of Iris Pollard.

'Hello, boy,' he said. 'What you belong about these days? I abmt seen 'ee for dammee years.'

'No,' I mumbled, 'I haven't been home for some time, actually.' I thought to avoid embarrassing him by any comparison between our achievements, and refrained from telling him what, in fact, I did 'belong about'. That I was something of an authority among those academics with whom I rubbed shoulders in my daily life. 'I usually go abroad for my holidays.'

He merely nodded. Then suddenly screwed up his face in a brief but intense expression of bewilderment, sipped his beer, and looked to the door for some way out of this conversation.

Oh dear! He had seen more countries than I would ever see. He could get by in Spanish and Arabic. He had been a merchant seaman for nearly twenty years and still could not understand why people thought him stupid because he could hardly read or write. He placed his glass upon the table, holding it by the handle still, leaned back in his seat, looked at me from beneath his languid lids and said, slowly, that otherwise I might not misunderstand . . . 'You . . . bleddy *shitbag*, Shimshai,' and began shaking with deep bellyborne laughter until I was forced to throw my righteous indignation overboard and laugh with him at what I had almost become.

'You tuss,' I said. 'You always were a bleddy tuss, Uncle.'

I was home. Brought down to earth with such a pride-shaking jolt that I feared ever to rise above myself again in case the second descent should shatter me completely. They would bring me down by contempt, should I rise too high, and Joe had used the kinder means, of ridicule.

When we had sipped a few more beers, and Joe had rolled a few more ragged fags, we strolled along the harbour to see who was who and what was what. Joe knew everybody, and lost contact with nobody, for although he spent much time away, his returning, unlike mine, was considered the permanent side of life. His excursions were trips away, but mine were journeys back.

It was May month, I remember, in the year before Cleo came, my favourite time for going home, and the harbour was bright with freshly painted boats and summer frocks. Warm, bright and light. On the wharf a child throwing bread to the eternally ravenous gulls. On the cock-bank a bent back vingling lancies.* On the slip a woman, young woman, sketching, long hair and legs, pencils in the mouth held by white teeth. There was a man carrying rope. A thick coil of rope over his shoulder. Sea-boots, in this weather! A peaked cap.

---

*An old man on a sandbank fishing for sand-eels with a hook.

Navy blue guarnsey. A black-bearded man, quite short for an Englishman, quite tall for a Cornishman.

'That's . . .' I wasn't sure. 'Looks like Steve Trevorrow, surely.'

"'Es, That's Ste'.'

'I hardly recognized him, with his beard.' Joe looked at me in astonishment. 'Didn't recognize Steve Trevorrow?' he said incredulously. 'How are you so?'

'I've not seen him more than a few times for . . . since just after he was married. He married Mary Trenowden, I remember.'

I wished Joe did not have the habit of screwing his face up like that. His thoughts were so open. The expressions on his face were fleeting, but if you caught them they were so often a reflection of yourself. The brief spasm which I saw then told of my affiliation by memory and recollection, as opposed to knowing and being, the chasm between observing and partaking. I had distanced myself by remembering the past instead of living the present.

Steve came up the slipway and we went back to meet him to have a yarn. He had always been quite good-looking and well built, not big and brawny, but well proportioned and fit, and now he was more handsome than ever. The years had improved him, for I always thought he looked too immature, too boyish, whereas now, with a touch of grey about him and the lines at the corners of his eyes, he looked his age. Yet there was something young in those eyes which indicated that a big part of him had refused to take life too seriously.

He took and shook my outstretched hand. Smiling at this unnecessary gesture between two so close.

Joe went off and left me with Steve, and I spent the day with him, feeling, as I have often done, a certain envy for his way of life which seemed so steady and uncomplicated. We went up to his loft, back down to the boat with some fishing lines and boxes, and finished up on the Platt, yarnin'.

The Platt is a vantage point, an observation post, from which may be seen everything that goes on in and around the harbour. Events behind the harbour are neither here nor there, and when the chaps lean over the railings they have their backs to them, for they are of little interest. Sometimes a good yarn is told about upalong, above the market-place, but you are getting into miners' country in the Stennack, and beyond that is nothing but a few farmers, and whoever heard of a good yarn about farmers? The best yarns are about the harbour and downalong, and about the people living in the small cottages crowded so close together that you can't fart without waking the neighbours.

The Fisherman's Lodge is on the Platt. Now the Lodge is like a club, with exclusive membership, where you can go for a game of dominoes, or euchre, or a bit of peace and quiet away from the women. Anybody can join, more or less, but yet they can't, if you know what I mean. Most members are old, for they have the time to spend there, and they exercise by walking up and down on the Platt in line abreast, pacing the quarter-deck in fours, or half dozens, coming about after twelve paces in either direction. You can go for a long walk, have a good yarn, get a bit of exercise and fresh air, and still see what's going on. It's a proper way to spend the time, can't 'ee see? Now, they are beginning to organize what they call 'day centres' for old people. In them, old people are made to feel even more old, useless and dependent than they are, with cups of tea provided by middle-aged people who approach old age with such fear and dread.

'When I was a boy,' High George said when he was eighty years old 'you used to see a pile of old men here on the Platt, but you don't see them now.'

Tommy Blue was there that day, so was Silas Rouncefield and James Perkin, and it was good to hear them yarnin'. Steve spoke with a broad accent which is so peculiar to the town, even Penzance people recognize it immediately, or Hayle people, or Camborne people for that matter, and they are a fine lot to talk. Calling each other 'Old Pal' and 'Pard'. What can you expect, from miners? Don't know a gurrie from a gurnard!

I had little to say, so listened to the others and caught up on the news. Steve was 'pleasuring', taking people to Seal Island or for fishing-trips in his boat. His wife took in a few tourists for Bed and Breakfast and Evening Meal. He still did a bit of carpentry in the winter. Robbie Stevens was getting frail, and High George had passed away. Tommy had settled down and Quizzy Maggie had become more quizzy than ever, ferreting around in other peoples' lives because she had none of her own. More and more people coming on holiday every year, and more and more of them coming here to live.

Martha and Freddie Curnow were married just as everyone expected, especially Martha. Steve wondered how Freddie had managed it, but never asked. Freddie was not the sort you could talk to about these things, though I found out a brear bit, later on. People lose their pride as they get older, even Freddie.

Martha and Freddie didn't have the luck of Steve and Mary, they went in for a smaller house as this was all they could afford, but she was a worker; by God, she worked. Well, Freddie wasn't getting bran-for-ducks working in the grocer's shop so they pushed away in the summer, all three crammed into a single room so that the rest could be let, and before long their house was on the market. They sold it easily, at a good profit, and they asked Tim Penberthy, who was setting up as an estate agent, to keep an eye open for something which might make a guest-house. They made three moves altogether, finishing up with a ten-bedroomed guest-house and a car park and a mortgage which inflation was to swallow like a gannet swallows lancies. That's where they were smart, Freddie pointed out; they ignored the sea views and went for the car park. He packed up his job at the grocer's and worked at home. They did very well out of the rising property market, and why not, he said, they were local. Not one of their buyers was.

In the early years Steve put money from his mother's house to pay off the mortgage and saved for a boat. 'Do what you like,' Mary said, 'it's your money.' But she saw the money to be made from taking in people and couldn't resist adding, 'But if it was my choice, I'd go in for a bigger house.'

'A bigger house!' Steve said. 'We've got four bedrooms now. What more do 'ee want?'

'I mean a guest-house. A proper guest-house.'

'I don't know anything about taking in damned lodgers,' he said. 'Besides, I had enough of that with Mawther. It killed her. We should be content with what we have.' And, to remind her where her primary duty lay in those days, 'We d' have two cheldern t' bring up.'

'I wish you wouldn't talk so damn broad,' she said, 'make me say such words. How will the children learn to talk fitty if not from we?'

The fifties swung into the sixties. The seventies loomed and Steve's hair became grizzled here and there with grey. The children grew away and the time for looking forward, by some insidious trick of age and memory, became the time for looking back. It came upon them by stealth, this fortieth year. While they were looking forward, it crept up from behind, catching them unawares, like tickled trout.

They had fallen into the trap of happiness, a routine, a way of life without memories. In looking back they saw only a void, years of empty days running into each other without distinction, and an unspoken suspicion grew in their minds that the past twenty years had been stolen by time. Somewhere in the receding years Steve and Mary had grown apart, repelled by the same magnetism which had initially drawn them together. They had become so alike in their shared lives that the differences now appeared as irreconcilable rifts. During the winters Mary complained of poverty, and in summer complained of work. She had lost the ability to go out to play, had become irrevocably adult with the responsibilities of motherhood, and saw relief from work only in even more work, to ease the struggle in the future. She saw how Martha and Freddie were so much better off financially, while apparently living an easier life; they could convert their guest-house into self-contained flats, if they wished, and have no work at all. The great rift in their lives had become centred on the question of a guest-house.

Steve had acquiesced, reluctantly, in so far as he agreed that they should let their best bedrooms for the peak three months of the season, but adamantly refused to consider selling their home and buying a guest-house. From time to time Mary might read an advertisement in Tim's long column of property for sale in the *Echo*, or mention that so-and-so's place was up for sale, hoping to tempt him, but he refused to consider it. Mary became reconciled to Steve's indolence. He had no ambition, no go in him, he was too easy-going, she told Martha.

Steve realized that the time had come for an assessment of their lives, and he looked back with a vague sense of unease which he could not define. He felt guilty for feeling unhappy when there was no cause for unhappiness, when they had achieved everything they had dreamed of in the early days, and more. They had radio and television, high-fidelity tape- and record-players, washing-machine, refrigerator, deep-freeze, central heating, carpets on the floor, their own transport, possessions which were unheard of, much less dreamed of, in his mother's day. What more could you ask? When there was so much poverty in the world about them. 'We have everything,' he told Mary. 'Why can't you be content? The boy is doing well at college and the maid is likely to follow him. We are blessed.'

Continually he reminded her thus that their lives were good and they should be happy, yet in his own mind there was a growing disillusionment that somehow his own life had been unfulfilled because of his own contentment. He saw Tim on the road to fortune, Shimshai the successful academic, Freddie with enough collateral to retire when he wished, even Uncle Joe had travelled the world. All his contemporaries had achieved something with their years, but he was unchanged after the passage of twenty which he could not remember. There was a feeling that he should have done something, accomplished something, extended himself and reached some hypothetical peak from where he could look down and review his achievements.

There had never been a peak he wished to climb, no goal he wished to reach, he had been content to travel through life and watch the scenery, with no thought to the journey's end. There was not even satisfaction in his work any more. He was a skilled carpenter who had been taught that his work was a lasting monument to his craftsmanship and would last for a hundred years, like the work of the old men in the fine houses around the town, but now his conscientiousness was an embarrassment. Nothing was permanent.

23

Time was money. 'Just a quick job. We're moving soon. It's only for the season. Patch it up. That's good enough.' It was with a sad heart that he would go into some fine old houses and divide up the rooms for extra accommodation, tearing down the beautiful plasterwork and intricate joinery to make space for cheap partitions and hardboard doors.

The town had become commercialized and degraded, and the people corrupted by greed. The few tourists who had provided a bit of extra hard-earned cash for his mother and her sisters before the war had became a mass of sprawling humanity crowding the beaches and streets like sprawling emmets.* He preferred fishing.

Steve liked the early mornings with the sun rising over the eastern shore before the harbour became crowded with tourists, and the air was clean from the wide Atlantic. And he was catching more fish every year, they were coming earlier, the mackerel, and he took old James Perkin on with him for a share. James stayed with him for the summer to act as skipper while Steve touted for passengers ashore. Bleddy job! Nothing was ever right for James. He grumbled at everything, from the weather to the passengers, and enjoyed every minute of it, for he had becme bored with retirement and being a spectator of life outside the Lodge, and was secretly tickled to death when Steve asked him to lend a hand. He had been fishing and grumbling about fishing all his life. Taking passengers to the Western Carrack and catching a few mackerel was an A1 way of spending a few hours. Provided the fish were there, mind. He saw no point in going out like Steve did, hour upon hour, fish or no fish. There was no sense in it. James was a small man, with a suntanned face and arms, lined and sparkling eyes, and an old cloth cap that never left his white bald head unless it was whirled around by finger and thumb as an aid to thought.

'They're goin' in for new boats,' he said, 'round Land.'

'So I hear.'

'New gear, echo-sounders, radar, radio.'

'These things cost money, James.'

'I edn sayin' they don't. I knaw they cost money. And fish is bringin' a good price. We always kept up with the times, in our family.'

They were always right, in that family, but James was hinting at the very decision Steve himself knew would soon have to be made. The mackerel shoals were getting bigger and more predictable every year, and they were coming earlier, in the winter. So, should he sell the

---

*Literally 'ants', but derogatively refers to holiday makers in general.

Mermaid and go in for a bigger, better-equipped boat and stay fishing full time? That's what he wanted, but it was a big step. A lot of money. If the large shoals were becoming more of a winter phenomenon and were a long way out or around Land, in Mounts Bay, it would take a bigger boat to make money at it. A boat with all the gear. A lot of money. He had a yarn with Mary about it.

'I'm bestin',' he told her, 'to go in for another boat.'

'Another boat?' she looked at him in amazement. 'What other boat?'

'A new one. Have one built.'

'Have one built!' she said. 'Just like that! Where's the damn money coming from—make me say such words—that's what I'd like to know. You tell me that. Where's the money coming from?'

'There's grants. From the Government.' He hesitated, before continuing, 'And I can borrow.'

'Borrow!' Mary said, 'I thought you didn't believe in borrowing money.'

'It's business,' he said, 'fishing is business like any other. You have to borrow if you're going to get anywhere.'

'When I wanted to borrow on a guest-house, you raised merry hell. Make me say such words.'

'I've told you before. I don't know anything about taking in bleddy lodgers.'

'You don't *want* to know. Damned boat. I'm fed up with it.'

Mary was scared. So much had been lost in boats before. Thousands to lay out and no certainty that the fish would be there next year. Not one of them. And now, here was Steve, who had never got off his ass to achieve anything in life, talking of going thousands in debt for what she saw as nothing but a gamble. And she was right. Fishing had always been a gamble. Fortunes have been made at it, but the small men always suffered in the hard times, the men who had put their own money, their own lives, into it. If the gamble turned sour on them they could lose everything. 'Besides,' she said, to test him, 'how can you borrow money?'

'On the house,' he said.

It was the worst row they ever had, and kept them apart for weeks. Worse because, as in all truly bitter arguments, they said so little to each other, and kept the most pointed and vicious comments to themselves, for in their utterance would have been inflicted unhealable wounds. The conflict was, for each of them, internal and unspoken. The quarrel was a silent battle of wills, the resolution of the dormant battle of dominance which Mary was sure to win, for her arguments were sound, the logic sure. They had only to look around them to see where prosperity lay. Where were the big cars? Who

25

went abroad for a holiday each year? Whose investments were rising in value each year on the growing property boom?

But Steve looked not upon these things. He saw the hands of the women, the eyes of the men. He questioned the mad philosophy of success which demanded more, *more*. He knew that he might be wrong, selfish, in his intention to buy a way of life by putting all their achievements at risk, but he also knew, by some undefinable instinct, that he was right in refusing to become emasculated and a servant in his own house, like a shuffling eunuch catering to tourists who demanded two weeks' pampering to compensate for the very despair he was trying to avoid.

He could tolerate them in his boat, if only for the money it brought, and most of them were all right, he had to admit, but there were so many of them. Pushing and shoving in the streets, with noisy transistor radios, and aggressive eyes on them. Come Sundays he went off and wandered the cliffs, away from the unbearable crowds, to spend his leisure in solitude and get his bum brown.

Chapter Three

If it was a dance they were going to, why couldn't they call it a dance and have done with it? The Hotel and Caterers' Association Annual Ball. It was only a dinner and dance, call it what you like. Yet when he was there, he had to admit, he did enjoy himself. It was always held in the winter, of course, in the 'off season', usually in January when a few deposits from early bookings put a few bob in a few pockets and there was hope springing again for another prosperous season ahead.

That year, when Steve and Mary went to the Annual Ball with Martha and Freddie and Tim and his wife, Cleo was already living in the town, though Steve had not met her. He had seen her, but that's all. Tim knew her, for he had sold her a cottage, High George's that was, down in the Rows. There were not many newcomers that Tim didn't know, for they were his business.

The dance was to be held at the big hotel, with the sweeping drive through avenues of elm trees, on the outskirts of town. It had been a seat of landed gentry in the last century. The family had been among the first to suffer the crippling benefits of the Welfare State. First the great house became a hotel, then the lesser houses, descending through the scale of opulence by way of manors and villas and the large Victorian terraces of granite, until finally, the private houses of the common people were the last to get chopped about to accommodate the new prosperity of tourism. There is now hardly a building larger than a cheap bungalow which can afford to stand as a dwelling-place in its own right. Those who formerly maintained the grand parlours and servants' quarters—the professional men, doctors, lawyers, fish-buyers, and mine captains—are either extinct or live in former fishermen's cottages and farm labourers' hovels done up, and spend their surplus, when they have any, on machines instead of people, and do their own washing-up.

Steve and Mary went by taxi, for Steve intended getting a little under the weather, three sheets to the wind, as you might say; and besides, Mary wouldn't go to the Ball in a beastly old van. Sam Pascoe was coming to pick them up, and he would bring them home when the grand celebration was over. 'Carriages at One,' it said on the ticket. Carriages at One! Did 'ee ever hear anything like it?

'I don't know why you don't get a dinner-jacket,' Mary said. 'Everybody else will have a dinner-jacket.'

'Never mind me. Sam will be here d'reckly and I don't want to keep him waiting. He's got other people to pick up besides we.'

She would use too much make-up. Sure as eggs is eggs. And too much scent. And Martha would be gaggled in the bleddy stuff. He went down to the front room and filled a glass from a bottle left over from Christmas. He was on his second drink when Mary came in to be complimented. She was not as bad as Martha in the way she dressed, but, perhaps because she tried to outdo her, she always looked not quite right, somehow. Steve could never figure it out. The more she spent on clothes, the worse she looked, it seemed to him. Martha was worse. Must cost Freddie a bleddy fortune. But Martha made the money in that house and she could spend it as she wished.

He couldn't see why, but Mary had done it again. There was something not quite right and she had too much make-up on. She never wore make-up years ago. Why did she have to go smothering her chacks in it now? If he didn't compliment her she would feel neglected and sulk. He had long ago learned not to try and suggest things. What did he know about clothes and make-up?

'Let's have a look,' he said. 'Yes. That's O.K. You look very nice.'

'Is that all?'

But she was reassured. She knew Steve well enough to know that he would soon tell her if there was the slightest little thing wrong. She slipped her coat on. Her best coat, a coat for Chapel, over all her finery. Sam rang the doorbell and they went out to his taxi. 'You're not going tonight then, Sam?'

'No, Iris is waiting at the dinner so I thought I might as well earn a bob or two. You've got to make 'n while you can, boy.'

The taxi-driver, the waiters, the chef, the mayor, the guests of honour. They had all gone to school and played Pumperino* together. How can you put on airs and graces?

'And neow,' said the toastmaster, obviously a damn stranger as soon as he opened his mouth. Sounded like a cockney trying to be posh. 'Pry silence for His Worship the Mighor, Alderman Timofy Penberfy.'

---

*Pumperino: A rough-and-tumble wall game.

Loud applause. 'Good old Tim,' said Freddie, to inform the gathering that this great man was a friend of his.

Tim was a good speaker, though no good at yarns. He kept them amused for five minutes, told a few jokes at the expense of the tourists, and went on to say how welcome they were and that we should all work together to ensure that this jewel of a town became a resort to rival any in the world. He told the yarn about the tourist who said, 'Oh, I think I'd better have the salmon,' when the waiter asked if he would like the salmon hors d'oeuvre. But he made a balls of it, and was unaware that this joke had been circulating in the catering industry for years.

He welcomed the strangers among them, knowing full well that nearly half the people here tonight were strangers, and would remain so even when they took the town over completely, as they were well on the way to doing, with Tim's help. Always shrewd, was Tim. He knew the mentality of money.

When the coffee was drunk and the speeches made they went into the ballroom, a new addition to the old building. Steve had worked on it when he was an apprentice and he looked around at his handiwork as they entered. Steve and Mary and Martha and Freddie sat at a table together, and Tim and his wife joined them when Tim had done his duty and made clucking noises to all the right people he hoped to use and be used by in the future. Then he took off his chain of office and put it in his pocket. 'You ought to wear it all evening, Tim,' his wife said, 'it is expected of you.'

'I don't want that thing breaking my neck all night. How can I dance with that thing clunking against people's tits?'

There was a tone of irritation in his voice which betrayed secrets of his marriage never discussed, for it was essential that Tim should appear to succeed in all his ventures. He stuffed the heavy chain into his pocket where it bulged weightily, counterbalancing the other bulge where his wallet strained the tailored lines of his expensive dinner-jacket. He called a waiter and ordered drinks. He was in his element. Recognized as the leading citizen of the town, and reassured by his financial training that in these times of high inflation the man who owed the most was potentially the richest. He was set to make a fortune. Money was his life and his hobby. He enjoyed wheeling and dealing in finance as others enjoyed sport, fishing, or solving crosswords. A good many of the people here tonight, he thought, looking around the room, owed their prosperity to him. It was his ability to draw finance from a seemingly bottomless pit of debt which helped them through the long hard winters between summers of plenty. He was one of those rare people who knew what he wanted from life, and he was fortunate in the limits of his desire, for he wanted only money, and a taste of the power it brought. In this most mundane of desires he had been gratified and he also had the ability to enjoy his success, another rare quality.

However, he was not deluded by success and knew it to be but relative. 'It's better to be a big fish in a little sea than a little fish in a big sea,' he used to say, for he knew that the big fish in this little community would be swallowed whole by the sharks of commerce in the cities.

Wealth is comparative. There are those who have the power of life and death over their fellows by reason of the possession of cows, or cowrie shells. We thought Tim was rolling in it, but some spend more on coming-out parties for their daughters than Tim would earn in his life. Steve was hard up in some ways, but his family ate well, and lived in a warm, dry house: untold riches for some.

Steve watched the waitress approaching with a tray of drinks, and leaned back in his chair as she put them on the table. 'Thanks, Iris,' he said, and as she took their empty glasses away Martha said, 'I heard she's in the family way again. Thought she ought to know better, come her time of life.'

'Thought she was past it,' Freddie said.

'I expect she thought so too,' said Mary. Mary was getting tipsy. She didn't know how to drink. Either drank nothing, or too much and lost control of her tongue.

'Damn hard lines,' Steve murmured, to no one in particular, 'if she is pregnant. Come her time of life. I 'spect it's just a yarn goin' round.'

' 'Es,' Martha said. 'I expect it's just a yarn.'

Freddie asked Mary to dance when the group played a quickstep. The majority of people there were too old to let themselves go in the gyrations of the latest dancing, but the group were too young to have known the sensuality of dancing with a partner in your arms, so the few quicksteps and foxtrots they played were brash and rhythmless.

'Who are the band?' Martha asked.

'They're a group,' Tim reminded her.

'Group of what?' she said, and let out the first of the night's many shrieks of laughter when Tim leaned over and whispered in her ear, 'Group of sillybuggers.'

Freddie and Mary stood facing each other awkwardly before joining hands, and Freddie placed his right hand on Mary's waist, waiting to catch the beat before moving off. Always the gentleman, was Freddie, in public. Steve was well tanked-up by this time, and his eyes were bright and heavy-lidded, as always when he had been drinking, but he was not so drunk that he would dance with Martha. He nodded at the floor to Tim's wife, who rose immediately, not wishing to dance with her husband, and she stood waiting for him to take her hand. She was from up-country, a bit aloof. Steve didn't talk much while dancing but concentrated on the music, trying to remember the steps and unable to get into the swing of the thing while holding his partner so far away. He had never danced with anyone the way he had danced with Iris. She used to melt into his arms as light as a feather and look at him as if they were the only people in the room. He saw her going from table to table in her too-short black-and-white waitress's uniform designed for a younger body and less weary legs. He wished he could dance with her, talk to her, but he avoided her as always, for the sake of memories . . .

Tim's wife wasn't with him, the dancing was difficult. 'How do you like being mayoress?' he asked her, by way of being polite as they stood waiting for another tune to be played.

'I'm sick of it,' she said. And there was an end to it, he could think of nothing more to say.

Tim was dancing with Martha. He had to, after being left at the table with her, and he was forcing her into intricate steps and sequences which were completely his own invention and bore no relation to the music being played. He was much shorter than Martha, and as he shoved her round the floor he pushed his shoulder into her great mullocks* now and then, to give her a thrill and ensure that she wouldn't dance with him again. He was grinning all over his chacks at his own mischief, and he came back to the table long after the others, after stopping to greet people, shaking hands and slapping backs. He stayed in conversation with the hotel manager for a few minutes, and had a few words with Wally Buller, the bright young solicitor from up-country. When he sat down he removed another bulge, which was his pipe and tobacco, from his pockets. 'I wish you wouldn't smoke that thing,' said his wife. He grinned at her, filled the bowl and tapped his pockets, looking for matches. Steve threw some across the table.

'Fancy a contract,' Tim said, 'to build a block of flats?' He leaned back in his chair and puffed clouds of smoke all around him. 'Wilkins, or Wilson, whatever he's called, the manager, is applying for planning permission for the hotel grounds. Accommodation for the staff. Nice job. Set you up. What about it, eh?' He anticipated Steve's hesitation. 'No problem. No problem. You can employ masons and plumbers and people, on sub-contract. You know everybody—all the good tradesmen. Terry Tuttle and people. Why not? Set you up.'

'I'd have to think about it.' Steve said, 'it's a big job for one man.'

'Employ people, for God's sake.' Tim would have no hesitation at all. 'Expand! 'You can't go wrong. A man of your experience.'

*Mullocks: fishing-floats made from inflated pigs' bladders.

Steve was still reluctant. 'I don't have the money to lay out on big contracts like that,' he said.

'No problem. No problem. Don't worry about the money. I can arrange that.' A chance to make a pile of money and Steve was turning it down. They couldn't understand him.

'Somebody has to build the bleddy thing,' Tim said. 'We can work together, form a limited company. I've got enough plans in my office to keep a builder going for years.'

'You can't go wrong,' Freddie said. 'I'd have a go at it. You've plenty of collateral.'

'Freddie would have a go at it,' Martha assured them, 'like a shot.'

'I'll have to think about it,' Steve said, and looked around the ballroom.

John Ashton was there, with that party from away, a blonde party with striking blue eyes and a slim figure in a long plain dress of a brownish sort of colour with just a little white frill around the neck. She looked right. Neither overdressed nor underdressed. John Ashton could pick them. He had grown taller than all of them, and was handsome-looking, with fair wavy hair and white teeth. From being the youngest, smallest of the boys, he had become the most elegant and self-assured of them all. He was unmarried, but never without a woman, a beautiful woman. He used them like status symbols of his masculinity and set them in his sports car, or wore them on his arm as accessories to his expensive clothes. When the music stopped he came over, for he had seen Steve eyeing his woman. He spoke to Tim, the mayor, to impress her, made brief acknowledgements of Freddie, and Steve, who looked at him in amusement, knowing that he was penniless and that he had probably borrowed money from his latest fancy woman to pay for the evening out. She stood away from the table waiting for John to rejoin her and Steve was aware of her looks and figure but didn't look at her directly, now that she was so close. He had seen her before, and knew her name was Cleo.

'What schemes are you hatching tonight, Tim?' John said. 'Making another quick fortune?'

'Make two, if I get the chance.'

'I want to see you about that deal we were talking about.'

'Sure. Drop in to the office. We'll have a yarn about it.'

John smiled at the rest of the table, showing off his good looks and returning to his woman. Tim wondered how long she would tolerate him. She was a fine bit of gear. He fancied her himself, but, as always, had kept business and pleasure strictly apart while selling her High George's house, in the Rows.

'Going to buy a house, is he?' Martha was asking him, wishing to be first with the news.

'He wants to buy yours,' Tim told her, to avoid answering and to change the subject. He knew Martha.

'Buy ours!' she exclaimed. 'He'll never have the money to buy ours. He's dammee penniless!' She was highly indignant that their property should be devalued by the likes of John Ashton, who was nothing but show and swank. 'Buy ours,' she said. 'Some hopes.'

The music became too loud for conversation so they sat and watched the dancers until the group, obeying some ancient ritual, played a waltz to signify the end of the evening. Tim waltzed with his wife and put the chain back on to clunk against her tits and annoy her, but she couldn't complain, and he was grinning at everyone as they shuffled around the floor, happy with the evening and the new deal to build the block of flats which would more than pay for this, and a good many other, secret, evenings out.

Steve saw Martha and Freddie dancing regally together, with their backs too stiff and their heads too high, and thanked God he hadn't married Martha or anyone else but Mary. He held her close to him, concentrating on the *one* two three, *one* two three, of the three/four time so that she might relax and follow his lead. The drink had made him mellow and sentimental. No one was looking at him, so he put his cheek against hers. She drew away, embarrassed at this public show of affection, and spoke to other women as they circled round the floor. 'Had a nice time? Lovely dinner. Like old times!' Nodding to this one, smiling to that one.

'Do you want to dance with me, or with they?' Steve said.

'How don't you talk fitty? You don't have to talk so broad.' She jerked his arm. 'Stand up straight,' she said, 'don't hold me so dammee tight. I can't breathe.'

He relaxed his hold on her and she continued looking round at everyone else, to see who was dancing with who in this last waltz of the evening. Steve gave up. Dancing was for the young, and this would be his last dance. What was the point if there was always to be restraint, a concern for what other people were seeing or saying? He too began to gaze about him. He saw John Ashton with his blonde, holding her so close as if she was the most desirable, the most precious woman in the world, although she didn't appear too happy at being shown off in such a manner. Steve bumped into somebody, 'Sorry.'

'You're drunk,' Mary said.

The group were packing up their instruments even before the round of polite applause at the end of the waltz. This had been a good evening for them, with a good feed, free drinks, and they had not even worked themselves into a sweat. Not like the gigs with young people.

In the large, thick-carpeted foyer by the main door of the hotel, everyone was wishing each other a good night. Tim shook hands in his Official Capacity, as he liked to call it, with all of the important men of the town as they left for home, and with all of those who liked to think that by shaking hands with the mayor, they too might become important. Strangers, mostly, people who didn't know him. Martha and Freddie were among the last to leave, taking advantage of the public occasion to display their popularity to all. Steve was waiting to go, tired and sleepy, but the women were gathered in a cluster, chattering and giggling at brash jokes among themselves.

The taxi-driver entered and stood waiting at the door. 'We are coming now, Sam,' Steve said wearily. He had been up at five that morning.

Outside, the cold air crept stealthily under their clothes, and drove out the accumulated heat of the night. Steve shivered as the sweat cooled and chilled the skin of his back. Mary shed the jocularity of the preceding half hour as soon as they were sitting in the taxi and said nothing but a few pleasantries to Sam all the way down the main road and over the throbbing cobbles of the streets to their own front door.

They sat in the kitchen drinking a cup of coffee before going to bed. Mary had enjoyed herself, let her hair down, said a few daring words, she was relaxed and still a little stimulated by the drink, the dancing, and the company of so many old friends. She thought that Steve was the handsomest man there, and wished he had a bit more ambition, like Tim and Freddie, so that people would look up to him.

'Do 'ee think Tim meant it? About the flats? I thought he might have been drunk.'

'Tim never talks business when he's drunk.'

'Will 'ee do it? Take the job on?'

He pulled off his tie, glad to be rid of the restriction round his neck, and threw it on to the back of the chair. 'I would have to give up the boat.'

Here was an opportunity at last for him to be something. He could be a master builder, with his own firm, with men working for him. He could go to work best-changed, in a suit. He could make a pile of money. If he wouldn't run a hotel, then he could be a master builder. There was money in it.

'The boat!' She thought, Boat, boat, boat! But she was careful not to chide him. 'If you made a pile of money you could have two boats,' she said. 'I can't understand you. Why not? I can't see what you have to lose.'

Steve sighed deeply. 'If I wanted to expand and take on men, go in for big contracts, I could do it on my own.'

'You said you didn't have the money to go in for anything big. Tim said he would help 'ee. Tim's got plenty of money. He said he would.'

'He said nothing of the kind. I wasn't that drunk. I know what he said.' He laughed and shook his head. 'I know Tim Penberthy, the crafty bugger. He's desperate for a good builder. Everybody is as busy as hell on the new estates and extensions and one thing and another. What he said was . . .' Steve looked directly at her to ensure she would understand, '. . . that he could *arrange* the money. Arrange the money. Our bleddy money.'

She looked at him, blinking. 'Our money? We haven't got any.'

'The way Tim thinks, we have. We own our own house, don't we? He would raise money on our deeds.' He shook his head again. He must think I'm a bleddy tuss.'

'Well, it's business,' she said defensively.

'Mary, my 'ansome, if I go into debt, I shall do it for myself. For us. Not for Tim. Tim's a good old sort, do anything for anybody, but in business he's as hard as nails. By the time I paid interest to the bank, and he had his little cut from all hands, he would get more out of it than me. And I'd have all the worry.'

'Cut? What cut?'

'His "reciprocal", that's what he calls it. Commission. Call it what you like.' He drank the last of his coffee.

'One day they are all going to come undone, all these smart asses, sure as eggs is eggs. And they're not taking me with them. And don't go outside saying I said so.'

'I shan't say anything.'

'No,' he said, doubtfully.

'I was only thinking it was time you did something. At your age.'

'At my age I'm going to do as I belong to do. Go along comfortable.'

She was sobered by his good sense, annoyed that he was too cautious to move into the big money, yet relieved that he was not the sort to gamble everything they owned for the sake of prestige and ostentation. She was surprised that he had thought so much about this offer of Tim's, while apparently too slow in the head to make a quick shilling when it was offered to him on a plate. They hadn't talked so seriously for ages.

'Let's go to bed,' he said.

As they went upstairs and along the landing to their bedroom, Steve ran his hand affectionately over Mary's behind, feeling the ripple of muscle as she walked. 'What's that deal John Ashton was talking about?' Mary said, still thinking of the financial juggling among their contemporaries.

'John? He's trying to buy a house down the Rows. Ephraim Pengelly's house. John couldn't buy a bleddy gurrie. Spent all his money on cars and fancy women.'

'Who's that party he was with tonight?'

'I don't know. A stranger. She's bought High George's house that was. Artist, so they say.'

'One of that crowd,' Mary said.

He was in bed by the time she finished in the bathroom, and he watched her undressing. She undressed before him like they do on the beach, leaving nothing uncovered, but slipped her night-dress over her head before taking off her underclothes. She had a nice pair of tits and her shoulders were smooth and round. Soft, she was, not like Martha and a few others, gone hard and muscular, though she had a few lines beginning to gather at the neck. She was still the best of the bunch. She reached into her nightie and slipped off her bra, put it on the chair with her other things, then slipped her pants off, hiding herself from him by lifting the back of the nightie while facing him. 'How are you lookin' at me like that?' she said. 'No good you lookin' at me like that.' She combed her hair at the mirror and it was in her voice that she wanted him, but she could never take the initiative, begin. 'I'm tired,' she said, 'no good lookin' at me like that.'

Why couldn't she throw off the nightie and come and kiss him, sit on top of him? Mary Wary Quite Contrary, will she or will she no? Things we used to say, Steve thought . . . Annie, Annie, how's your fanny? Boys and girls come out to play, we will have it away, away. Touching them up after Chapel with hands in folds of Sunday frocks fighting for handfuls of black balsh.* Always the fighting for it, for the girls must be innocent and unwillingly defiled. Except Iris, poor Iris in the family way again.

'Look at the state of your clothes,' Mary said. 'Thrown everywhere.' She picked them up and hung them on hangers, her breasts swaying loosely under the thin material of her nightdress. Steve wanted to get his hands around them and kiss her on the lips. He rose at the thought of it. 'I don't know why you don't wear your 'jamas,' she said, 'you've got two pairs of 'jamas in the drawer.'

'I don't know why you bother to put that nightie on when you know I'm going to take it off again to-once you get in bed.' He ran his hand over her as she reached for the switch.

'We'll see about that,' she said, and he kissed her as she settled on to the pillow and turned to face him. 'Kiss me,' he said.

'I am kissin' 'ee.' He ran his tongue along her lips, trying to open

*Balsh: fine tarred string.

36

her mouth. 'I don't like that,' she said. 'You know I don't like that.' He kissed her neck, shoulders, lingering on her breasts, ran his mouth down over her belly. She turned over on her side, lying on his arm. He ran his fingers through the fur.

' "His left arm is under my head and his right arm doth embrace me," ' he quoted.

'No need for blasphemy,' she told him.

'That's not blasphemy,' he said, 'Solomon knew what he was talking about. "Let him kiss me with the kisses of his mouth." It's beautiful.' 'Don't be crude,' she said.

'Crude? Solomon? Haven't you read the Bible?' Of course she had read the Bible. He took hold of her hand, placed it upon him. 'Ecclesiastes,' he said. 'Chapter Seven, Verse eighteen: "It is good that thou shouldest take hold of this . . ." ' he held her firmly as she tried to pull her hand away. ' "Yea, also from this withdraw not thine hand".' He rolled over on top of her, pushing her legs apart with his knee. 'Get that damned nightie thing off,' he said.

He never saw her naked in the daylight, but in the gloom of two o'clock in the morning by the dim light creeping through the curtains from the half moon hanging over Tregenna Woods she pulled the nightie off over her head and lay for a minute or two while he caressed her breasts with both hands. She drew him down on her, that he might not see her face or her body as she made love to him in the dark, and she opened her legs.

Chapter Four

A howling gale. Flying spume. Twin quays drenched with spray from breaking waves, slates clattering from some roof in Fore Street, boats straining at the moorings until they threatened to part, a dustbin lid clanking past the Lodge where they huddled in the doorway, watching the give in the ropes. A newcomer. A nod.

'Hard weather.'

'Hard weather.'

No more is asked. No opinion sought. Superfluous comment, it is said, is a sign of inferior intelligence, and no comment on the weather, other than a bare statement of fact, is required at a moment such as this. If the moorings are secure, the boats will ride it out. If not, then they'll part and scat their sterns agin the quay. It is obvious. And all they who didn't see to their moorings at the proper time will get all they deserve. So some watch with confidence, some with apprehension. All watch without expression.

They stay until the ebbing tide, moving against the wind, ceases to break over the quay, and to one unfamiliar with the harbour the worst seems past. But the boats strain even harder at the moorings as a vicious, swirling ground swell drags them now to this quay, now, with gathering strength and speed, to that. The boats, held at bow and stern, give against the pressure and heel over as the tide pulls their keels until the gunnels dip below the surface. The slacker the moorings, the more they drag away, and the more they dip their gunnels. There were some boats shipping water already, and the more they shipped, the lower they rode, they became less buoyant and consequently shipped more and more. One was obviously going to sink. Her moorings were very slack and she floundered with the swell, rubbing her starboard side against the sharp bow of the boat next in tier.

'Ha!' said James, 'no fenders nor nawthen. And March month here.'

'Where is he?' somebody said.

'Up the country.'

They watched in silence as the boat sank lower and lower.

'These people don't understand, Steve. They don't understand.'

The harbour was treacherous. These people did not understand that this was not some anchorage in a quiet estuarine backwater where they could be left for months on end. Safe in gales of any force as long as there was no ground swell, the mooring ropes of the local boats would hold battleships in other harbours, just for occasions such as this, when a moderate gale accompanied by a swirling swell strained the chains and ropes to breaking-point.

'Her keel's too deep,' said a voice. 'Too deep.' They all looked at the sinking boat. Standing with their hands thrust down in pockets, some leaning forward at precarious angles with shoulders jammed against doorposts and walls.

'He ought to be here.'

'He's up the country.'

When a swell came in, it started at the old quay, in a great slow surge, crossed the mouth of the harbour to the west pier, and, swirling in an arc, swept around the harbour like a maelstrom, sweeping everything before it, and died away, leaving the boats riding quietly at anchor to await the next onslaught. As the tide receded the danger was increased, for the whole harbour might suddenly empty in a swirl, leaving the boats high and dry with taut moorings. Then, from around the quay would come another rush; circling the harbour, it would pour towards the gunnels left lying exposed and vulnerable, facing the tide and with insufficient depth to float. The swell would pour aboard until they floated off, or filled with water and sank. Deep-keeled boats were particularly vulnerable at this time.

Steve looked at the *Mermaid*. 'Were all right,' he said, with a glance at James.

'Yes. We're all right.'

Steve always knew when James was mad at him, for he said 'yes', instead of "es". Like the rest of them he never pronounced the 'y' unless he was being polite or talking proper to strangers. Or like now, being downright bloody sarcastic. What he meant was: 'Yes. We are all right. But no thanks to you. You should have been here at five o'clock this morning when the tide was out, and unlocked the door of the loft so that we could have got the kedge anchor out and saved all this worry.' Well, Steve had been home in bed. His moorings were all right.

'We can get our anchor from the loft,' he said, 'take it out in the skiff. Drop it well to port of that boat. Take the rope aboard of her with the skiff. Make fast and take up the slack between the runs. We could do that.'

'The harbour, Steve, is like a boiling pot. A boiling pot, I tell 'ee.'

'Been out in worse than this. Many a time.'

'For your own, Ste', for your own.'

'The skiff might capsize, Ste'.'

'He ought to be here, Steve.'

'He's going to lose his bleddy boat, whoever he is. For Christ's sake.'

'Now, there's no need for language, Steve,' Silas Rouncefield muttered. Silas swore like a bloody trooper when he felt like it, as everybody knew.

' ''Thou shalt not take the name of the Lord thy God in vain . . .'' ' James said, angrily.

'Don't quote the Bible to me, James. I know the Book better than any of 'ee.'

'That's what it d' say, Steve.'

'I know what it d' say. And I'll tell 'ee something else it d' say . . . ''But the stranger that dwelleth with you shall be unto you as one born among you, and thou shalt love him as thyself . . .'' Leviticus, Chapter nineteen, Verse thirty-four, as told to me by old Robbie Stevens when my wife started taking in bleddy lodgers. Now, come up with me to the loft to get the bleddy anchor.'

(And the Bible says a lot of other things, like 'An omer is the tenth part of an ephah', and 'Thou shalt not committ adultery.')

They trudged up the narrow street to the loft in stony silence, holding their heads low against the wind and rain, where the gusts swirled around the corners. Steve knew very well that he couldn't stand by and let a man's boat sink without making the slightest effort to save her, and James knew very well that they might lose the skiff, be capsized into the sea, still not save her, and not have a ha'p'orth of thanks from him, whoever he was—a stranger!

He said once more as Steve inserted the key into the worn lock and shoved the door open with his shoulder, 'He ought to be here, Ste'.'

'Yes, yes. All right. He ought to be here. Now take the painter, I'll bring the anchor.'

James stopped in his tracks as they rounded the corner once more and saw the harbour at the bottom of the hill.

'My shoes, Steve, is wet leakin'.'

'Yes.' Steve could feel the water creeping into his own socks.

'Wet leakin',' James said. 'What a crant.'*

What he meant was . . . they should have had their sea-boots on,

---

*A to do, a mess.

40

but by the time they went home for them it would be too late to do anything for the stranger. And that it was all Steve's fault if James got double pneumonia and died as a result of this tomfoolery.

James let out a deep and resigned 'Aaaaagh' and trudged on down the hill.

Reaching the quay steps, Steve brought the skiff alongside. He kept her close, but clear of the granite corners, while James climbed aboard with the anchor and rope. Then they took an oar each and pulled out towards the stranger's boat in the middle of the harbour. They tried to pull together, but they were thrown against each other as they reached the rough backlash where the waves were rebounding from all sides of the harbour and breaking against themselves in a mad confusion of chop and spray.

'Like a boilin' pot.' James shouted against the wind, while in the Lodge a row of faces peered at them through the rills and raindrops running down the windows, and on the lee wall a huddle of humped shoulders and hands in pockets watched in silence.

Steve glanced over his shoulder and saw the first swirl of a ground swell coming towards them. 'Ground say!' he cried in James's ear.

When the inrush caught them the chop was flattened, but the skiff was taken astern so fast that they had to row with all their strength to prevent her from being dashed against the other boats moored around them, and James muttered fiercely under his breath as they strained against the oars.

'Damn strangers!' he shouted at the top of his voice.

'Language, James,' Steve laughed, 'language,' as he shook his head to clear the wet from his eyes.

After each inrush there was a lull in the turbulence and now they rowed hard to clear the moorings of the large fishing-boats riding it out solidly in the middle of the harbour, and gained the far side of the stranger's boat before another swell reached them. They strained against this one, held their ground, and when it had subsided James took both oars while Steve took the anchor and, judging the distance to the boat, cast it overboard.

The stranger's boat was dragging badly, and would part her moorings or capsize sure enough if they didn't make the new painter fast pretty soon, so James unshipped the oars and rowlocks, payed out the anchor rope, and let the skiff be taken by the waves and drift alongside her, all the while tossing like a cork and shipping water whenever a wave caught the bow on the dip. James bailed out the water which was now swishing over the bottom-boards and into their shoes. 'Sink, d'reckly,' he said.

As they bore down on the boat Steve poised himself in the stern to make the jump when the two boats were quiet enough. They had to get close enough for Steve to jump, but not close enough to touch, for in this swell the skiff would be forced under if the larger boat's gunnel came down on her. And either could have a plank stove in if they were driven together by the waves. Steve had the coil of the anchor-rope in his hand and stood with one foot on the stern, balancing himself against the unpredictable lurching of the skiff, and as the boats came together he stood up, and in the brief moment when they were on an even keel and steady, he jumped. James rowed away and, keeping the skiff bow-on to the weather, came round to the stranger's lee-side while Steve made a loop round a stanchion and took up the strain. Each time there was a lull in the swell he hauled the boat on to the new rope, holding her there when the swell dragged her keel, until the old moorings were sinking uselessly and the new anchor holding the full strain. He felt a thud as the keel struck bottom when the bow was lifted by a wave. 'Just in time. Now we have to moor the skiff again.' He made fast with a final clove-hitch and waved to James.

James bent his old back and pulled alongside, close enough for Steve to make another jump. The water in the bottom came up to his ankles as the skiff dipped her bow under his weight but he ignored it and took his place at the oar and they rowed back to the quay, letting the skiff anchor overboard before they reached the steps. Then, with Steve on the oars, James clambered ashore. Steve stowed the oars and waited his chance to follow. As he jumped, a sudden wave, up from nowhere, lurched the skiff and his wet shoes slipped sideways, thrusting him forward, so that he fell full length on the steps. The skiff surged on to him, jammed his foot between steps and stern. The waves swept over him, but he hung on to the railing. James grabbed his arm, steadied him as he limped clear up a couple of steps and hung on, grimacing with pain.

'Make her fast,' he said, 'I'm O.K.'

James ran up the steps with the painter and made fast to a bollard while Steve, clear of the sea, turned and sat on the wet steps, removing a soggy shoe from a rapidly swelling foot.

'Ooo hell,' he said, 'Here's a bleddy crant.'

Mary was furious. 'I should like to,' she said, 'for a damn stranger. Make me say such words. You're dammee soaked.' Steve limped upstairs to the bathroom with Mary following and complaining about the wet. 'You'd never think I paid forty pound for that carpet,' she said.

'Pull my shoes and socks off. What's a carpet for if you can't walk on it?'

'If it was left to you the place would be like a pigsty.' She pulled off the sodden sock. 'Oh, my Lord!' she cried. 'Oh, my soul.' The swelling bruise discoloured his ankle in a throbbing ache. She knelt before him and removed his other shoe and sock. 'Oh, my dear soul.' Steve told her not to make a fuss. Go down and put the kettle on. He had a hot bath to drive out the chill and gave himself a good soaking before going down to the kitchen where Mary, seeing that his foot had come to no permanent harm, began scolding him again.

'Damn strangers!' she said as she cut the saffron cake. 'See any stranger doing it for you? You're dammee soft. Time for 'ee to give up the old boat. There's any amount of work and you're down there muckin' about in that damn boat, make me say such words. There's no sense in it.'

'No,' Steve said, 'No sense in it. But I get my living at it.'

'Your living! What sort of a living? Martha and Freddie are going off to Spain at the end of the season. Where are we going? Nowhere. And if I didn't work all summer, we wouldn't have bran-for-ducks.'

So, that was it. She'd been talking to Martha again. Listening to her going on about their holidays and their possessions. Being made to feel inferior and falling for it, hook, line and sinker. 'That woman,' he said, 'gives me a pain in the ass.'

'If you didn't spend so much on that boat, *we* could go off on holiday too,' Mary said. 'There's any amount of work. Robbie Stevens has been asking when you are going to do his job, and that there artist, that Tony, has been asking about his windows. There's plenty of work. I don't know how you don't give up that boat and go in for building proper, or buy a guest-house, like everybody else.'

'I thought Robbie was laid up.' Steve had heard all this before, so he ignored it.

'He is. I saw Sarah. They are both laid up. She's looking after them. She d' want the job done.'

'It's only a gate to mend.'

'Don't matter what it is. She d' want 'n done. She said it blew right off in the wind last night.'

A couple of days later his foot was almost as good as new. He had a look over the stranger's boat, tightened up her moorings, and took his anchor back to the loft. Then he took his tools up to Robbie Steven's house. On the way, he met Terry Tuttle, the plumber, struggling on his short, bandy legs beneath the weight of an enormous tool-bag. 'What a game, boy,' Terry said. 'What a bleddy crant.' His cynical view of life was well known, and he wore a permanent smile as if amused by the futility of it all, but he was a good tradesman, so Steve often passed work on to him.

'Hear any more about Tim Penberthy's job for the flats, did 'ee?'

'No. Best left alone, I thought.'

' 'Es, best left alone.'

Sarah Stevens had grown into a neat an tidy spinster with her hair more grey than brown. She was known to be 'very nice'. A very nice woman. Very pleasant, but you had to be careful what you said to her—no 'darns' or 'hells', or anything remotely concerning sex. She was never seen with untidy hair or smudged shoes. She had a ready smile for everyone. A nice smile. No one ever saw her laugh. Her face looked as if it had just been washed, a minute before you met her. She was correct. Still one of the regulars among the diminishing congregation at Chapel, she turned out in all weathers to walk downalong to take her place in the family pew. Usually she was alone since her parents were not able to walk so far, though sometimes, Easter perhaps, or Harvest Festival, say, they would have Sam's taxi to take them there, for the singing. Oh, the singing. It used to raise the roof.

She let Steve get on with the repairs, it was only the screws come adrift from the jambs and the hinges twisted a bit, while she worked in the scullery, washing sheets, going upstairs occasionally to see to her parents' needs. He put on new hinges and used longer screws. That's all it needed, the timber was sound. Robbie always looked after his property. He packed his tools back in the frail* and leaned over the hepse door† to call into the house. 'All finished, Sarah. I'm gone.'

'Gone, are 'ee?' she said. 'That was quick.'

'There wasn't much in it.' He stepped aside to allow her to come out into the back court and inspect his work.

'That's better,' she said. 'Better than it was before.'

' 'Es.'

She stopped him from picking up his tool-bag with a gesture of the hand, and said, '*He* d' want to see 'ee. He d' want a bit of a yarn for a few minutes.'

Steve didn't want to go up there, into a room of sickness.

'I'll go up and see him d'reckly,' he said. 'Let me put the tools in the van, out of the way.'

He said 'd'reckly', meaning later, some other time, not now.

'How is he?'

'Oh, he's all right . . . You know. He's very weak. And he d' have trouble with his water. But he's all right.'

There was no need for Steve's fear of sickness, no need for his revulsion, his dread of the deathbed. It would be all right. Sarah said so. 'Might's well go up now,' he said.

'Come in. I'll take 'ee up. He'll be glad to see 'ee.'

*Frail: A rope-handled tool-bag.
†Hepse: A half-door or stable door.

44

There was no mention of her mother. No 'they', only him. He. Father. He was the household, the unquestioned head. He was a man of a totally man's world, and considered his family to be an extension of himself, his character and beliefs. Sarah led Steve through the house to the stairs. 'Course,' she said as they approached the bedroom door, 'he's nearly ninety, you know. Only to be expected.' Steve nodded. 'I mean,' Sarah said, 'the age is there.'

She opened the door and said 'Steve is here, Father, Steve Trevorrow.'

'Come in, my son, come in.' His voice was strong. 'Set 'ee down.' Indicating the wicker chair beside the bed. It was an old bed of satin walnut, matching the dressing-table and wardrobe which stood against the walls. A high bed, with an ornate head and foot, and a white bedspread of handmade crochet-work. On a table by the window stood bottles of medicines and little boxes of pills. Below it, under a clean white towel, the outline of a bedpan. On the floor was lino, with rugs of the kind made from dyed sackcloth and strips of old material from discarded clothes, another with heavy wool sewn into hessian. They made their own rugs in the old days and they lasted well. Sarah had new carpets downstairs but up here everything was as it was, as it belonged.

Robbie's wife lay beside him, propped up on a pillow, a tiny figure who had passed her stature on to Sarah. Steve glanced at her, self-consciously, and saw the vestiges of her youthful beauty remaining only in the bones, the high cheeks and forehead, the small nose and chin. Her skin was deeply lined and yellow. Her lips were mouthing words but there was no sound, only an occasional chuckle or a sigh.

'Don't pay no account to she,' Robbie said. 'She's . . . gone. Gone.' He looked at her, with his lips pursed. 'Course,' he said, 'she's nearly ninety, you knaw. Only to be expected. I mean, the age is there.' He turned to Steve with a rueful smile, 'We cain't be first and last too, that's for sure.' Steve agreed with him. 'We cain't be first and last,' he said.

Sarah went downstairs, leaving the men to talk alone. Robbie looked again at his wife. 'She's be'n a good hard-workin' woman,' he said, 'a good hard-workin' woman.' Steve nodded. ''Es,' he said, 'a good hard-working woman.' Robbie regarded her in silence for a while and then turned to Steve and said, 'Well now. And how are you, my son?'

'Oh, I'm all right, Mr Stevens, considering my age.' They laughed together.

'How old are you, 'en Steve? I d' forget.'

'Gone forty, now.'

'Gone forty! 'Es, I s'pose you are . . . Sarah's in her thirty-eight.

She's a good hard-working woman,' he said. 'She's be'n a good daughter to we. A good Christian woman.' He paused in thought. 'She's like her mawther.'

They had a yarn about this and that, and one thing and another. Steve told him all the news from down the Lodge. About the fishing and the weather, and how the west pier was falling down for lack of maintenance and how all the shops were being bought by people from up-country. Strangers taking everything over. The youngsters going away. You didn't know half the people in town now. Didn't know who they were, nor what they were. How everybody seemed to be making a pile of money. It wasn't like it was. Tommy Blue was failing.

'And what about you, now?' Steve said. 'How are you?'

'Well, you can see how I am. No need to ask. I'm waitin' to be called. Me and she.' He gave Steve one steady nod, looking him in the eye. 'Waitin' to be called.'

Now, one of Robbie's race would have had the right thing to say to that, but Steve could only nod in silence. Robbie helped him.

'I'm ready. I'm a fortunate man. I'm ready to go. "There is a time to be born and a time to die." You know that one. "The bitterness of death is past." Here, give me the Book!'

Steve took a worn and faded Bible from the beside table and handed it to the old man, who held it in both hands, looking at it in silence for several minutes, while the steady ticking from the gold pocket-watch, lying with its chain coiled on the table, counted away, counted away . . .

'It's all in here,' he said, eventually. 'If you've a mind to look for 'n.'

'Yes. I suppose it is.'

'Now, I can talk to you. You understand? You d' think upon these things. I can tell. You're like your grandfather. I mean your *great*-grandfather. He was like you. You d' look like 'n. He was a fine man. A tall man. Taller 'n you, but the same build as you. A fine sailor. He was a fine sailor. Now, we was all fishermen but we wudd'n all sailors.' He looked at the sky through the lace curtains. Casting his mind back . . . back . . . 'We was fishin' in the North Say, one time, and when all hands were beatin' back to Scarborough in a north-east gale, they were nervous of it, don't 'ee see, he decided to up and race for home. Sail with the wind and race for home. Yes. Seventy-two hours sailin' as hard as they could sail. Landed their herrin' in Newlyn, fresh.'

Steve smiled. 'A good man, eh?' He'd heard the yarn before, from old Robbie and his own grandmother.

'He was a good Christian man. And he had Scarborough rock for all

46

the children. Always brought Scarborough rock for the children when was away to the North Say.'

'I've heard them say so.'

'They used to go down to the quay to meet 'n.' He laughed and nodded his head. 'But he wouldn't give none away until he had been home and put on a clean guarnsey.' They laughed quietly together, and the old woman joined in. Steve looked at her, wondering how much of her mind was left.

'Now,' said the old man through Steve's speculation, 'are you ready, my son?'

'I'm not as ready as you, Mr Stevens.'

The old man looked at him. 'You're a young man. You d' have time.' He tapped the cover of the Bible with the flat of his hand. 'Plenty of time.' He gazed above the lace curtains to the infinity of the sky, oblivious for the moment of Steve, who regarded him anxiously, or the wife who compressed her mouth over toothless gums in spasms of mute, long-forgotten conversation. Steve felt hot and uncomfortable in the room and wanted to leave. Robbie's gaze was vacant. He was, thought Steve, either reliving some moment of his past or anticipating the eternal bliss of the heaven he was soon to see.

Steve was extricated when Sarah came up and told her father it was time to rest, and he went down with her to have a dish of tay in the kitchen. She paid him for repairing the door, for there could be no debt in that family.

Her mother passed away soon after, sleeping in the old man's arms.

Chapter Five

Cleo stood back from her painting, wiped a brush on a piece of rag, and sighed deeply. Tony sat in her armchair and studied the picture without comment. He was a man whose most noticeable feature was his bald head. On some men a bald head passes unnoticed, like eyebrows, or upper lips, say, but Tony had such fine eyes, such a thick grey beard, such a well-shaped nose, such good looks, in fact, that a bald head appeared somehow incongruous, as if this one concession to his age was contrived, like a wig of skin. His remaining hair was fairly short by the standards of the time, though long for a man of his age, so that by wearing or not wearing a hat he could add or subtract twenty years at will. He was, still is, a successful artist. Successful in the sense that he could paint, and was doing the one thing in life which meant anything at all to him. As Tim made money, Tony painted pictures. You could live with one of Tony's pictures and see something new in it every day, but he sold so few that he could not afford that most essential comfort to a lonely man, a wife. He had known women in his youth, and had loved more than one, but he loved his job most of all. His job was painting pictures, and he did it every day of his life.

Women adored him. They thought he was past it . . . Lust. They were wrong. He lusted after them all but was not prepared to risk premature demise in a heart attack during the struggle for physical ecstasy at a time of life when there were still so many ideas to be committed to canvas. He lusted after Cleo. He loved her too, as did all compassionate men.

'No one will understand it,' Cleo said, looking at the picture, 'but I can't help it. That's the way they always develop.'

'Can *you* understand it?' says he, being Irish. 'That's all that matters, is it not? Never mind this No One fellah, whoever he is.'

She was pleased with the painting. It was of a great rock emerging from the sea along the cliffs just west of town. But tomorrow, or the day after, she would see defects in it, some area ill-defined or some fault in composition, and she would despair. This elation after some successful achievement was invariably followed by disillusionment, and the two emotions had been symptomatic of her personality for as long as she could remember. She had come to fear elation as the precursor of some dreadful depression which was forever looming to shatter her happiness.

'But, if no one else understands it, if there is no communication, then surely it can't be art,' she said. And added, wistfully, 'Certainly no sales.'

'By Jesus, woman' (he said 'Bejaysus') 'I understand it. I can see what you are trying to say. It's a style you are developing. A style it is. Can you not see that? It's *you*. It's a Cleo, all right. Unmistakable.'

She laughed and kissed the top of his head. But Tony had not finished with her. 'You are an artist, woman,' he said. 'Now for God's sake, just get on and paint.' He had, in that gentle way of his, told her before the plain truth of creative art, which is this: Don't think. Do. Paint, he told her, until the colours swim before your eyes and shapes loom up and entwine you in your dreams. 'Don't come to me and talk about art. Come and show me some pictures.'

'Do you know how long I've been painting, Cleo?'

'Nope.'

'Over forty years. I began in my twenties. And never sold a damn thing until I was over forty.' He chuckled to himself. 'What I lived on all those years, I dread to think. Now, the other day this fellah walks into my studio and offers me five hundred quid for a painting that no gallery would take, or look at, ten years ago. Five hundred quid! After hanging in my studio all that time. I told him it's not for sale. I kept it, you see, all that time. I know it's a good painting and I wouldn't sell it now for a thousand.' He laughed into his hand. 'A thousand and one I might consider. I just moight.'

'You must have had great faith in it. To have kept it all this time.'

'Faith!' he cried. 'Faith!' and thought for a few minutes before saying, with a deep note of sincerity in his voice, 'The great thing, Cleo. The great thing in life, as well as art, is to be true to yourself.' He leaned his head to one side, 'And that's very difficult. Self-knowledge makes difficult learning, even for an old man like me.' Thinking for a few moments, he said, 'I should heed my own advice, should I not? And get back to my own studio and do some work instead of sitting here, chatting to you.'

'I like to hear you wandering on. You are good for me, Tony. I need someone to talk to sometimes. Someone to listen to.'

'Well. That's good. Yes, that's good. I'll come around, now and then. I know what it's like, you know, loneliness.'

'But you have so many friends.'

'Oh, yes. Oh yes,' he paused, 'but I'm talking about loneliness . . . loneness. You know.'

Cleo looked at his face, and into his gentle and understanding eyes. 'Yes,' she said softly, 'I know.'

They sat without speaking for several minutes. He was looking at her painting. She resisted the temptation to ask, once more, his opinion of it. Finally he turned to her and said, 'You need to fall in love.'

His words were so unexpected that for a moment she was silenced with astonishment.

'Really, Tony! What's love got to do with it?' Although that is obvious enough. 'Besides, I, I've . . .' she faltered.

'John?' he asked, raising his eyebrow. She didn't answer him, but lit one of her infrequent cigarettes as he sat silently in the chair, looking down at the floor, with the slow drumming of his fingers on the arm the only indication of his anxious solicitude.

She blew a vicious cloud of smoke to the ceiling. 'What are you?' she said. 'Some kind of clairvoyant? A mind reader?' She was angry with him for knowing her so well, a reaction I have often seen. 'I thought no one knew about that. What it was like.'

'He's a strange man,' Tony mused, 'A strange man.'

'Strange? He's more than strange!'

Tony reached for her hand and drew her close to his chair.

'Did you love him?'

'No. Yes . . . Oh, I don't know. I thought I did. When I first came here and was all alone he took me over. At first he was kind and helpful. But after a while he seemed to have a power over me. I couldn't resist it. I was afraid of him yet afraid to leave him. To leave him! And we didn't live together. You know . . . we didn't . . .' She had difficulty in saying it. '. . . even make love. He was concerned about what people might say, he said, my reputation, if he spent the night here. Yet he often stayed till midnight. He said he didn't like to stay out too late because his mother would worry. His mother! At his age. I thought he was trying to impress me by showing concern and restraint.' The pain came back to her . . . 'Why couldn't I see it? What he was like?'

'He's a strange man.' He looked up at her as he fondled her hand, 'I've not met a man like him before. And a local man too. He's not like the others. You will find them a difficult people to know. They keep to themselves still. It's true. Even now. I've lived here a few years now and I don't know many locals. But I understand them. It's the same at home, don't you see? In Ireland. Oh, they talk to you . . . in the pubs, say hello in the street, but you can't get close to them. It's not intentional. They have their own friends, their own families, they don't need anyone else. We have no right to demand friendship simply because we come here to live. They probably have difficulty enough coping with the friends they already have, do they not?'

There was, she thought, a smug look about that grin. 'You might not find it so easy to make friends. Among the locals, I mean, because of the art business,' he went on. 'I mean people tend to think of artists as being "different". From what they are different I wouldn't like to guess. Nevertheless I feel at home here, being a Celt.'

She missed the humour in his eye. 'John knows everyone,' she said, 'yet I met so few locals through him. He seemed to keep me apart, as if he wished everyone to know of me, yet not meet me. He's so popular. Do you know, he still comes to see me? Yes. He's . . .' She shook him playfully by the back of the neck, suddenly laughing. 'You crafty old devil. You know everything about me.'

'I wouldn't want to know everything about anybody. It's a great responsibility, knowing people . . .' he trailed off, as if appalled at the prospect. 'I know one thing; it's not me you'll be after fallin' in love wit'.' She knew, without looking at him, of the rueful look that appeared on his face, and anticipated the continuation of his remarks. 'An ould fellah like me.'

'Don't you be so sure,' she said. 'Now, what about that coffee you came in for?'

They went into her kitchen. 'It's a lot tidier than mine,' he said. 'You've been decorating, I see. Lots of white. Hmm. Yes. It's a great colour, is white. A great colour. I think I'll do mine white . . . my kitchen. It's a bit of a mess, my kitchen. The walls are a sort of spattered muck and smoky brown colour.'

'Your kitchen? I thought it looked quite nice. Mushroom, I would call it.' Tony ignored her.

'It's that ould gas cooker,' he said. 'I'll have to get rid of it. But I'm quite fond of it, y'know. Quite fond of it. It's been a good servant. You get fond of ould servants, at my age.'

She was only half listening to him musing aloud, and concentrated on putting coffee and sugar in mugs, watching the saucepan.

'I painted it the other day. I mean I painted a picture of it. I'd been getting my breakfast, quite late you know, I don't get up very early, and somebody came to the door . . .' His lips pursed as he remembered the occasion. '. . . I think it was Arnold or somebody, you know, the poet, returning a book or something, and we got chatting, there on the doorstep, you know the way you do.

'The milk was boilin' over,' he went on. 'The kettle was spittin' water onto the eggs in the frying pan, great bubbles of porridge were

51

creeping out of the saucepan like lava from Vesuvius. A good breakfast sets a man up. I loik a good breakfast. The stink of burns mingled with the steam. When I came in the whole thing looked like some terrifying great fire-breathing monster. I was afraid to go near the bloody thing, but I saw all the colours in it, you know. Those lovely flashes of electric blue where the spitting fat was being ignited in a kind of sparkling halo round the frying pan, and the shapes of porridge runnin' down the cooker, bubblin', you know. The kettle began to whistle and the porridge to spit and fart; oatmeal turned to black, crimson-lake crept out and raped the yellow ochre, indigo danced with emerald green, vermillion killed chrome-yellow with a purple cloak . . . it's a great painting. I had great fun painting it too, great fun.'

'Oh Tony. You're joking.'

'Oh no. Oh no. I'll show it to you. I had to turn the gas out you know. Risked me bloody life. But it's a great painting. I was afraid the house would catch alight, so I had to turn it out.'

Cleo laughed as she pushed past him and took their coffee into the studio, and thought what a lovely man Tony was. There was no malice in his make-up at all. If you kicked him in the guts he would be sorry for you . . . sorry that there was such a defect in your character.

'My kitchen is not that well organized,' she said. 'I want some shelves put up for the pans and things. Do you know anyone who could do it for me? Someone who wouldn't charge the earth.'

Tony said, 'It's no use me attempting it. I can't hammer a nail in straight. What about Steve Trevorrow? Do you know Steve? He's a great man with the woodwork. Does his carpentry in the winter and works his boat in summer. He has the look of a fisherman, don't ask me why. I've had a few talks with him. He's an intelligent fellah all right. Quiet. I think he's read a lot. I'm sure he's read a lot. He told me he's read a lot. He repaired my studio after the gale. Replaced some glass. But I reckon the whole place is ready to collapse.'

And, before she could reply, 'It's a comfortable chair, is this. You don't get comfortable chairs these days, they're all these plastic and chrom t'ings, bloody terrible for the backside. My ould mother had a good chair. A great big t'ing you could curl up in. I used to curl up in it as a child, and I reckon oi could still curl up in it. It's the oddest, strangest t'ings that stay in the mind. Irrelevant t'ings.'

She decided to ignore the sudden bursts of his old accent.

'You haven't told me much about yourself at all,' she said.

'Have I not? Have I not, now? Well, now, let me see . . .' he mused, exaggerating his Irish brogue again, 'I was t' delicatest of t'irteen childrin. I was so small that oi was reared in a sock on the hob. Would you believe t'at. They t'ought I'd nivver live. But I did. I've lived all me life. Which goes to show, does it not, that you should never listen to other people. Or to be sure, you'll be dead before your time. Or never live at all.'

'Is that all? Is that your life's story?'

'Will you get a job in the shop, selling the pottery? You looked great in the shop last year.'

'It was only for a month. I was lucky to get it. I hope to work all summer this year.'

'What nonsense. He was lucky to get you. I'll give him the Divil if he doesn't take you on, the ould skinflint. He's damn lucky to get a girl like you selling his bloody ould pots.' He smiled at her and nodded his head to emphasize his words.

'You're a very beautiful girl, Miss Cleo.'

'I can almost believe it when you say so.' She smiled at him wryly, for so many had told her.

'And that friend of yours, Barbara, she's a beautiful girl, she has a lot of character. I'd like to paint her portrait.'

'Why don't you ask her? I expect she would be flattered.'

'Do you now?' he said. 'A pity. I shouldn't have thought that.'

Cleo was amused at the expression of disappointment on his face and the repeated raising of eyebrows as he let her apparently highly significant remark settle in his mind.

'Surely, she said, 'any woman would be flattered if an artist asked her to pose.'

'They would. That's the trouble! And they expect the artist to flatter them. I gave up painting the human figure for that reason. They expect too much. They demand too much from an artist. They demand more than his art. Could you believe that? More than his art. But there's some great paintings in faces, Cleo, some great paintings.'

'And why not me?' Cleo asked, frivolously.

'Oh come now. You're not pretending to be jealous, are you?'

'Of course I'm jealous. First you tell me I'm beautiful, and immediately after say you'd like to paint a portrait of Barbara. I think you are an old lecher.' She came and sat on the arm of the chair and put her arm around his neck.

'But you are a lovely old lecher.'

'You haven't painted portraits,' Tony said, 'since you came here.'

'No. I'd like to, some of the locals have very interesting faces, but I haven't the nerve to ask them. I can't afford to pay models, and people never seem to like my portraits, anyway. They would never sell.'

'Sell. Never mind the sell. You'll soon get to know the people, now.' A reference to John again. 'How long have you been here?'

'I came last summer . . .' she paused. 'Actually it was because of a local man that I came here in the first place. I met him in London, a long time ago when I was at art school and he said he was in love with me. I didn't know he was Cornish until one day someone was asking about his accent. And his name. It was awful, because I thought it was his real name for years, but it was only a nickname.'

'Oh!' Tony cried, 'They're great ones with the nicknames.'

'I thought "Shimshai" was a bit odd . . .'

'Shimshai! Bejaysus, do you know Shimshai?' He leaned back in the chair with his arms and legs spread in an attitude of amazement.

'Careful. You're knocking me off the chair.'

'Well, fancy that. Now fancy that. And he never said a word. I get a letter from him now and then and he never said a word. He's a dark horse, that Shimshai. He's coming back. Did you know that?'

'Yes. At Easter. He writes to me too. He was very kind to me in London. He's very nice.'

'Nice? He's a dark horse, I'm tellin' you. I'm raving jealous that he knows you and never said a word. Aye, it's like him, not to say anything. He would find it amusing to keep us in the dark about his relationships. He's . . . close!' He thought about it for a while. 'Introspective.' And he added suddenly, 'He's a great friend of Steve, the fisherman, or carpenter, or whatever you like to call him. They grew up together. They went to school together, but Steve left to learn a trade and Shimshai went on to college. A great shame, that, about Steve. He should have had the education, though I doubt it would have done him much good if he was to stay here. You'll have to meet him. You'll just have to meet a few more people.' He leapt from the chair. 'Tell you what. We'll have a party. There hasn't been a party for months. God, when I first came here we had parties all the time. I don't know what's happened to the bloody place. We'll have it in my studio. God, we've had some parties there.' He calmed down, remembering some disastrous nights. 'But it gets a bit hectic for an ould feller like me. Everybody comes, that's the trouble. But there will be no time for parties in the summer. Time you met a few people, and time I did too, I'm becoming a recluse in my old age. Yes, we'll invite ten people each and no gatecrashers. I've had a hundred in my studio before, and I didn't know who the hell they all were and couldn't find myself a bloody drink. Finished up stone-cold sober trying to throw them out at three o'clock in the morning. And trying to paint next day, you know, with a terrible buzzing in your ears and the whole place smelling of smoke and stale booze.' He shook his head, 'You don't mind if you've had a great time yourself, do you not?'

'Calm down, Tony.' He had been pacing up and down the room quite carried away by his enthusiasm. 'You'll bring on that heart attack you are always anticipating. I had thought of asking a few people here, but it's hardly big enough. Although, I suppose we could manage twenty.'

'No, no. We'll have it in my studio.'

'I'll invite Barbara. And . . . I don't know who else.'

'Shimshai! We'll invite Steve. And, oh, we must be careful or we'll have a hundred again.' He laughed aloud. 'Oh, we'll have a great time.' Excited as a child at the prospect. 'It'll do you good. Now I must be off. I want to paint. We'll have a great time.'

'But when?'

'Oh! Yes. On the Friday. Good Friday, eh? Shimshai won't be home until Easter. T'at's a good idea, an Easter party, is it not?'

He put his hat on and went to the door with his mind full of enthusiasm for life and his art, walked off down the road and came back.

'The shelves,' he said. 'I'll be asking Steve about the shelves. He's a great man with the woodwork. And he has an interesting face. Now there's a face you could paint. A lot of character.' He nodded in affirmation of his statement. 'Now I'm off to work. And remember what I said.'

He had said so much, more than he had ever said to her before, that she would never know to which part of their conversation he was referring. She watched him striding happily away before returning to her painting.

Tony's mind was toying with an idea for a composition depicting a fair-haired creature at the feet of a god. Cleo had the ability to stimulate him through her own self-doubts and questioning. That her torments regarding art were his own also he had not mentioned. He saw her as his disciple. He needed her adoration, and felt free to exploit her in furtherance of his art.

'Jesus Christ himself had twelve,' he muttered, 'I ask you for only one.'

Chapter Six

Cleo's cottage was High George's that was. It shared a common scantle-slated roof with the others in the row, with chimney-pots adorned with cowls to stop the down-draught when the east wind eddied and rebounded from the roofs and attics round about. Externally there was nothing, apart from the yellow door, to distinguish it from the rest. They are all small, with small windows and small doors, and granite lintels which wave with irregular undulations from house to house where they have settled down after the initial levelling by the builders. The lintels are now at rest, and will remain so, if undisturbed, for a thousand years, though doors might need rehanging, or windows easing when the sash-cords squeak.

Steve knocked on the yellow door and turned his back to it. Sure enough, Quizzy Maggie emerged from the adjacent house. She grunted with effort as she bent to place an empty milk bottle on the step.

'Jest puttin' a bottle out,' she said. She had never found out who had done that terrible thing to her brand-new hat, that time by the station steps. Steve nodded, said nothing. She went in and emerged again carrying a flasket of clothes to take up to the Island and spread on the grass to dry. To dry in the traditional way, spread in the sunshine on the grass of the Island, though visitors' kids ran all over them, and their dogs pissed on them. She only went up there to see who was who and what was what, using the old ways as an excuse, spreading a few towels or an old sheet on the grass while doing most of her washing in the new laundrette, down to the Ropewalk, where the Networks was. She had been alone for a terrible long time.

As she passed, she smiled, but only with her mouth, and her eyes were all inquisitive. She nodded slowly.

'She's in,' she said. 'I knaw she's in.'

'Good!' said Steve, and without expression stared her out, forcing her off up to the Island.

The door opened behind him and he turned to face Cleo. She saw the bag of tools on his back, the lengths of timber leaning against the wall.

'Oh. It's you,' she said. She was wearing jeans and a pale blue sweater, both bespattered with paint. Her sun-tanned feet were bare.

'Steve Trevorrow,' he said. 'I thought you were expecting me. Didn't Tony tell you I was coming today?'

'No. I mean yes, but I didn't know it was you. Come in.'

Steve took his tools into the kitchen, came back for the timber, shut the door and looked at her. 'Who were you expecting?'

'You. But I didn't know it *was* you. I mean, I've seen you around town, but I didn't know you were Steve Trevorrow.'

'I've seen you around too. It's surprising we haven't met, as you know Tony so well.'

They had not 'met'. In this town one rarely 'met' people. Not: 'I'd like you to meet so-and-so. So-and-so, this is Steve.' One saw them in passing. A new face among so many other new faces which came and went, and one saw them again without recognition, and again, until someone might ask 'Who's that fellah?' or 'I've seen her around, who is she?' and the recognized face became the familiar face, the nod a greeting. And they would say 'I've seen you around, but I don't know your name.' Then, so often, they disappeared—gone no one knew where. It was as if their total existence had been but that part of their lives lived around this harbour.

Cleo had come the previous summer, unnoticed among the general influx and swelling crowds of tourists. One of the many faceless faces, and Steve became aware of her as one becomes aware of spring—suddenly it's summer, and you try to recall when spring began, too late to live with the warming grass and the unfolding bracken, so that he could never remember when he first saw her. He remembered one day last September when he had walked up the sand in the sheltered corner of the harbour where a few late visitors were absorbing the last of the summer sun. He was carrying the skiff's oars over his shoulder, and he walked right past her, looking down at her as she lay in the sunlight, so close that sand from his footsteps fell upon her towel, and he had looked along the whole length of her brown body in that little black bikini. She had opened her eyes as his shadow fell across her face, and he had looked away and trudged along up the foreshore to his loft, remembering the fine grains of sand adhering to her temples and that her eyes were blue. Blue enough to swim in.

But there were so many girls to look at in the summer and at that time she was just another body lying in the sun. They come on to the sand in the harbour now, where years ago the smell of fish and tanning kept it clear, and the old men lean over the railings by the Lodge and watch the bodies oiled and cooking in the sun.

'That's a fine craft,' they say. Or, as the oil is rubbed on youthful skin, 'Giver her the lotion, boy. Giver her the lotion.' Watching hands massaging backs and bellies of warm young flesh.

'I'd rather be on that than on the dole, Silas.'

'I'd rather be in bed with she naked, than with you in your best suit, Tommy.'

'Now, there's a fine Porthleven stern. A fine starn-board, Ephraim.'

'Had a good look there, Steve. Comin' up the foreshore, jus' now.' They didn't miss much, up there on the Platt by the Lodge.

'A fine craft, Steve.'

'I've seen she before.'

'She? She's one of these here hartisis. She be'n and bought High George's house. Must have plenty of money. Young woman like that theer. With no man.'

'I 'spect she's got a man somewheer. Young woman like that.'

'Well, that's what they d' say, Steve, tha's all I can tell 'ee. Tha's what they d' say.'

They'll say anything in this bloody place. 'They'll say any bleddy thing,' he said.

'What you comin' to, Steve?' Silas Rouncefield grumbled. 'Swearin' so like that.'

She said, 'I've cleared everything away for you.' He was aware that she wore nothing under her blue sweater. 'I've put all the stuff in the studio.'

He tried to hide a smile, but she saw it, for her eyes were on him all the time. 'Why are you smiling?'

'Studio?' he said. 'You call it a studio, do you? We always call this the kitchen. What you call a kitchen, we call a scullery. The lounge, before it was all knocked into one like this, was the front room. It was always called that, even if it was at the back.' He looked around him. 'I've been in this house before. Never thought to hear it called a studio.'

There was little furniture; a deal table (now called 'pine'), with two bare wooden chairs tucked beneath it, a small dresser with a few bits of cheap china, and a big armchair with worn arms and a cushion squashed into a corner of the seat. There was a low divan against a wall, and near the window a colour-splashed arrangement of boxes held paints, jars, brushes, old rags and a stack of bare canvases. Standing on an easel in the centre of the room was a half-finished portrait of a man wearing blue dungarees and a guarnsey. He was tying a rope to a bollard and his face was effectively hidden. That rope wouldn't hold pussy, Steve thought.

The kitchen was hardly big enough to hold the cooker, sink and cupboard, all on one wall, and he had little space for his tools on the floor.

'We can move the table into the other room,' she said, and he noticed that she refrained from using the word 'studio'. It was always easier to do things alone, but they will help, these women. When they were in the other room he lifted the table over the armchair and placed it out of the way.

He began work, plugging the walls and fixing brackets, while Cleo stood watching him from the doorway, occasionally handing him a piece of wood or a tool, and asked him questions. She asked him about the bay, the rocks, where did he fish, about his family, his mother and father, were they all Cornish? Steve wished that she would get to hell out of it and let him finish the job in peace.

The sun came through the window in a sudden shaft of brilliance as a break in the clouds passed overhead, and the dust from his saw was transformed into a million dancing stars as it fell on to Cleo's bare brown feet. She spread her toes to absorb the warmth but Steve grew hot with the effort of his work and stopped to remove his guarnsey, dragging it over his head, ruffling his hair, and pulling his shirt out with the stretching of his arms, exposing his back and stomach, so that he had to stuff it down again before resuming work. All the time, she watched him, making him feel uncomfortable under her scrutiny, but finally the brackets were fixed and he placed the shelves on them. 'Can you hold them in place,' he asked, 'while I drive the screws up?'

She came and held the top shelf and he tried to ignore the outline of her breasts between the outstretched arms. He concentrated on fixing the shelves and finishing the job as soon as possible, conscious all the while of her shape, her hair, and those intense blue eyes. She was a fine craft. She was lovely. She made him nervous. 'Well, there we are,' he said as casually as possible. 'All done.' He bent to pick up his tools, catching sight of her brown feet and dirty toenails. 'I'll just clear up the mess.'

'Never mind that,' she said, 'I'll do it later.' Why did she keep looking at him?

'Would you pose for me?' she said.

'*Pose*?' He felt his face flush uncontrollably.

'Yes. You have a strong face. A lot of character. I'd like to paint you.'

'Oh. I don't know about that.'

'It wouldn't take long, for a portrait. In fact I would like to do three portraits of you.' Steve laughed a nervous laugh of quandary, but she decided to push him to the limit. 'One portrait, one in your fishing gear, and a nude.'

'Nude?'

'Yes. You have a good body. The muscles are well defined. I'd like you in a working pose, or swimming perhaps. In clear green water. Do you swim?'

Steve felt again the hot flush in his cheeks, and turned his back on her in embarrassment, pretending to look for more tools on the floor, picking up an old screw and a bent nail. She had touched him in an even more tender spot than she realized, for it was his own morality which was put to the test, that day there in her kitchen. How many times had he told himself, 'It is not indecent. Nudity is not indecent.' But pose! Bleddy hell. Not bleddy likely. Oh no. She would look at him as no one had ever looked at him before; seeing the veins in his arms, the muscles of his abdomen, the hairs on his ass and his dangling balls. All scrutinized with searching eyes and put in a picture to be placed before the world. His face. Oh no. Not bleddy likely. And by a woman? Painted by a woman. He would get hard. Sure too. Ah—yeah. Pose all right. That's good, that is. These bleddy artists were all the same. Pose all right. Over there on the bleddy bed. His blush turned to fire as the initial embarrassment flared to anger at her affrontery, and he turned to face her.

'No need to be embarrassed,' she said.

'I'm not embarrassed.'

'Good.' She leaned back against the sink and folded her arms. 'Most men would be embarrassed. Some of them would be angry.' She was smiling. 'They would think I was a "brazen hussy".' Her head tilted slightly to one side as she regarded him with outward calm and watched his reactions. 'They would think,' she continued, 'that I wanted them to have it away with me,' with a jerk of the head, 'over there on the divan. And a lot of them would try me on, even though I didn't mean that at all.'

'I didn't think anything like that,' he said defiantly, obviously lying.

'Good,' she said.

A pause, then, 'What do 'ee mean, "Good"?'

'I mean you have a fine body, you're not embarrassed, you won't make a pass at me . . . the perfect model. They are hard to . . .'

'I just don't want to, that's all. Pose!' he scoffed at the idea.

'You *are* embarrassed.' She shrugged and picked up the broom. 'Never mind,' she said, indifferently. 'I oughtn't to have asked.' She rolled the mat with her foot and swept the dust and shavings into a heap. She stooped down with dustpan and brush. Steve watched her. He was stuck in the corner of her little kitchen, holding his canvas tool-bag in front of him with both hands on the rope handles. He wanted to go, but he would have to squeeze past her, and she made no attempt to let him by. The dust was swirling again in the shaft of sunlight, settling on her feet and coating her toes in grime. She seemed never to wear shoes.

Pose! He was flattered by her request. Through the door he could see her stack of canvases and the boxes and jars of paints and brushes. The bits of rag. Two paintings were visible on the wall, they were frameless and stood out sharply against the whiteness of the room. He didn't like them, but he could not determine why. Both were of places he knew, the Harbour and Maen a Mor. All the artists painted them, time and time again, tide in, tide out, figure in blue, patterns in the moorings, ripples, reflections, and the bleddy sun always shinin'. At least these were not like that. 'The glass is fallin',' he said to himself as he switched his eye from one to the other, trying to see what was wrong with them. Come to think of it, Maen a Mor did look a bit like that sometimes. He narrowed his eyes, concentrating on one picture, and there was no blue in it. Two-thirds of it were sea and sky and there was no blue. It was nearly all in tones of brown. Purple bleddy sea! And the rocks were dark green. It was Maen a Mor all right, he knew every foot and hand-hold of the towering mass. He had climbed all the faces of it as a boy, progressing from the easy route on the landward side to the almost sheer cliff over the sea when he was a young man, egged on by the voices of Tim and Sam, already at the top, while Mary and Martha watched from the cliff-top opposite. They pretended to be picking sea-pinks, but they were watching all right. Freddie never did climb Maen a Mor. The cracks and crevices were all here in the painting, and, mentally, he climbed it again, placing his hands and feet in the time-shattered fissures, following the way up over the taut canvas.

Everything he remembered of the scores of ascents was here—the slight overhang half-way up, the ledge at the top, everything. There was even the sensation, somehow portrayed, of the vertigo he felt after his first climb, when he stood upright at the summit trembling with fear as the blood from his knees trickled down and congealed in his crumpled socks. But this was not a painting of the rock as he knew it. It was not just a cold irregular pinnacle emerging from a swirling sea. From the drab browns and yellows a strength emerged, a straining skyward, and, although she had captured the mood of thrusting defiance he had beaten as a child, there was a movement and a threat of eruption in the long-cooled masses which he could

T.S.E.—E

not understand. It was as if the ancient smouldering heat was still molten beneath the cool surface crystals, threatening to expend its power in a last explosion.

She took an age to sweep up the dust, and all the time he was standing there, waiting to go, looking down at the sunlight striking her hair. Then he realized that she was embarrassed. More than he was. He saw that it had not been easy for her. Asking him. That she had put on a mask. At last she could make no more pretence of sweeping up the few specks of remaining dust, and stood up, facing him, seeing the silent laughter in his face, sensing the tension between them slipping away. With a shy smile at first, lest his laughter be derisive, she joined him in mirth, sitting on the floor with her head back against the door. They laughed together like children running from mischief.

'I didn't do that very well, did I?'

'No. I really did think you were a brazen hussy.'

'That's what becomes of trying to be something which you're not.' She gave a sigh and flopped back against the door, exhausted. 'I promise never to do it again. It's all Tony's fault. Suggesting I use you as a model.'

They were silent for a while, appraising each other afresh. Then she rose and said she would make some coffee, and they sat drinking it on the floor of the kitchen while Steve looked through the door at her paintings again.

'I was never any good at art,' he said, 'I don't understand your pictures.'

'Don't you like them?'

'I didn't say that. That one, of Maen a Mor . . .'

'What?'

'Maen a Mor. It means ''Rock-in-the-sea''. It looks . . . well, phallic.'

'It's meant to.'

'Oh.' He turned to study it again, then turned back to her and studied her face. There was a long silence while they simply looked at each other, smiling a little. 'I would like to paint your portrait,' she said.

'I'll think about it.'

'I can do it here in the studio. No one need know—if you are shy.' She smiled as if to say that being shy was the finest attribute a man could have.

'Studio!' he said. 'High George would die laughing if he was alive.'

'Well, that's what I call it. Who, did you say?'

'High George. He lived here.'

'High George? Was that his name?'

'He was called . . . eh . . . um . . . dammee, I can't remember. High George was his nickname. That's what everybody called him. He was quite a character. There was a model for you.'

'What a splendid name.'

'Most nicknames are.'

'He didn't look after the place very well.'

'Oh?'

'Look at that beam over the door. It's full of woodworm. You would think he would have done something about that.'

Steve grinned, but tried to hide it. He looked at the holes in the beam. 'Have you been treating it?'

'Of course. I bought some stuff to kill them.'

'I shouldn't bother.'

'But, it will spread.' Steve was killing himself with laughter, but kept it back long enough to say, 'High George kept his house like a ship. He even had ship's names for everything. He called all the rooms after parts of a ship. That's the galley, this is the cabin, upstairs was the fo'castle. He lived alone for a long time. When he'd finished his washing-up he used to stick his knife and fork in that beam. Any woodworm in there have been stabbed to death long ago.'

The sat on the floor drinking their coffee slowly, she wanted him to stay, he not wanting to go, sensing a mutual attraction. There was something about her dirty feet that fascinated him, and his eyes kept straying from her face to those grimy toes. They were small, dancer's feet, and he thought how sensual they were, stretched out towards him, within reach of his hand, and he wanted to take hold of them to feel the strength and sensitivity of them.

They felt a tension slipping away and were totally at ease together and he returned a look as frank as hers, a questioning searching look which neither wished to end.

The coffee was gone, and he rose from the floor, for there was no excuse for staying longer. She rose too, and made some conversation, asking about where he acquired his skill in woodwork if he was a fisherman, and he told her that he had served his time.

'It is my trade,' he said.

'It must be useful to have two skills.'

'Yes. Sometimes.'

'Which do you like best?'

'I . . .' He stopped himself, recognizing this conversation for what it was, and shook his head, grinning widely.

'Sorry,' she said, 'I'm asking too many questions.'

He nodded. Still grinning. 'I must be going.' Put his hat on. 'Promised Mary I'd paint the kitchen window this afternoon.'

'Mary?'

'My wife.'

'Oh.'

They went to the door where Steve stopped and looked back at the painting of Maen a Mor. 'I like that one,' he said, 'now that I know what it's all about.'

They said goodbye, fully aware, both of them, that it was not, and Steve slung his bag over his shoulder and wandered up through Fore Street to home. He stopped at the gallery in Will's Lane, with his bag on his back, his jeans all scruffy from muck and many washings, the tops of his shoes scuffed off from much kneeling on concrete floors, and he looked through the window at the paintings.

Some of Tony's paintings were in the gallery. You can tell Tony's paintings a mile off. Cleo's were like them in a way. She was lovely. Though they tended to be quieter in tone. Had such beautiful hair. Whereas Tony's were bright, bold. And those neat little tits under her jumper. Though that was hardly surprising from someone who had been painting as long as Tony. Those eyes looking at him. She had looked at him with expressionless eyes, yet searchingly, and he had returned an equal scrutiny. Bland, uncompromising. He had given away more to Cleo, in a glance, than he had revealed to anyone else in his life. There had been an understanding in her look which disturbed him, and he went back through the whole incident in her cottage, wondering why he had felt so uneasy and nervous in her presence yet, on the other hand, he had never felt so much at ease with a woman after they had laughed together.

Bit of a nerve, asking him to pose—just like that—no preliminary enquiries as to whether he might even consider it.

'Pose? Bleddy hell.'

What a crant.

Chapter Seven

Mary greeted him with, 'About time,' raising her voice above the grinding of the washing-machine. She was in a bad mood.

'What do you mean, "About time"? How can I get to the window with all this stuff in the kitchen? Everything is full of steam. How can I paint on wet wood? You're not ready for me.' He saw that her scolding was just an excuse.

'You don't have no trouble painting that old boat. It's a funny thing to me, but every time I want something done, you find some excuse.'

'I'm not finding excuses. I thought you said I could have the kitchen to myself today. The mats will have to come up, and the table be moved.'

'More trouble to paint a little window. Lord knows I've been waiting long enough.'

'Look. You didn't want it done till the spring. For the past month I've been on the mackerel, and before that getting the boat ready. I can only do one job at a time.'

'Be'n on the mack'rel! And what for? That's what I want to know. What for? There hasn't be'n fifty pounds in all of it. And I've got lodgers coming in next month. Everything is left go till the last minute with you.'

'Last year I made enough. You were glad to have it. You have to keep trying.'

'Keep trying! Huh. You could be like Boney Enny. Don't see he out every day. He d' just wait till somebody else d' start catching a few, and then he d' go out.'

'Yes. Well, I like to keep trying. Get them first, while the price is high.'

'You like to keep trying! And while you are muckin' about in that old boat, I have to struggle to make ends meet. You have no idea what it's like. Wouldn't be so bad if you helped me in the summer with the lodgers. 'Stead of that you're hangin' around down on the quay all day, yarnin' with that crowd down the Lodge.'

'Oh, Mary. You know very well that we do all right from the boat. I make as much as anybody else, and with the bit of carpentry in the winter, I don't see that you have anything to complain about.'

'Oh,' she cried impatiently, 'you make me sick. Look at your hands. Grouted with muck and grease. Your hair is full of dust . . . I don't know what you're like. Carpenterin'. You had the chance of a big job and turned it down. Don't forget that.'

There was no coping with her in one of these moods, but he made another attempt. 'I'm still earnin'. I can only be in one place at a time.'

She changed her tactic. 'When did we have a holiday, eh? You tell me that! Some people go abroad every year. Some people have a nice car. All we ride around in is a beastly old van.'

So that was it. She had been listening to Martha going on again. That damned woman had caused more rows in his house . . .

'I need a van for the gear, he said, 'my tools, and gear for the boat.'

'*Boat, boat, boat*! That's all I ever hear. Boat, boat, boat. I'm fed up with it. *Fed up with it*!' The washing-machine gurgled and went into a slow slopping of soapy water and suds. 'Martha and Freddie have booked to go abroad again this year. Where are we goin'? Nowhere, as usual.' She had revealed the cause of her discontent and now he could cope with it.

'They can afford it. Because Freddie has collateral,' he said, grinning openly. 'I haven't.'

'No. And never will.'

'No, s'pose.' Sometimes he doubted that she was so insensitive. That she could not see how she hurt him.

'If it was left to you, we should never have nawthen. Martha and Freddie make more money in six months than we do all year round. If you were to sell that boat we could . . .'

'No! How many times do I have to tell you? *No*. Now, no.'

'You make me sick.'

'Martha and Freddie,' he said contemptuously. 'It's never "Freddie and Martha", is it?'

'I don't know what you mean.'

'No, I don't suppose you do,' he sighed.

Freddie's hands were soft, his fingernails even and clean. The skin of his face glowed pink from many washings and was free of sun and salt-dried fissures, and had not known an unshaven stubble for twenty years. His hair was trimmed every fortnight, and showed no sign of receding but just a trace of grey which Freddie brushed into prominence, for he thought it made him look distinguished, befitting a man of collateral. He held his cigarette between finger and thumb, continually flicking the ash, and screwed up his eyes every time he put the filter to his tight-pursed lips. 'There's nothing worse than nicotine on the fingers when you are serving guests,' he said. 'People notice things like that, you know.' He liked to sit in his comfortable lounge, or go out on to the patio, and look at his property. The carpets, the furniture, the well-equipped kitchen, the car park and the imposing cut-granite front of the building gave a man a sense of achievement. He was a man of property, with negotiable collateral, and he had started with nothing.

'If you was to sell that boat . . .'
'Oh, assoles to 'ee.'
'Hm. That's all you are fit for—language! Language and drink.'
'Look, are you gettin' out of this kitchen, or aren't 'ee?'
'It's too late to start painting now. I've got pasties to make for this evenin'. So you can clear out. Go down and do that job for John Ashton's fancy woman. Earn a shilling or two.'
'It's done. Done it this morning.'
'Well clear out all the same. I don't want you hangin' around here all day.'
He swore softly to himself and went out. He strolled downalong to see who was in the Lodge.

There was an atmosphere of quiet preparation, an unhurried annual rejuvenation which descended on the town in spring, when the shops and cafés underwent a face-lift, with new signs and coats of paint, and along the harbour the railings were chipped free of the winter's rust and coated again with red lead and aluminium. A cleaning ritual of expiation to appease the gods of hope for the sins of last summer, together with a prayer, here and there, that this year might be more propitious than the last. Most hoped that this year they would achieve their target of gross takings, and if they did, another target would be set for the year after—for therein lies progress.

Others hoped and prayed that maybe a touch of paint here and there would bring in enough extra customers to stave off bankruptcy for another year.

There were some who viewed the preparations with trepidation, fearing that there would be even more litter in the streets, more fights after dark, and more puddles of beery spew drying on the pavements in the mornings—old people.

Strolling along the wharf, with his hands thrust deep into his pockets, Steve saw James, and he fell in with him there by Pollard's that was, and went along to the Lodge. Uncle Joe was giving her a coat of tar, to keep the water out.

'I see the cards is out,' he said, and they all read what they had to say. For several square feet the wall of the Lodge was impregnated with thousands of tin-tacks where the cards had been nailed up in the past. The wall was solid iron. There was so much iron in the wall that they couldn't drive another tack, and they have since put up some contraption with a glass front to slide the cards into, but at the time Cleo lived in the town they were still using tacks. You can see them in the wall of the Lodge, if you've a mind to look. Steve read the card aloud, for Uncle Joe couldn't read or write.

> The funeral of the late
> Mr ROBERT ARTHUR STEVENS
> Beloved Father of Sarah Stevens
> will be held
> At two o'clock on Wednesday.
> Friends please accept this
> the only invitation.
> (Family flowers only)

'Robbie's gone then, Steve.'
'I never knew that Robbie was gone.'
Strangers find it amusing. That the cards are tacked on the wall of the Lodge and placed in shop windows. 'Why not simply put it in the paper?' they say. 'But what if we die on Saturday?' 'Don't follow, old chap.' 'The *Echo* is out on Friday.' Why must they question such an honoured custom?
'When did Robbie go?'
'Af'noon funerals is a pest, Ste'.' James said, 'We d' always have mornin' funerals in our family. The proper time for funerals is in the mornin'. It's the proper time.' Nearly everybody had af'noon funerals, except for James's family, but they're a cussed crowd, that family. Everybody knows that.
'Yes'day,' Uncle Joe said. 'He went yes'day. There'll be a brear many theer. Everybody knawed 'n.'
They made their way around the Lodge to lean on the railings and have a yarn about old Robbie Stevens, where they could overlook the slipway and the harbour and see what was going on and keep an eye on things. A group of children were building sandcastles in front of the incoming tide, adorning them with shells and gulls' feathers and bits of driftwood gathered from the shore.
'That's the way of it, my lad,' James muttered. 'High George is gone. Now Robbie is gone—that's the way of it. "For we are but yesterday, and know nothing, because our days on earth are but a shadow." The Book of Job, Ste'. But a shadow.'

Steve nodded solemnly. 'Robbie knew the Bible,' he said.

'I did a little job for'n last month, too. Never thought he would go so quick.'

'Very religious, Ste'.'

'I suppose when the old lady went he gave up,' Joe said.

'Sarah will be on her own now. Funny how she never got married. She was a good-lookin' woman, years ago.' Steve watched the children dodging the tide.

'She must be about your age,' James said, 'She must be your race.'

'A bit younger. A bit younger than we. I could never understand how she didn't get married.'

'Some is like that, Joe. Stay home with the old people.'

''Es, I s'pose.'

'Thought she would have done you, Joe,' Steve said, still watching the children. Joe spat at a gull sitting on the sea below them, and said nothing.

The children shrieked with fright as an extra-large wave among the gentle surges of the harbour swept around their castle.

'Ha!' said James. 'Look out here.' Steve glanced at Joe, who was looking at the children. 'Wet feet, now. Wet sockers for all hands. Smacked backsides for they, d'reckly,' James said.

'That fair-headed one is Sam Pascoe's little maid,' Steve said, thinking of Iris with another one on the way.

'Pretty l'l thing.' They watched the children with amusement, seeing the tradgegy of life in their guileless faces and unfeigned reaction to the incident. A heap of sand was all that remained of their morning's work. Fort, sandcastle, houses and gardens with their decorations of shells and feathers all devastated in an instant. A second wave and there was no trace but a few bits of flotsam on the tideline. The children sat on the baulks to wring out their socks, stretching them out of shape, and were soon engaged in a pitched battle with the wet, soggy socks as weapons, slapping them across each others faces with hysterical giggles.

'Be screechin' d'reckly,' Joe said, and James chuckled quietly. 'We never had wet sockers very often,' he said, 'because we only wore boots to school and on Sundays. That's in the summer, mind. We had boots for the winter. I'm not saying that.'

'Don't see children wearing boots now,' Steve mused. 'We had boots for school and playing about in, and shoes for Sundays, then we had shoes all the time.'

'We called our boots "hob stankers",' James said. 'Hob stankers. Did 'ee ever?' He ran his hand over his face as if wringing some unpleasant memory from his mind. 'Things is defferent now, Steve. I was put away to sea when I was fourteen. Fourteen!' He tossed his head in disgust. 'One of the crew,' he said. 'Put away fishin' at fourteen. Like a man. My very first trip we went over to Ireland, herrin' drivin'. In the wenter, you understand. It was cold, Ste'. Oh, 'es, it was cold all right. 'Nuff to take your very life.'

'They are only children at fourteen now,' Steve said.

'Things is better now, my lad.' James straightened his back and rubbed his hand over the wool of his guarnsey tight across his chest. He greeted Tommy Blue and Silas Rouncefield, who turned up together after reading the card. 'Here we, now.'

'Have 'ee had your breakfast?' 'Here we.'

'Aaah,' said James in contentment as he turned to face the warm spring sunshine. 'Mind, we had some good times. I edn sayin' we never.'

'We had some good times,' Tommy said.

'But, things is better now, understand?'

'Some things is better,' Silas said ominously, unaware of the preceeding conversation,' and some edn. James ignored him; he was going to tell his yarn.

'The First War was bad times, Ste'. Bad times.' He passed his fingers over the grey stubble on his chin. He was going to tell his yarn all right. Tommy Blue leaned forward in anticipation. Silas Rouncefield, on the other hand, leaned back against the railings and peered from the shadow of his peaked cap, holding his folded newspaper in front of him with two hands. ''Es,' he said deeply, 'terrible times.'

'The First War was bad times,' James began, 'and people aren't the same, Steve, after times like that. Bad times can do terrible things to people. I remember, one time, there was no herrin'. Here with Christmas comin' on. As i' always was when the herrin' started. And in they days, no herrin' was no nawthen. You understand? No nawthen!' He leaned over the railing and also spat at the gull on the water. The gull cocked its head and regarded him with an eye of yellow contempt. 'Well,' James said, 'perhaps a gurrie or two, but no *herrin'*. No herrin' like it belonged. Anyhow. We was away over to the eastern shore. Light breeze, south-east. Dark! Muzzy owld night. Knaw? Nets all shut. Waitin'.

'Now, what was i' to be? Should us have a haul, or no? Waitin'. I had a pump-shep—I can remember that. Last of all, Steve, last of all, the say was boilin' with them. *Boilin'*. Come up all about us. Any *amount* of herrin'. And we started haulin', haulin'. Haulin' them, Ste', as hard as we could haul.

'Hen'y said, ''Put out the light, boys. Put out the light,'' and pointed away to the no'thard. We all looked, now, and lo and behold it was Joe Mully and they tackin' down towards us. And behind they

was Mathy Gezzah's party (what names we d' put upon people).
'Now! They might have seen we was haulin', or they might not, I don't knaw, but boats is like gannets—where the fish are, they gather, and if the others saw we haulin' they would be down upon us all hands. And that's a coddle! All fishin' too close, with nets foulin' and one thing and another. A proper coddle. Besides, Ste', we all knawed what a good catch all around the fleet would do. A poor price on the market, now that's what i' meant. Now that's the way it was, Steve . . . we doused the light.'

James stopped to draw breath, thinking of that dark night, and letting the yarn have the proper time in telling.

'Here we, now! Brear thing aboard. All hands haulin', and laughin'. They was comin' aboard fit 'nough to sink her. Joe Mully and they made away to the westward. Mathy Gezzah and they hove-to to shut nets at the back of The Bezzack. We had them to ourselves. I never *seen* so many herrin'. Young Dan'l aboard of we was nearly screechin'. Shakin' his head, he was, trying' to stop the tears. A grown man screechin', Ste'. "My little maid shall have a new frock out of this," he said, "as sure as the Lord's in heaven." "And a goose for we," I said. And all hands haulin' and they was comin' aboard fit 'nuff to sink her. Scads o' them, Ste'. *Scads* of them.

'Last, Mathy looked agin me, and he said, "What are we doin', James?"

' "Doin'?" I said. "We're haulin'," I said. "What do 'ee think we're doin'?"

'He catched howled of my sleeve, Ste', like that.' James took hold of Steve's sleeve and grasped it tight in his fist.

'Like that. And Mathy nodded across the bay to home, and then he said, "Theer's little cheldern in theer," he said, "with no shoes upon their feet and no meat in their bellies. That's what we're doin', James. *That's* what we're doin'. And the birthday of the Lord comin' on, here. That is what we are doin'."

'We, all hands, stopped haulin'. Lookin' agin one another from eye to eye. And we couldn't look one upon the other . . .'

' "I'll light the light," Hen'y said, "James, give them a blast on that horn." '

James shook his head, and shifted his cap with one hand, briefly exposing the whiteness of his scalp. 'We put out the light,' he said, 'We done that. We put out the light.'

They stared silently at the harbour, unwilling to intrude upon the respectful appreciation of a good yarn told. Steve had heard the yarn before, of course, as had Tommy and Silas, but he enjoyed hearing it again, savouring the pauses and emphases in James's voice, as one enjoys the second reading of a good book. James gazed at the sea, as if he still could not believe that they could have done such a thing, so many years ago. 'They must have been hard times,' Steve said.

They stared at the sea until their minds wandered from those old times and Tommy Blue said, 'He still habn't come, I see.'

'Who in the world is he?' Silas grumbled. 'Leavin' a boat so long.'

'A stranger,' James told them. 'An up-country man.'

'Nuff said,' Silas observed.

'They don't give it a thought,' Tommy reckoned.

They were still intrigued to know who could leave such a valuable boat in the harbour for weeks on end without so much as bailing her out. Even Tommy Blue had no idea who he was, and Tommy knew most of what went on around the harbour, for since retiring the harbour had become his sole interest. He had at last fulfilled his life's ambition. After a youth of poverty he had spent his life at sea, in sail and steam, fair weather and foul, and had finished up crewing for a millionaire in the Mediterranean.

'That was all right, that was, Ste'. Hee Hee. Nothin' to it.'

He had twice been fished from the sea after his ship had been sunk in two world wars and he knew the value of life. He knew exactly what he wanted to do when he retired. He had considered a bit of a garden, putting ships in bottles, doing a bit of fishing, and keeping pigeons, but had decided against all of them. Tommy Blue had taken a long time to make up his mind, but he had decided, in the end, that after a lifetime of hard work he would do absolutely nothing, and he did it with a determination conditioned by sixty years of striving. He had a few more years left to live, and after so long abroad he was quite happy to let them slip peacefully by while he sat in the sun on the seat by the Lodge. In winter he went inside and sat by the tall tortoise stove and gossiped and listened to gossip. And the yarns. Tommy's eyesight wasn't too good and he screwed up his eyes behind the wire-framed glasses as he peered at the stranger's boat lying safely at the moorings Steve had put down for her.

'Dicky Admiral,' he said, screwing up his eyes and raising his head in an attempt to see over the defect in his vision, 'Dicky Admiral said he d' belong up London.'

'Dicky Admiral!' said Silas.

'London!' said James, with contempt, as if London was some particularly insidious vice. 'London!'

Steve laughed. 'Quite a few people do live up London,' he said.

James turned to him with a face bursting with indignation. 'I knaw that. I don't want you to tell me that.'

Steve thought, Oh Christ, here we go.

'I have be'n to London you knaw,' James said.

Tommy Blue looked from one to the other with an expectant grin, winked at Silas Rouncefield, but Steve remained silent. He knew James well enough to realize that any remark or comment, however conciliatory, would be taken as an offence when he was in one of his sudden moods of aggression. Steve had had enough argument for one day, with Mary. There was silence between them, and Tommy Blue could see that there was no fun to be had here. So he shoved off.

'Gone up'long,' he said, 'to do me arrants.'

'And me too,' said Silas in a wavering tenor, 'before the shops are shut. Anybody would think I had nawthen to do.' His voice crashed into a resounding bass, 'Stood here yarnin'.'

'Hang on,' said James, remembering his own errands, 'I'll stroll up'long with 'ee.'

Steve was left alone. He went across the Platt and leaned on the railings by the road, watching them amble away up the Prom. Three old men. Silas, tall and upright, thin as a lathe. James, small and compact and wiry. Tommy Blue already showing signs of shrinking away in his loose reefer-jacket. They were all about the same age. The same race. The same race as Robbie, dead and gone.

Tim Penberthy drove past in his Jaguar and pulled up outside the pub. He left his car in a No Waiting area, right plonk on the double yellow lines, and left the key in the ignition. Freddie was with him. What was Freddie doing going into the pub with Tim at this time of day? They must have been 'doing business'. Martha wouldn't know, that's for sure. Unless Freddie had been seeking advice on the management of his collateral.

Steve heaved himself off the railings to follow them into the pub, grinning widely to himself at Freddie's new nickname. The name he would carry to his grave. Whether he liked it or not. Whether he knew it or not. Collateral Fred!

Chapter Eight

Af'noon funerals *were* a pest. A man had to go out working in the morning, and then come home to get all best-changed just for an hour. And it was hardly worth changing for work again afterwards. Besides, you never felt like working much after a funeral, especially when it was somebody like old Robbie Stevens. But most funerals were in the af'noons. Say what you like—most were in the af'noons.

Steve always felt uncomfortable all best-changed and never knew where his things were. His black tie and white shirt. Mary always had them somewhere or other, all ready, but he would have to ask for them, to acknowledge the fact that she had taken so much trouble in preparing them. The washing and ironing. He called down the stairs.

'Where's my clean gear, Mary?'.

She didn't hear. Steve went out on the landing and leaned out over the banister rail. 'Mary, where's my gear?' No answer. She was out in the kitchen. He went down to her, rubbing his freshly washed face in a towel. 'Where's my clean gear, Mary?' he asked.

'Aren't you ready yet? You'll be late!'

'Yes.'

'Your shirt is in the bottom drawer with the rest of them. Your tie is in the wardrobe. You don't look very far!'

'No.'

Shirt in the drawer, tie in the wardrobe, and Robbie in his box. He dressed slowly, tying his tie three times before he was happy with the knot, getting it creased in the process. He combed his hair, then brushed it with Mary's brush. He combed his beard, studying himself in the mirror. Here beginneth the funeral of the beardless ones. The two generations of shaven chins and haircreams. Robbie's father, and our grandfathers, all that race, they all had beards, and then they died out of fashion. Robbie never had a beard, and our fathers never had beards. Steve's mind wandered among the features of dead fashions as he stood motionless before the mirror, seeing his face framed in the successive progression of styles which had adorned the men of preceding generations. His mind recalled the evolution of his own features, and he stared at the eyes which studied his passive face from the misted depths of the mirror before him. The face of his childhood, unlined and pink; the down of youth and strong young teeth; the first faint lines and the salt-tanned skin. The laughter and tears all gone, and look at it now! Grizzled and creased and thin on top. He wondered if he was good-looking. If he had ever been handsome. And wondered how his face would age in the years to come, where the lines would go, and the hollows grow, and how the flesh would hang when the eyes were closed and lifeless in a silk-lined box as Robbie's were today. He tried to see what that artist party saw in his face. Why she wanted to paint his portrait. Pose! She was a fine craft. His face was ordinary, he decided, nothing special.

Time to make tracks. Knowing nearly everybody. Greeting his friends, people in the street.

'Hello, boy.'

'Yow!'

'All right?'

'A1.' They could see that he was all best-changed.

'Goin' to the funeral?'

''Es. Robbie's funeral.' He fell in with Tommy Blue.

'We were shepmates,' Tommy said.

Together to Robbie's house, to the little-used front door, where a crowd of dark-clothed men stood talking quietly in twos and threes, and greeted Steve and Tommy solemnly before resuming their subdued conversation.

'He was the first one to have an engine aboard, you know.'

'Kept up with the times.'

Inside the house to pay respect to Sarah. 'I should have thought,' somebody said, 'that it would have be'n a men-only funeral. I don't want no women wailin' after me.'

She was wearing a dark grey coat, with a black hat and black gloves, and she greeted him with a faint smile. Steve wondered what to say. For the old man had lived a good life. Had a good innings, as the English say, with their mania for sporting terms. He had lived his span. Three score years and ten. Plus another ten or more by reason of strength. And for the last five Sarah had nursed both him and her mother. She had little reason for sorrow in her bereavement, and now Steve saw the fatigue of sleepless vigil and the strain of the funeral showing in her eyes. He thought she had been crying a little and wondered why, for the old people could not be first and last too.

He said, 'Hello, Sarah. I was sorry to hear the news.'

'He was very fond of you, Steve.'

'He was a good man, Sarah. A good man gone.'

'We can't be first and last too, Steve,' she said.

'No, we can't be first and last too.'

Quizzy Maggie was there. She kept farting around with cups and plates in the back kitchen. Arranging. Doing that which had to be done. Insensitive as a block of elm through familiarity with death. Wanting the thing done right. 'He was my second cousin,' she said, and Steve nodded, looking at Sarah who observed him with a sad stare which he found disconcerting; which reminded him of forgotten fears and future dreads.

'I heard,' he found himself saying, 'that he passed away in his sleep.'

'He asked for the Book,' Sarah said, 'though he belonged to reach out for it himself. And when I gave it to him, he held it high up on his chest, under his chin almost. He was holding it with his right hand. With the other, he held on to mine.' She hesitated before continuing, in a small distant voice, 'It was as if he had decided . . . that it was time to go.'

And he saw that Sarah had been crying for the lonelines of it. The loneliness of the years to come.

Quizzy Maggie burst into a spasm of tears, and Steve remembered that time when he had kissed Sarah in the shadow of the lighthouse, behind the upturned stern of Taffy's punt, so many years ago, and he heard Maggie crying, 'He's gone to a far better place, Sarah. A far better place,' wiping her eye on a black-edged hanky. 'He's gone home to the Lord, Sarah, my cheeld. To a far better place.'

Sarah said, 'Yes, Maggie.' And Steve saw the intelligence of Robbie flash briefly in the daughter's eyes, for Quizzy Maggie cried floods of tears at everybody's funeral, and Steve had no time for her, but in Sarah's face he saw a compassion and understanding that was the direct inheritance from her father.

'*Tim Penberthy took 'ee home. A couple of times.*'

'*I never left 'n kiss me nor nawthen.*'

'Time,' the undertaker said quietly, 'to bring 'n down.'

Sarah nodded. 'All right, Peter.' And as Peter and his young apprentice went up the narrow, winding stairs, Maggie said, 'They'll have a brear job bringin' 'n down over they stairs.'

Sarah went into the back kitchen where she would not have to watch the coffin taken from the house. 'Come in here, Maggie,' she said. And Maggie followed, after glancing once more up the stairs, for there was an authority in Sarah's voice which was final. Steve had never heard her speak like that before.

They brought him down feet first, with the coffin's silver handles scraping the banisters and the papered wall. He was nearly upright, and Peter and his helpers were straining under the weight. A little plaster from the wall fell upon the stairs and was stepped into the carpet.

'Let's give 'ee a hand, boy,' Steve said. Nearly upright! Peter had most of the weight. He must be all slipped down to the bottom. 'He's some weight, you.' Peter whispered, and Steve helped to ease the box around the winders. Must be slipped down, all crumpled up. With his head lolling and his shoulders jammed in the taper of the box. There's no dignity in this, by God, but it doesn't matter, it's not Robbie. Robbie's gone to a far better place. They eased him down, and levelled him out, and Peter nodded a thanks and he was carried through the doorway of the house, where he had lived for sixty years, to the hearse.

Peter came back in, straightening his suit, nodding again to Steve, and calling softly through the door as he passed a palm over his straight, shiny hair, 'Ready, Sarah?'

She paused beside Steve. 'I want you to walk after the family,' she said, 'he would have wanted that.' She was the family. She and Quizzy Maggie, who insisted that she was some distant cousin of everybody in the town.

'Walk with Tommy Blue,' Peter said. 'They were shipmates.'

'Yes, walk with Tommy Blue.'

The people outside were silent as Sarah came and took her place behind the hearse. She had decided that they would walk, in the old way, all the way to Chapel and up to Barnoon. Sam slipped the hearse into gear and began the slow drive through the narrow streets of cobbles and scarred tarmac where the ancient mains had leaked their water and gas in years gone by.

There was an occasional murmur of conversation from the followers as the sombre procession rounded the corner and passed down through the streets to the Chapel, but apart from this and the distant shouts of children playing somewhere out of sight, there was only the sound of their black-shod footfalls, unhurried and out of step. They shuffled along the larger cobbles of the harbour, past the Lodge where the flags flew at half-mast, and came to the Chapel door. Some passers-by had raised their hats, others stood in silence as the black and grey procession ambled past, giving a few moments of their time to pay respects to the dead. Yet others hurried by, unseeing, avoiding the eyes of the mourners. Distant, unknown people, who lived in some other ghetto of the town where there were new exciting changes taking place, with clothes, music, experiments in cosmetics. Busy people, whose lives had no time for the dead. Young people.

The Chapel was full, for, besides those from the house, others had come to attend the service, and the minister saw faces which he had never seen in Chapel before.

'We are here today,' in a rather high-pitched voice and in an accent from the North, 'to pay our respects to a man who was a lifelong seafarer, a fisherman.' He said 'fisher man'. 'A man who spent his days toiling on the deep, casting his nets to reap the harvest of the ocean, but also a man who, like Peter, heard the voice of the Lord and became to the end of his days a true God-fearing fisher of men.' The minister was a man of metaphors, and they came readily to his mind in this community. 'I feel sure,' he said, 'that there are those among you here today, both among the faces that I recognize and those I don't, who have at some time or another been set upon a true course by this pilot who has now set sail to the harbour where the gales of sorrow blow no more.' Steve sighed into his hymn-book. The man must be a bloody landlubber to use such phrases. His accent began to jar on Steve's nerves, with all the s's pronounced as z's. 'I remember when I first came to this lovely little town, and Robbie said to me "You'll have to take us (he said 'tek uz') as we are." You'll have to take uz az we are! And it was in thoze words, I think, that Robbie soomed oop the strength of his own character and of hiz own faith. Tek uz az we are! For he knew that many of uz are not as we should be, or az we should like to be, boot az we we are. And it waz az we are that Robbie took uz, for he saw that we are like boats adrift in a storm, needing guidance back through the jagged rocks of folly and the sandbanks of sin. Back to the moorings of security in the haven of the Lord.'

Surely, Steve thought, it hasn't always been like this. This religion. Surely men with the intelligence and courage of Robbie's generation would never have come flocking to the Chapel to hear such stuff as this?

They sang *Eternal Father Strong to Save* and *In Heavenly Love Abiding* and the basses came through strong and resonant, the way Robbie would have liked, with the tenors not too overpowering and the women sounding mellow and sweet. It was good, proper singing, which drained the emotions and let the sorrow and grief express themselves to one and all. A brear many men blowed their noses as they sat down and said their own prayers for Robbie and Sarah, and the women dabbed their eyes in clean white hankies bought special for the job.

Then they went up the long hill to the cemetery at Barnoon, where the minister said what he had to say about ashes and dust, and the breeze from the north-west stirred the hair of the capless men as they stood on that bleak slope above the wet sand of the deserted beach.

The sexton, whose name Steve didn't know, threw a fistful of earth onto the box where it landed with an empty thud, and turned away. Steve wondered if it was possible to be a sexton and still believe in God.

Sarah had arranged for Sam's taxi to take her back to the house, and after a few words of thanks to some of those who had come, she sat in the back seat and was taken away. The people drifted away after her, some back to their own homes or for a round downalong, and some to Sarah's house for a cup of tay. Steve walked downalong with James and Tommy Blue. Down the quick way, the steep way, down Barnoon Hill, but walking slowly and talking.

'He was a good old shepmate,' Tommy said, with an old man's grin. 'Used to be a hard case, years ago.'

'Robbie did?'

''Es, so sooner fight as eat meat in they days.' He paused for a moment, hanging on to the railing by the steps, peering through his thick glasses at the roof-tops in the valley below. Remembering his youth. 'He was a brear bit older'n me. A good old shepmate.'

At the bottom of the hill all three continued walking in the direction of the west pier where they would stand for a bit of a yarn, and James asked, 'Aren't 'ee goin' down to the house then, Ste'?'

'No. No, I don't think so.'

'I understood you was. I believe Sarah understood you was.'

'Oh?'

'I believe she's expectin' 'ee to go back there, Steve. For a cup of tay.'

'I don't want no tay.'

'Well you knaw what I mean.'

'You should ought to go down there, Steve,' Tommy Blue added, pausing again in his stride. 'You sh'd ot to. Seein' there's no family. No close family, and he was like a father to 'ee.'

Steve said, 'Well, 'es I s'pose. I s'pose I should, really.'

'She'll be expectin' of 'ee, Steve.'

''Es, I'll go down there. I'll go down there dreckly.'

After a few more steps he left them and went down to the Lodge, where he stopped for a while, but there was no one there to talk to, and he began to feel cold in his suit, wondering if he might go home and change into his guarnsey. But he decided that he'd better go in his suit. He couldn't turn up in his guarnsey after a funeral. Not very well. The flags were still flying at half-mast and would do so for the rest of the day.

The flags were not flown for everybody—only for those who belonged here and nowhere else. For those who were as much a part of the harbour scene as the twin quays, and as much a part of the town as the narrow streets and cobbles. Mind you, there were some who were born here, and lived all their lives here, but who passed away as strangers, for they lived the lives of suburbia and were unknown. The obscure ones. The flags proclaimed not merely the passing away, but the very existence of those men and women of whom the community had been aware. These flags, thought Steve, wer the obituaries of the local characters and those who had truly belonged. For some, like Robbie, they were a token of respect. For some they were a send-off, and damned good riddance, while for others like the simple and feeble-minded, who had perhaps been the butt of bawdy humour while still alive, they represented the genuine mark of sympathy and compassion. It is better to be loved, and laughed at, as the village idiot, then left to languish with loneliness in a madhouse.

Strangers find the flags amusing—and so often remark upon the clannish Cornish. They feel ostracized and rejected by the heart of the community (not realizing that even we do not know whether we really belong, until the flags go up and we look behind and count the black procession following us up to Barnoon Hill). They cannot decipher this secret semaphore.

There had been a brear many there today. Everybody knew him, respected him, though he had been nobody of any consequence, nobody of importance, merely respected. And that's a fine thing.

'Course,' Maggie was saying when he arrived at Sarah's, 'we was second cousins, you knaw,' and she chewed on her saffron cake with a few spare crumbs rotating fiercely in the hairs of her sparse moustache. 'Yes, he was first cousin to my mawther. Robbie's faether and my grandmawther were brother and sister.' Maggie knew who was who, all right. No doubt about that.

'I believe we're related somewhere,' said a woman whom Steve knew by sight.

'Why, yes,' Maggie exclaimed in her best English. 'Why, yes. Why, your mother was a second cousin to en. Why yes!'

'Well, we've always been very friendly,' said the woman. (She was a Pollard, from Carbis Bay.)

'Why, yes. You ot to have walked with the family.'

'Oh, I didn't mean that,' she said hastily. 'You and Steve are related too, aren't 'ee, Steve?' Bringing him into the conversation.

'I'm sure I don't know,' Steve told her, trying to keep the irritation from his voice. 'Do 'ee mind if I have a smoke, Sarah?'

'No, that's all right. I'll get an ashtray.'

'Why, through your mother's side,' Maggie said, 'of course we are.'

'I suppose we are all related somewhere,' Steve said, for once in his life trying to be patient with Maggie, and by his disinterested tone extricating himself from the conversation, blowing smoke to the ceiling and watching it curl around the banisters and drift upstairs.

Eventually all but Maggie and Steve were gone, and Steve was about to rise from his chair and leave also, but something in Sarah's eye said plainly . . . Stay. I want to talk to you. So he merely turned in his chair, to lean on the other arm, and returned her look.

'Maggie!' she cried suddenly, 'I've just remembered. I've got hardly any tay in the house. Can 'ee drop in and get some for me? On the way up? And drop it in here tomorrow?' Pausing, 'I don't want to go out.'

'Why yes,' Maggie said. 'But I sh'll have to run. The shops is nearly shut.'

She struggled with her coat and Steve thought that perhaps he could help her. But if he did, she would only say 'No, that's all right. I can manage. It's only the lining,' or 'These old sleeves,' or 'It's catching at the elbow,' or any bleddy thing but 'Thank you.' He let her struggle.

'Now, cheerio, my dear,' she said to Sarah, 'and don't go upsettin' yourself.'

'No, I won't. Cheerio, Maggie. And, thank you.'

Maggie went up off the road, still fumbling with the buttons of her coat, and almost running in her haste, although there was plenty of time.

'She's not a bad old soul,' Sarah said to Steve.

Steve didn't answer her, and wondered why she had kept him.

'I want to clear away the clome* a minute,' she said, and he waited while she removed the few cups and plates which had not been taken out by Maggie. He realized that she was unaware of using this old word, and that she must be suffering intensely to allow it to slip out, for Sarah never used 'broad' expressions intentionally. After removing the dishes she went upstairs and came down with a small blue box which she placed on the table beside him, then she went again to the kitchen and returned with a tray. A small black-lacquered tray, bearing two full glasses.

'A drop of sherry,' she said, and hesitated before continuing. 'I'm glad it's over, Steven, I'm very tired.' She sat in a chair opposite him.

'I'm sure you are,' he said, fumbling with the stem of the sherry glass, running his thumb up and down it, brushing the slight dew which formed from the heat of his hand. 'It's not been easy all these months.'

'No,' she said, and sipped her drink in quick little gulps, as women do who are unaccustomed to alcohol. It was obvious that she had something to tell him, but her face was inscrutable, bland, blank. She was not attempting to hide anything, it was simply that her mind was numbed by this awful finality.

*Crockery.

Eventually she reached for the blue box lying on the table between them and opened it with her thumbs, slowly, reluctantly, with the box on her knees.

'Father wanted to you have this,' she said and took the old man's gold hunter in her hand. 'His watch. He bought 'n when he retired. He said that as he had always been his own boss, he would have to buy his own retirement present. He's had it over twenty years.' She put the box on the table and sat looking at the watch, which she held in the palm of her hand, with the gold chain swinging in a loop between her fingers. 'He never spent a lot on himself, you know. Very little, really. But I remember him bringing the watch home. Two, he had. This one, and this one.' She touched the silver case which hung from a black ribbon round her neck. ' "I don't suppose you'll be retiring, Mawther," he said, "at least, I hope not"—laughing, he was—" but I got one for you too!" I can remember them now, sat in these chairs, looking at their watches. Asking me to listen to them. "I've always wanted a good watch," he said, "a good watch." It was just after he sold the boats that he bought them . . . He had them engraved.' She opened the case, and Steve could see the black-and-gold Roman numerals and the engraving inside the cover. He knew the watch.

'Wanted *me* to have it,' he said.

'Mawther was going to ask how much they cost, but I caught her eye and stopped her. He never bought much for she, neither.'

'But, I don't see how . . .'

'Father put his arm across her shoulder—he never showed much affection, you know—and he said . . .'

Steve was sure there was a bead of moisture in the corner of her eye, but she blinked and it was gone.

'. . .he said to her, "They'll come in for the grandchildren".'

Steve could see the second-hand, jerking minutely, and it passed almost in a full circle before he could look at her.

'But . . . you might . . .'

'No, Steven. Now now,' and by way of explanation, which was unnecessary,' not at my age.' She passed the watch over to him and, mechanically, he reached for it, feeling the heavy weight and the chain coiled in his palm.

'We had a talk,' she said, 'and Father said if that was the case, I should give it to you. He was very fond of you, Steve. Ever since your Father was lost. Very fond of 'ee, he was.'

'But, Sarah, you might still ge . . .'

'There was a time, Steven, when I had high hopes of getting married. But, there we are now . . . P'haps it was meant to be.'

He could not return the slight smile with which she said this, for Sarah had been unable to hide the wretched sorrow in her voice, and he didn't know what to say. He lifted the watch to his ear. 'It's a good watch, Sarah. Thank you.'

She rose and went to the window where she could see the sea, dull and without sparkle under the cloudy nor'wester. Its waves rose slowly, silently, without anger, and rolled away unbroken to the eastern shore. 'Can I have a cigarette?' she said.

'I didn't know you smoked, Sarah.'

'I don't,' she said, still looking at the sea, with her back to him, 'but I want one now.'

He stayed with her for a while, and told himself that he ought to drop in and see her now and then to make sure she was all right, now that she was all alone. But how could he? It would only lead to gossip and speculation, which Sarah would find unacceptable. A woman all alone.

'I'll drop in now and then,' he said as he left, 'to make sure you are all right.'

Sarah smiled and closed the door behind him. She knew that she would see even less of him now. Now that her father was dead and there was no reason for Steve to call except to see her, and she couldn't have that, for he was a happily married man. If he came she would have no alternative but to discourage him, or his reputation would suffer.

Steve went home, to get out of his best suit, but Mary was in the kitchen when he arrived, and she had the kettle on. Steve slumped into a chair, staring vacantly before him.

'You ought to take that suit off, Steve,' Mary said. 'It's getting all creased.'

'Aye. I will in a minute.'

'It's the only one you've got. Cost a fortune for a new one. Clothes are dear as saffron.' She placed a cup of tea before him, and he stirred it absently.

'Many theer?' she asked.

'A brear few.'

'I thought there would be. Everybody knowed 'n.' She sat opposite him, still wearing her pinafore over the jumper and slacks she wore for doing the housework when they had no people in.

'I hardly spoke to 'n, more than to say hello. Never hardly spoke to 'n at all, really,' she mused.

'He wasn't a woman's man.'

'No, I s'pose.' She wasn't sure what he meant. 'How's Sarah? Upset I s'pose.'

'Not too bad.'

Sarah wasn't upset. She was resigned to a life of loneliness and melancholy. If only she wasn't so damned religious; got out a bit. Mixed with people a bit. Steve reached into his pocket. 'He left me his watch,' he said.

'Left you his watch?' She returned the cup and saucer to the table and was silent for a few minutes. 'See the will, did 'ee?'

'No,' he said, irritably. 'I didn't see the will. How should I see the will!' He passed the watch over to her. 'It's a good watch,' he said. 'Gold. Though I don't know why he should have left it to me.'

'How did he come to leave 'n to you?' she asked, not listening to him.

'He used to like talking to me. I b'lieve he thought I was religious. Couldn't get away from him half the time.'

'That's Sarah, that is,' she said, decisively.

'What is?'

'Why, leavin' you the watch.'

'Sarah?'

'Why, yes. He would never have left *you* his watch. He never had no reason for leaving you his watch.'

'Sarah said he was fond of me.'

'She was, more like.'

'?'

'Now don't say you didn't know! My dear Steve, I'm not that daft.'

'What the hell are you talkin' about?'

'Chasing your ass off. Hangin' around after Chapel. Followin' 'ee out to Clodgy and all. As if people didn't know.'

'When, for God's sake?'

'Why, when we was courtin'. You took her home enough.'

'I...I took her home once. But that was years ago. Christ Almighty, woman, you're talking about twenty-odd years ago.'

'Twenty years, twenty minutes! What's the difference? She was mad after 'ee.' Mary put the watch back on the table. 'You never saw nobody else take her home. And mind your language!'

'Tim Penberthy took her home a couple of times. If I remember right.'

'Only because you were taking somebody else home.'

'Some of the others took her home.'

'Well, who? Tell me who?'

'Oh, I don't know. Anybody. Everybody. Everybody took everybody home at one time or another. There was nothing in it.'

'Not Sarah, m'dear. Not Sarah. There was only one for Sarah. And he was courtin' somebody else. Now, don't tell me you didn't know, Steve.'

He gazed at her wearily. Would she never let it go? The past. We are not the same people as we were. People mature, they change. Even Sarah, for all her cloistered life within the Chapel and her father's strong, believing hand. Or had she? Sarah! Was she the same as the lovely little Sarah of twenty years ago? Was she the same Sarah as that trembling, yielding girl whose passion was so intense that she made him fear his own? Was she? Was she the same one whose lips had almost exhausted him in a single kiss? And, would she have gone all the way—would she have cast aside her religious morals and done it with him? With him, and no other? She who was so prim and proper, and demure and sickly sweet. Would Sarah Stevens ever have lain naked on her back and opened her legs for a man? Never! Or, had he alone unleashed such passion in her that she had been terrified of ever revealing it again? The thought of such passion and desire suppressed for a lifetime was obscene, disgusting, and he was appalled that he might have been in any way responsible for her frustration. A preposterous, vain notion, and he cast it from his mind.

'What damn silly nonsense you d' go on with,' he said.

Chapter Nine

The small panes in the glass partition were new, but as the pub was old and quaint the alterations were 'in keeping', the new glass was irregular and crude, with the result that passing figures in the outside passageway were seen as dismembered evanescences which flowed together and formed faces of grotesque proportions as they peered into the room. The outside windows were clearer, being genuinely old, but to me, sitting inside, the figures strolling along the harbour in their bright holiday clothes seemed unreal, fantastic.

In going down for Easter I avoided the great milling crowds of summer, but there were still a few early visitors to remind me that this was now a holiday town, and these early ones were lucky that year, for the weather was kind to them. How different things might have been for Steve and Cleo if Good Friday was pissing down with rain.

''Ullo,' somebody said. ''Ullo again.'

''Ullo, Steve.' I had not seen him enter, being distracted by the passing figures, but turned on hearing his voice. The bar was half-full and Steve greeted those he knew—nearly everyone in the place. 'Mornin', Tim, John, Joe . . .' He stopped to speak to Terry Tuttle, the plumber, about some job or other, then he brought his drink over to the corner where I sat alone.

'Didn't know you were home.'

'Came down a bit early this year. Just for a few days. I like coming at Easter, it's the best time of year.'

He asked about my life away. My work and travels, as always. And I brought him up to date, knowing that the stories of my misdemeanours would go no further. Thus we shared our lives, briefly but intimately, while drinking a pint of beer, or sometimes while out in his boat, for we occasionally went fishing together—on fine days, for my stomach is no sailor. I enjoyed those times together, out there in the bay, fishing for mackerel on the first of the flood-tide, with only our laughter reaching the watchers on the shore.

The bar was filling up and during our conversation we had nodded to the arrivals we knew, but now Collateral Fred came in and the voice of Tim was heard above the vocal confusion of many conversations.

'Yes, that's right, boy. I'll see you're all right. What are you having anyway?' George came and waited for the orders. 'Don't see much of you these days,' Tim said to me. 'Half of the Best for Steve, George, and better see what these other buggers want. What about you, Freddie?' His big round eyes became half closed in an inquisitive smile. 'Better make his a half too, or I'll be in trouble with Martha. Got enough troubles right now.' His smile beamed wider, and his pipe-clutching hand rubbed over the rotund belly struggling to escape the confines of his belt. He was putting on too much weight. The good life would kill him in the end. 'A touch of acid,' he said. And his eyebrows rose in exaggerated nonchalance while his voice became confidential. 'One or two little financial problems at the moment. Not to mention certain difficulties on the matrimonial side. Nothing that can't be resolved, however. I shall sleep on it tonight. The problem, I mean.'

More laughs, and full glasses. Steve could see this developing into an expensive morning, and he could ill afford it. He felt in his back pocket to check the notes there. Tim saw him. He missed little. 'Skint again, Steve?' He was hinting, as Steve knew very well, at the contract for the flats. Steve had no need to be hard up, if only he would get off his ass and move with the times.

George was totting up the round, leaning with both hands on the bar and interrogating each drink in turn with a quizzical eye, when Cleo came in.

I can never look upon that woman without admiring her. Now that she was living here I hoped to see more of her, and was envious of all these who could enjoy her company while I was away making my living in that academic desert where I thirsted more and more for the company of my childhood friends.

'Ah,' said Tim. 'Hello, my han'some.' He reached out his arm to her, and like a magnet drew her to his side. 'Come and have a drink.'

'Oh, thank you, Tim.' She saw me and gave me a little wave with the tips of her fingers. 'I have a friend with me. Where is she? Come in, Barbara.'

'Oh,' Tim said, 'I know Barbara. How are you, my love? How about a kiss?' He had one on either side of him and was grinning fit enough to burst. 'I'm in the chair, as bleddy usual. Something for the girls, George.' He drew another note from his wallet and added it to those already on the bar. 'Have one yourself,' he told George.

'And Jesus said, "Who touched me?" '

'What's that, Shimshai?' But I shook my head.

'Nothing.'

Steve had heard me, and he chuckled. 'Luke, Chapter eight, Verse forty-five,' he said quietly. 'Tim's a bleddy beauty. How does he do it? He knows everybody.'

That was the way they invariably spoke of Tim. 'He's a bleddy beauty,' they would say, 'Tim don't care,' or 'He's a bleddy rogue.' But, watching him now, I saw that they saw him exactly as he wished them to see him. He projected his image with the calculated accuracy which was the essential part of his superficial personality, and adjusted the focus to infinity so that the more remote people were from him, the clearer they thought they saw him. He was an actor too, as the fishermen touting for passengers on the quay were actors, but Tim's acting was superb, for he lived the part. His ability to convince people that the part they saw of him was the genuine part was a subtle as it appeared to be blatant. They left him, after an appointment in his office or an earnest, pipe-waving discussion in the bar, feeling that despite his effulgent volubility they had seen through him, that he wasn't so deep after all, when in fact he had allowed them to see only through the polish on a double veneer.

Because I had not made a pile of money through my education he thought I was a fool. 'No!' he said, 'I don't think you are a fool.' But old Shimshai had known him for a long time.

John Ashton, predictably, had moved in on the women at the earliest opportunity. Now that they were here he would buy the next round of drinks, there was no doubt of that. He would order the drinks with that air of haughty disdain that he had cultivated to perfection, apparently forgetting that he had gone to school with the barman, George. His blond hair and handsome features, together with his height, a little over six feet, and elegant clothes, contrasted sharply with the tubby and rather untidy Tim. John chose his clothes with great care after looking through *Country Life*, or *The Shooting Times*, or *Estates and Gardens*, not at the adverts, he was too clever for that, but at what all the people with money wore in the photographs. He then copied them perfectly—cavalry twill and Harris tweed, heavy brogues, a dainty little hat; he looked a country gentleman, and was broke.

Tim too spent a lot of money on clothes and assumed that therefore they would be right, but they, and he, were wrong of course. But if he knew, he didn't worry, as long as they were comfortable. He could always buy some more if he felt out of place in them, or if he got fed up with them.

These two were so different, yet each in his own way had an air about him, an aplomb. Together, they were inevitably the centre of attraction in the bar and all conversation was directed to their corner.

I loved these sessions, for when everyone came in, all the gang, and we had a drop too much, the façades which each of us had built around us dropped like crumbling masonry at our feet and were kicked under the table. We were boys again, with the same ones getting the best toys, and the scars from old fights, though well healed by the years, occasionally opened to reveal sores beneath the new tissue.

Soon these communal experiences, a growing up and a growing old with the sons of our fathers' friends, will be no more, for the concept of permanency is dying. Very often I wondered if we were the last to share this intimacy, a complete knowing of each others' lives, if not our thoughts, from childhood to a black-framed card tacked among the thousands of tarred-over nails on the wall of the Lodge. How little we had all changed, now that we were about half-way, and I saw little chance of change in the future.

Cleo, while joining in the jokes and laughter, was letting her eyes wander around the bar, studying the faces, and watching the men playing euchre in the opposite corner. She looked at me again and smiled. I called her over and indicated the seat next to where I sat. She sat close to me, and squeezed my arm. 'Thanks,' she said, 'Tim gets a bit exhausting.' She turned to Steve . . . 'Hello.'

'Hello,' he said. They were sitting opposite each other, on benches each side of the long table, and the smiles they gave each other were too brief, too casual. They looked at me, both of them, and then had another quick glance at each other, and smiled again.

One can see people converging, on a collision course like ships in a fog, and disaster looms inevitably for want of a change of tack. As a spectator one is not sure whether the impending disaster is but a hallucination, a trick of the light in the mist. A signal is flashed *you are standing into danger* but it is unseen, or ignored. Steve and Cleo were on that collision course before I was able to warn them. Or was it I who set the gyros?

'I didn't know you had met?' I said. 'You're a bleddy dark horse, Steve.' They both laughed, a little too readily, I thought. Their eyes kept meeting, Cleo's and Steve's, and they would look away, quickly, turning to me.

'How's the painting going?' I asked her.

'Very well. I'm working every day now, for I'll have to get a job when the season gets going. That's the worst of it. At the very time when you see things at their best, in the summer, you have to work at a job to enable you to paint in the winter. But it's going very well; I'm getting the feel of the place now.'

'It's all been done before, as I told you.'

'Yes. And you know very well that it was a foolish remark. Everyone sees it differently.' And she added, looking at Steve, 'An artist's job is to show people things they had never seen before. And to make them see themselves.'

'Artists!' Steve said, shaking his head. But I noticed a slight flush come to his cheeks.

'She's good, you know,' I said. 'You ought to see her work. I think you would like it. I think you two would see things the same way.'

'Well, I have seen some.'

'And?'

He shook his head. 'I don't know much about it,' and his eyebrow went up. 'I'm only a simple fisherman.'

'You might be a fisherman but you are not bleddy simple and you know it.'

Perhaps it is because I had never been in love, or had been in love too often, that I felt so sympatheic towards Cleo. And Steve too. 'You are too intelligent,' I told him on one of the few occasions when we spoke of it, 'You are too intelligent to know better,' and he had smiled wryly, with that characteristic raising of one eyebrow.

'You are trying to be clever again, Shimshai,' he said, and rose to replenish our glasses, adding ambiguously, 'My turn, I think.' Steve was obviously enjoying himself and drank all the beer placed in front of him. He spent his money with a laugh. 'I've squandered too much of my money in the past,' he said, 'on wild necessities.'

I could see that he was a little tipsy, as most of us were, by the extra sparkle that alcohol invariably brought into his eyes, though he rarely became drunk. I said, 'You're looking tight, Ste'.'

'Tight be buggered,' he said, and turning to Cleo, 'Sorry.'

'For people who are supposed to be narrow-minded Methodists you use an awful lot of bad language between you,' she said.

'We learned it from the English,' Steve said. 'We learned our English from the English.'

'But you *are* English.'

The last remark had been said with emphasis and her voice had broken through the general hubbub of conversation. 'No. No,' they all cried. 'English be damned,' and the whole pub exploded into laughter. Somebody sang *And shall Trelawny live!* to which everybody replied *And shall Trelawny die!* singing loud and clear, *Here's twenty thousand Cornishmen will know the reason why.*

And they were away—there would be no stopping the singing now, and no conversation was possible, until closing time. The men's voices were melodious and blended in a natural harmony. Nobody shouted or hurried the pace, singing was serious enjoyment, rounds of drinks were ordered in mime, with raised eyebrows and nods, wrists flicked to indicate 'Drink up, another one coming'. George, the barman, would stand holding his hand out for the money, but with eyes closed and head thrown back as the notes rolled off the tongue and he became oblivious to all but the music, and whoever happened to be buying a round would stand with him, singing for the sheer love of music and melody.

'They are like kids,' Barbara said.

'Happy kids,' Cleo replied with her mouth close to Barbara's ear.

The ship's bell hanging over the bar clanged out as George jerked the turk's head hanging from the clapper. '*Time* my lucky lads!' he called. It was half past two already.

Outside in the warm spring sunshine they clustered round the door talking for a while before making their way off for a belated lunch or back to a fuzzy afternoon of work. Freddie went off home as soon as George called 'time', hurrying his drink and leaving half of it unconsumed. Tim stayed talking animatedly to Wally Buller, the solicitor, for a while, then they left together in Tim's Jaguar. A traffic warden was hanging around outside the pub, but no one expected him to book Tim, and he drove off in a volley of banter: 'It's all right for you! It's who you are! Money talks!' Tim waved his pipe through the window, grinning all over his face.

Cleo said, 'I wonder where Tony is. He usually comes in for a quick one at lunch-time.'

'A quick one?' I asked.

'He's been very good lately,' she said, and I reassured her that I was not implying that he ever drank too much.

'No,' she replied, 'I didn't mean that. I meant that he has been working very hard.'

'Let's go round and see him,' Barbara suggested, and, turning to John, who had joined our cluster and was keeping close to her, 'Would you like to come?'

'To Tony's?' he said with a trace of a sneer in his voice. 'No thanks.' And he went off, up through Fore Street, sauntering elegantly, adding as he left, 'Hardly my idea of the ideal way of spending an afternoon off.'

Steve shrugged and Cleo said, 'You'll come, Steve?' and turning to me, 'And you, of course, always ready for a chat.' So the four of us went up through the narrow cobbled street to the old conglomeration of wooden studios backing on to the shore. Steve, I could see, had drunk enough to be affected by it but he needed very little to make him tipsy as I knew from past occasions when we had been drinking together. 'You *are* drunk,' I said. He nodded amiably in agreement, and laughed.

Tony was not at the studio, so we carried on to his cottage. I noticed that Steve was much more relaxed now, he was talking to Cleo about some book which they had both read, and, as I do on these occasions, had dropped much of his accent, or to be more correct he had dropped the dialect. The long vowels, with the broad 'a', taken to and retained by America, were still there and Steve, unlike John, or myself, to some extent, was too fiercely proud of his heritage to deliberately cultivate a false pronunciation.

'Have you known Steve for long?' Barbara asked.

'All my life. We grew up together.'

'And John?'

I looked at her. 'Him too, though he's a bit younger. Younger than Steve and me.' She was a lovely girl. Her colouring was incredible, and I found myself looking yet again at the roots of her hair to find some trace of a dye-line. Steve had called her ginger-headed but her hair was saffron-coloured, a beautiful fiery red. Like Cleo she had intense blue eyes, but Barbara's were darker, as were her eyebrows, but I suspect that these may have been touched up with something or other. I wanted to warn her: 'John's quite a man with the girls,' I said.

Tony lived in a tiny cottage with two up and three down. One of the downs was a kitchen, one a bathroom, and the other a lounge which, like one of the bedrooms, overlooked the beach and the broad rollers grinding in from the Atlantic. The outsides of the windows were nearly always encrusted with salt, while air-blown sand, driven by the north-west winds, infiltrated through the whole place with a persistence which had worn down Tony's house-pride. 'It's a funny thing to me,' he once said, 'but I can always get a half bucket of sand off the floor here if I sweep up three times a day. So I do it once a week and put it in a sack. That's 'time and motion', is it not?'

His voice came from the bedroom as we entered the front door. 'Come up,' he said, recognizing our voices. He was lying on the bed, fully clothed but with his left foot naked except for a huge bandage swathed around his big toe. We stood around his bed in amusement.

'What's happened to your toe?'

'I stubbed it,' he said.

'I've warned you,' Cleo scolded, 'about wearing sandals all the time.' And they laughed, for her own sandals were little more than a strip of leather and a sole.

'Oh, it's not the sandals,' Tony said. 'It's the dogs. A terrible place for dogs is this. A terrible place for dogs.'

'Dogs?' we all chorused.

'Were you bitten?' Cleo asked.

'Bitten? Oh no. Not bitten. I'd been for my groceries and I was carrying them in a bag, y'know, or a box—a box it was, and I couldn't see exactly where I was going y'know and as I stepped on it my foot went away from under me as if it was a banana skin I'd stepped on, so it did. Flat on my backside I went, smashed a dozen eggs, and stubbed my toe on the kerb. It's a terrible town for dogs, is this. I think it must have been one of these bloody great well-fed poodles. You know the ones, with a hand-knitted coat on their backs to replace all the natural fur that's been cut off in those comical rings. It must have been well-fed poodle-shit. I'd like to shoot the bloody lot—take it up as a hobby, y'know, dog-shooting. It would be great fun, would it not?'

We all sat on the bed, laughing with him, and he said, 'And how are you all?' reaching out and shaking me by the hand. 'Back for the summer, are you?'

'No,' I said, 'just the Easter holidays. Three weeks.'

'Of course, it's Easter next week. One day is much the same as another when you don't have holidays, y'know.'

'Get away with you. You are on holiday all the time.'

'Aye, that's what everybody says about artists. But I've been working hard lately. I have a one-man show in May, and hardly anything done for it. Time just goes, y'know. I have to force myself to work to a routine or I find I've done nothing at the end of the day, or even a week. You can waste a terrible lot of time. Are you coming to do my window, Steve?' he asked. 'I can't use the studio, y'know.'

'Can't use the studio?' Steve queried. 'I thought you only had a pane of glass out.'

'Oh, I did. I did. In the skylight—you know, the big rooflight with all those hundreds of small panes in it. But I tried to patch it up, y'know, with a bit of old hardboard. Got up there on a step ladder—I swear to God I only touched it. In fact I don't think I did touch it. No! I didn't, I hardly breathed on it. But just as I got to the top of the ladder, all the bloody lot fell in. Glass crashin' to the floor all around me, and splinters of wood flying—you would have thought that the great Crystal Palace itself was disintegrating around me, you would. If I'd been down on the floor instead of up the ladder under the original hole, begod I'd have have been cut into a thousand pieces. I reckon I hung on there for twenty minutes afraid to move, shakin' I was like a leaf. Me old heart can't stand it, you know. The doctor told me to take it easy. Take it easy! What with dogs and gales and showers of glass, exploding stoves and my house half buried under the sands of time—why the hell can't I have a quiet life? It's all I ask, y'know. Peace and quiet to get on with my painting, and the occasional enlightened individual who'll buy one. That's all.'

'Oh, Tony, you poor old thing,' Cleo said. But she saw there was a twinkle in his eye.

'That skylight has been ready to go for years,' Steve said. 'Just as well it's down—as long as nobody got hurt.'

'Nobody got hurt!' Tony exploded. 'I got hurt! Do you think that there are no other hurts but cuts and broken bones?'

'You might have been killed,' said Cleo.

'Take no notice of him, Steve,' I said. 'He's fishing for sympathy.'

'Tony burst into laughter. 'It means that we can't have your party there,' he said to me.

'My party?' I asked, for I knew nothing of this.

'Not a party,' Cleo said. 'We thought we'd ask a few friends around for an evening—next Friday—Tony thinks it's time I widened my circle of friends, so he's asked me to invite all the people I know.'

'In my honour? What a good idea.' I am not above flattery.

'You can come, Barbara?' Tony asked.

'And you, Steve?' said Cleo, with too much enthusiasm for my liking.

'Good Friday?' He was doubtful. 'Can I bring Mary?'

'Of course.'

'I 'spect she'll be going to Chapel. We'll come after Chapel.'

'Don't forget the Regatta!' I said. 'I don't want to miss that.'

'My place is not very big,' Cleo said.

'Big enough,' Tony told her. 'We'll just have a few around for a drink and a chat. Let's leave it at that. I hate organizing good times.'

'What's that about a regatta?' Barbara asked. 'I love sailing.'

Steve and I laughed. He was about to say something, but I interrupted. 'Are you entering your yacht this year, Steve?' I asked.

'Oh yes.' He was still a little tight.

'Do you have a yacht too?' Cleo asked in astonishment.

'Oh yes. Bermuda rigged racer.' His eyebrows rose as he grinned sheepishly.

Tony looked from one to the other of us, but he said nothing.

'Have you a crew yet?' I asked.

'No,' Steve chuckled. And I thought his air of innocent modesty was a little overdone.

'Well, what about the girls and me?'

He nodded. 'O.K.'

'Right,' I said. 'You still have your van? Then pick us up by the lifeboat slip, ten thirty, Friday morning. That O.K. for the tide?'

We grinned at each other. 'Just right,' he said.

Tony leaned forward and nursed his toe.

Chapter Ten

The April sunshine had barely penetrated the high cirrus which was slowly drifting away to the north-east when Steve drove his van up to the lifeboat house. He got out and opened the back doors. 'Perfect day for it', he said, as I climbed in clutching my boots by the heels. Barbara came in after me, and Cleo sat in the front next to Steve, who closed the rear doors before getting into the driver's seat. He turned back to us. 'Bit of a squeeze,' he said, and drove off, turning the van on to the slipway before accelerating along the wharf.

'Where is your yacht?' Barbara asked.

'There,' he said, 'under that oiler, right next to you.'

Barbara pulled Steve's oilskin off the long shape beside her. 'It's a toy!' she said.

'Toy?' cried Steve. 'That's not a toy.'

Steve drove progressively slower as they approached the pool, for the road became almost blocked with a straggling procession of people making their way to the same destination. There were groups of boys, fathers with their sons, and grown men, most of whom were wearing wellington boots or the long thigh-boots of fishermen, and carrying an infinite variety of model yachts and long bamboo poles. Some of the boats were already rigged, and their sails flapped loosely in the light breeze, while others were bare hulls with the sails wrapped around spars and carried separately. Clusters of girls, wearing their new Easter clothes, made way for the traffic, and waved to the boys who waved in return and joked with them, but were mainly concerned with the safe transport of their boats to the annual Good Friday confusion.

There were a few cars parked on the road when they reached the pool, but Steve found a place to pull in to the grass verge. After laying his model on the grass, he took a long wooden box from the van. In it there were three sets of sails, and Steve had a look at the pool before deciding on which set to use. The breeze was steady, from the south-west, not too strong, but with the occasional puff which rippled the surface of the pool and fluttered the stems of arrowhead and pondweed emerging from the surface near the banks. He stepped the mast and adjusted the stays, shipped the bowsprit and set the sails.

'It's huge,' Cleo said.

Steve laughed and sat on the bank, pulling on his long boots. 'Some toy,' he said. The model was three feet long, plus the bowsprit, and the mast stood some five feet above the bottom of the lead-weighted brass keel. Under the transom stern was written in an ornamental scroll the boat's name, *Wraith*.

'Where do you buy models like this?' Barbara asked.

'Buy them?' said Steve. 'You don't buy them. You make them.'

'Make them?'

'Yes. I made her nearly twenty years ago. Found just the right bit of yellow pine in an old house we were altering down'along. It was a lintel over a doorway—God knows how old it was, but it was well seasoned, no doubt about that.'

'You mean you design them and everything?' said Cleo. She ran her hand along the sides and under the stern, feeling the smooth curves. 'It's a beautiful shape. How do you decide on the lines and things? The shape of the keel?'

'Oh, a lot of it is knowing what the performance of other boats has been. There's a sort of traditional shape emerged over the years, just as each harbour had its traditional shape in the fishing-boats. I copied this from a model an old chap made for me when I was a boy, with one or two improvements, in the keel mainly—better balance, I thought. But she still didn't go as fast as his.'

The clouds had moved on so that the sunshine now struck their backs with penetrating warmth, and, with the promise of a fine day, more people were continually arriving at the pool. The boats ranged from little six-inch pieces of cork with a few feathers stuck in for sails and a slate for a keel, to elegant three-foot-sixers which sliced through the water with the grace of swans. There were yawls and ketches, one-masters, two-, three- and four-masters, schooners and barquentines—all manner of craft battled their way to and fro across the pool.

Boys raced around the banks to meet their ships and turn them about, feet wet and socks hanging in limp mud-smeared crumples round their ankles. There were cries and cheers as boats collided, capsized and righted themselves before sailing on with wet jibs flapping heavily on the halyards.

The brilliant colours of the women's clothes, emphasized by the sunlight, the fresh spring grass, the glinting cars lining the road, the reflections of hulls and mainsails, the sparkle of the water; Cleo saw it as a painting, but it wouldn't work, for there were also the cries and laughter, the sound of running wellingtons squelching with wet, the movements in the breeze and the gliding of the boats, the meandering crowd upon the bank. There was too much here for a single painting.

Steve picked the model yacht up by the keel, and clambered down the bank, wading out until the water was deep enough, then he adjusted the sails for the straight run across the pool, holding the boat back by the stern.

'Enjoying yourself?' Cleo asked.

'I don't know yet. If she strikes one of those bowsprits she might have a hole in her.'

'A hole? I thought they were all solid.'

'No, my 'ansome, they're all hollowed out. The idea is to make them as light as possible. She was built for racing, we used to have proper races once, over on the estuary, but it died out, so I made the hull very thin. When I make them for the cheldren I tend to leave a bit more wood in them.'

'My handsome!' Cleo said, with a teasing look in her eyes. Steve smiled and turned to her from watching the speeding yachts. She was looking at him with that look again, the look she gave him in her cottage when he did the shelves. Steve saw her blue eyes, and the strands of flaxen hair straying from under the scarf and winnowing across her mouth.

'Yes,' he said quietly, 'you are 'ansome. Bleddy 'ansome.'

The road was lined with cars now, and I saw Tim standing on the bank, puffing at his pipe and smiling benignly at the boys wading out into the water. He came over to us, smiling and waving to a score of people on his way.

'Hello, girls,' he said, 'enjoying the local traditions?'

'Seems to be the event of the year,' Barbara commented cheerfully. 'What's it all about, how did it start?'

Nobody knew. It had been going on for as long as anybody could remember; it had no beginning, no recorded traditions, or associations with pre-Christian rites of spring. It simply happened that on Good Friday everybody went to the pool to sail boats, or to watch the boats, or to meet people, or to get covered in mud, or to fall in.

'We could make quite a thing of this, you know,' said Tim, looking around the crowd.

'It's all right as it is,' said Steve.

'No,' said Tim, 'we ought to get the thing organized, with classes for the different-sized boats and a course set out for races with a starting-gun and prizes. We could form a committee to get it going properly. Raise money for prizes easily enough—small entrance fee. Be a bit of a boost for the season, coming at this time of year, we could get the council to let out a stall or two—touch of the ice cream and pop. Little bit of advertising.'

'It would die out,' Steve said, with barely concealed annoyance in his voice. 'To hell with the bleddy tourists.'

'No good saying that, man. You have to advance with the times.' He looked over the pool. 'Look at the confusion,' he said. 'With properly organized races we could get rid of all these small models in the morning—let the kids enter first. And the afternoons would give you chaps with the big boats a chance to have real competitive races. Yes, I reckon we could bring in a bob or two into the town.' He smiled at Barbara. 'I reckon I could make fifty quid out of it for myself, even as it is.'

'It would die out,' Steve repeated with emphasis.

'No,' Tim insisted, 'make a big thing of it. Get a bulldozer in here, clear the reeds, widen the pool.' He was carried away with enthusiasm for his ideas. 'Maybe have competitions for the best design too. Best model built by the competitor.'

'We all know which are the best boats,' Steve said, 'and if it's organized, well, I wouldn't be up here for a start.' He too looked at the mad confusion of yachts sailing their way in all directions up and down to and fro across the pool. The collisions and capsizings. 'It would die out,' he said. 'As soon as things are organized around here, they die out. You ought to know that. We don't like being organized.'

'You're too old-fashioned, Steve.'

'Yeh. Maybe I am.' He turned to Cleo. 'Coming?' he said, and they went on round to the opposite bank, with the thigh-boots flapping against his legs.

'It seems that Tim knows how to get you annoyed,' Cleo said.

'Oh, I'm not annoyed. It's just that Tim sees everything in terms of profit and loss—everything.' He stopped and looked at the boats again. 'This is for kids,' he said, 'the kids in all of us.'

'Yes,' Cleo said, 'I agree.'

They spent a couple of hours chasing around the pool while I renewed acquaintances with old friends and enemies come up for the annual excitement. The breeze died away and the day became glorious with colour. The new greens contrasted with old rusty bracken on the hills, and the bright boats on the pool flashed their reflections on the water like brilliant birds.

There was the sound of a heavy splash and a shout from the opposite bank. Then a brief silence before a crescendo of shouts and laughter. We looked to see a man, in up to the top of his long boots, fishing a small boy out of the water by the scruff of his neck. The kid was dripping wet, but laughing, with mud and ooze running from his hair.

'Number one,' said Steve. 'Most of us have been in at some time or another.'

'John is here,' Barbara said, coming up behind them,' and wants to know if we are going down to the ''Miners'' for lunch.'

'Tell him to come over,' Steve replied. 'Where is he?'

'Over on the road. He doesn't want to walk on the mud.'

'God,' said Steve. 'It's bleddy pathetic. Him and his clothes. But he's always been the same. You'd never see him fall in.'

'Shall we go?' Barbara asked.

'Aye. Aye, all right. I'll have to pack up the sails . . . Tell you what, you and Shimshai squeeze into John's car—don't get any mud on the seat for Christ's sake—and we'll follow you down later.'

John looked at Steve and the other men with their model yachts and long poles. He gave them a friendly wave but said, 'My God, they'll never grow up, some of these people. Look at Steve—he's got mud all over his clothes. Mary will be pleased about that.' He opened the car door, with just a trace of an elegant bow, and we clambered in. John drove off with the appropriate amount of roar belching from the exhaust pipe.

After dismantling the sails Steve packed them away in their box and loaded them and the yacht in the Mini. 'I'll have to dry them all out later,' he said.

As he was opening the van door a trim little woman with brown hair walked past. She looked at Cleo getting into the passenger's seat.

'Hello, Steve.'

'Hello, Sarah.'

He drove slowly along the three miles of winding road to The Miners' Arms, talking easily and naturally to Cleo, who managed to curl up comfortably in the passenger seat. As he drove, and spoke of trivialities, he was aware of the rounded form of her body and a faint perfume, and he glanced at her occasionally, wondering about her.

Cleo Nisbet—artist, young, beautiful—what else? Blue eyes, fair hair. Not blond exactly, straw-coloured almost, streaky, with a slight curl where it fell from her ears in an untidy tumble to her shoulders. A fine bit of gear, Steve. A fine bit of gear. Didn't know her—didn't know anything about her—damn strangers, you don't know who they are or what they are. She was full of life, vitality—her body, even when quite still, was suggestive of latent celerity, and her eyes roved continuously over the bare hills and granite-enclosed fields through which they were passing. If he were ten years younger . . .

John was bringing a tray of drinks to the benches and tables outside the pub when they arrived, and Steve went inside to fetch a pasty and a drink for Cleo and himself. In the shelter of the forecourt outside the pub we sat and chatted about the yachts and the local traditions, most of which had died out or become sick with commercialism since the advent of tourism and prosperity.

'Thank God that Good Friday comes too early in the year for the visitors,' John stated. 'It makes me sick the way everything is being destroyed by the locals in order to make money. The old tradition of the model yachts is something really worth having. I look forward to it every year.'

'Do you have a model yacht?' Barbara asked.

'Oh God, no. I'm too old for that sort of thing myself. I have more interesting hobbies now,' he said suggestively, and glanced at Cleo, who looked away.

'Not bad pasties,' I said, putting on the accent, 'for boughten ones.'

'Well,' said John, after a while, 'what shall we do this afternoon? I thought of going to Truro. Anybody like to come?'

I declined. There was room for only one passenger to ride with comfort in his car, and in any case I thought I'd walk back over the fields, though I did wonder whether to sound enthusiastic about going to Truro, thereby dissuading Barbara from taking up the offer, for it was obvious that it was directed at her. And she accepted.

'Walk back?' John said magnanimously. 'Don't be silly. We can all squeeze in again, just to get you back.' I saw, and was the unwitting accomplice in his plan—John and Barbara, Steve and Cleo—for the announcement of my intention to walk the return journey would be interpreted by him as collusion, for there was plenty of room in Steve's van. But I had not walked that way for years, and thought it would be a pleasant way of returning—I enjoy walking.

'You can't walk all that way,' John said scornfully. 'Through the farms? The yards will be full of mud.' He couldn't believe that I meant it, and was determined, as I see it now, not to let me remain with Cleo and Steve, but I, foolishly perhaps, was equally determined to show him that, despite his scorn, I would not only walk the four miles, but thoroughly enjoy it.

'My boots,' I said, 'are in Steve's van.'

'Very well,' he said, 'you must like punishment,' and rising, he brushed the seat of his pants with the palm of his hand, quite unconsciously, and motioned to Barbara who rose also and, after saying goodbye, sat beside him in the low seat of his old sports car.

Cleo, who had been quiet all through our pasty lunch, called, 'Don't forget tonight, Barbara,' as they waved and drove away. Steve sipped the last of his beer, and watched the glint of sunlight on chrome as the car wound through the lane and passed behind the Zennor hills.

'I wish I hadn't said that,' Cleo mused.

'Said what?'

'About tonight. He will want to come.'

She fiddled absently with a box of matches on the table while Steve looked at her questioningly. He envidently knew nothing of the reason for Cleo's parting with John. Probably thought it was none of his business. I thought it time to make a move, if I was to walk back in time for our 'do' that evening.

'What are you doing this afternoon?' I asked them. 'Why not come as far as the headland with me?' I said it more out of politeness than anything else. Well, I admit that I hoped Steve would decline, saying that he had to get back for some reason, and that I would have Cleo to myself, for I had not seen her for months.

Once a man has become close to a woman—once they have become intimate friends, without love or sex entering into the relationship, once they are able to cry on each other's shoulders and stay out of bed—then their association tends to stay that way. Furthermore, their friendship frequently outlasts the fickle, if more passionate, affections of a love affair. So it was with Cleo and me. And often, as now, seeing her laughing as she frequently did, with her flaxen hair straying untidily across her cheek, I wished it had been otherwise. She really was exceptionally beautiful, and one remained conscious of her beauty, unlike those women who attract men by a glamour which, on acquaintance, becomes negated by defects in their personality. She never told me her age, one of the few innocent secrets about which I used to tease her, but she must have been about twenty-seven at the time, perhaps a bit less. Although she had a mature and expressive face there was a certain childlike quality in her features, an open curiosity, and her blue eyes invariably looked straight at anyone to whom she might be talking. I remember saying to her once, when we were sitting over our coffee after a dinner she had cooked for me, and my mind had been wandering along these lines, 'I could never tell a lie to a face like that.' To which she had replied in a hurt voice, 'Why should you be thinking of telling me a lie?' Oh yes, I wanted her to myself, that afternoon.

'I'd love to walk to the headland,' she said. 'What about you, Steve? Do you have to get back?'

'No hurry,' he said.

'Well, let's go.' She stood up. 'But I mustn't be late back. There are still a few things to prepare for tonight.'

She couldn't walk back with me, for it would take too long. Steve couldn't drive straight back to town or she would be deprived of her walk. And I couldn't back out of walking . . .

They walked with me as far as the end of the lane, over the cattle grids and through the mud where the last of the winter's rain filtered from the fields and trickled across the path to join the stream, hidden and gurgling, in the thick vegetation at the bottom of the valley. It was warm now, and the sea was sparkling in the sunshine. We sat for a while on a grassy mound where the paths diverged, mine to the east, and theirs on out to the headland. I was reluctant to leave them, and talked too much, forcing conversation when none was required. Cleo hardly spoke. She was looking at the sea, and I felt superfluous, unwanted. Steve too was quiet, and I suspected that they wished to talk to each other, and not to me. I had never known Cleo so distant, and smarted under the slight, for we were normally so close. After several more futile attempts at conversation, I said my goodbyes and left them to it. Before dropping down behind the rise I turned, and saw them making their way out to the cliff at the end of the promontory. I felt a momentary pang of jealousy that it was Steve, and not I, who was to spend the rest of this lovely afternoon with Cleo, for I was very fond of her and afraid for them both.

At the cliff-top there was a slight declivity in the thrift-studded turf, and Cleo threw herself into it to lie full length upon the grass. She cupped her chin in her hands and gazed at the surge of foam and water over the rocks below. She kicked off her sandals and grasped little shreds of grass between her toes. Steve sat in the hollow, leaned back, with his head resting on his hands. Her jeans were tight over her legs and hips, and her feet swung lazily in the air, releasing shreds of grass from between her toes and tensing the buttocks tightly under the faded blue denim. Those dirty, brown feet. He ran his eyes over her again and again, but trying to force himself to look away, to look at the sea, to look at the sky, the rocks, cliffs, to look anywhere but at those twin mounds which tempted him to just reach and gently—just to touch—to feel, the firm round curves of them. He moved closer and lay beside her where he could not see her, and together they watched the sea, in silence. She turned to him, smiling, but said nothing, and looked down again at the swelling sea. The waves rose and fell with a heaving regularity, mounting in an accumulation of power to engulf the flat-topped rocks and recede in a cascade of rills and waterfalls.

'It's like the breathing of a great deity,' she said quietly, still gazing at the waves, 'lying eternally at the bottom of the ocean . . .'

He turned to look at her, as she went on, dreamily, '. . . sending its message to all the shores of the world. Surging breakers when it's angry, and slow, pulsating swells when it is at peace. Sleeping perhaps.' She inclined her head towards him, looking at him over the fingers cupped along her cheek.

'I would never have thought of it that way,' he said. Their eyes, having met, refused to part, and they gazed at each other, studied each other's faces as one studies a flower or a rare gemstone, admiring the beauty or the hard strength, yet searching for flaws. A party of oyster-catchers, disturbed from their pickings among the rocks by an encroaching wave, flew off around the point, their shrill 'kleep kleep' piercing the sea's roar and the minds of Steve and Cleo, drawing them back from the abyss.

'What are those birds?' she asked.

'Oyster-catchers.'

'You didn't look at them.'

'Neither did you. I know the call.' Her eyes! Her eyes . . . were looking at him. Seeing him. Oh, sea-blue eyes. In them a sorrow. I see a sorrow. A longing. A crying. A longing to see them filled with peace and love. A longing in them. A void in them. A void. Avoid! 'They spend the winter here,' he heard himself saying. 'Soon they will go away to breed. Though there's usually a few around in summer too.'

Close eyes, and look away. There will never be another blue. After those eyes the sea is mud, beneath a murky sky.

'I like you, Steve,' she said.

'You're a very—frank sort of girl.' He sat up, and fumbled in his pockets for cigarettes, needing something to do, to take his mind from those bewitching eyes.

'You are shaking, Steve. Your hands are trembling.'

A trembling. I see a trembling. A longing and a yearning. A helpless drowning in the depths of those sea-deep eyes. A touching of hands—cool fingers. 'You're not cold?' No. A gentle clasping. Looking. Touching her long fair hair. A trembling caressing. Of smooth cheeks a touching and blue eyes perceiving. Lips brushing, and parting. The sadness and the yearning. A closing and a kissing, with soft lips moisting, bodies yielding, hardness, trembling and arms enfolding. Murmuring, 'You're lovely, you're lovely. Oh, Cleo, you're lovely.'

'Brown eyes,' she whispered.

They kissed again, lying in the hollow, out there that day on the cliff at Zennor. A long soft kiss which drew waves of emotion swirling over them from such depths as neither had fathomed before. Their lips barely touched, but their hearts raced frenziedly together, and they were overwhelmed by the swelling emotions surging over them before parting with a sigh, exhausted. They saw in each other's response all the anguish to be suffered in the coming months. The folly and the sin of it. The joy and agony of it. And they both knew they were powerless to resist it.

'We must go back,' she said, simply, and rose and walked to a boulder, where she sat watching the turbulent swell and the oyster-catchers dodging the showers of spray, the weak spring sunshine still warm upon her back.

'Why?' Steve said.

'I don't know. It seemed inevitable. From the day you came to my cottage.' He came up behind her, and placed his hands on her shoulders, feeling the curve of her neck. 'I mean, why must we go?' He kissed the top of her head.

'Because,' she said in a voice barely audible over the surf below,' I am afraid of falling in love with you.' She reached and took his hand. Held it against her cheek.

'You mustn't do that,' he said.

Chapter Eleven

'But we've been invited to a party.'

'Party? What party?'

'Tony Connolly and—you know. I told you.'

'That arty crowd! No thanks. I know what their parties are like.'

'You've never been to one. Come on—let's go, and have a change. Meet a few new faces.' And he added, 'Shimshai is going.'

'Oh, he would! Always mixin' up with that crowd. Always did. None of the local maids were good enough for he. We wudn't *exotic* enough for he.' She grinned in satisfaction at her choice of words. 'And what do I want to meet new faces for? My friends are quite good enough for me, even if you don't think so.'

'Just because you meet new friends doesn't imply that you have less regard for your old ones.'

'Oh no?'

'No, of course not.'

'That's what you say. But I notice you have less time for some of your old friends since you have been knockin' around with that lot. Before, we used to go out with Martha and Freddie, but not now. Not since you be'n knocking around with that lot.'

Steve was silent. They would go up to Martha's. Martha's and Freddies's, for Steve did not wish to see Cleo that night. He was glad that Mary had arranged for them to see Martha and Freddie tonight. Cleo must be pushed from his mind. They would be in high spirits at the party, and the wine would flow. Steve was afraid of his own behaviour there. Afraid lest the wine dispelled the guilt and nervousness, and lest he and Cleo should be left alone. For if they were . . .

But then again he felt that perhaps he should go, and let Mary go to Martha's alone. Why not? After all, he had only kissed her. And he had kissed one or two since he had been married, especially in the early days. He had even kissed Martha. Oh, Jesus. Martha of the wooden lips—and the sweetness of Cleo, the warmth and moisture. A peck at a party and the revelation of his secret self of which until today even he had been unaware. The two actions of the same name which bore no more semblance to each other than . . .

And where were Mary's kisses? Where were the kisses of their youth? They had never been, for their kisses had nothing to convey, there was no message in them and they had said nothing, as they had ever since. I only kissed her, he said to himself over and again; there's nothing in it. But tonight we will go to Martha's. And I can listen to Freddie's stereo and his incessant chat about all their possessions, while my mind will be thinking of nothing but Cleo's lovely mouth.

'I'll come to Chapel too,' he said.

Mary paused from her offices at the table. 'You're going to Chapel! What are you going to Chapel for? You haven't been to Chapel since I don't know when.' She tried half-heartedly to persuade him to attend Chapel every Sunday, and now he was going of his own free will. She was incredulous. Steve smiled at her.

'Well,' he said, 'I shall go this evenin'.'

'Then you'd better get your beard trimmed. It's looking awful. I don't know why you don't shave it off.'

Steve chucked her under the chin. 'I shall trim my beard. I shall comb my hair. I shall have a bath and cut and clean my fingernails —and my toenails. I shall clean my teeth. I shall adorn myself in all my finery—that is to say, I'll get best-changed. And I shall go to Chapel and I shall sing—they still have hymns, I suppose.'

Martha and Freddie were in Chapel when Steve and Mary arrived, already sitting in their family pew. Steve led the way forward to the pew where his family had sat for three generations, to where he had stood as an infant, barely seeing over the back-rest of the seat in front, just tall enough to see the great painting of the old men at prayer in this very place. But the pew was already occupied. He led into the one behind, but Mary indicated that they must not go there, it was the Trebars' pew, they must sit in the one behind that.

After sitting down he bowed his head in the customary prayer, and he said the prayer he always said, 'Dear God, I thank you for my good fortune'. He always said that, and often wondered what other people said. Perhaps they asked for things, but Steve thought that was more for Father Christmas. He always had.

'Who are they?' he whispered to Mary after his devotions.

'Shhh,' she said, 'strangers.' And as an afterthought, 'They don't know.'

Steve nodded indifferently and looked over to the great painting. It *was* a painting. Look at the old fella's face. There was a Christian man. You could see it in his face—and in his hands, the gnarled old hands clasped together with the cap screwed up in them. You could see the tension in the cloth where the old man's hands were wringing together in supplication. Poor as a church mouse and devout as an angel. We can never go back to that, Steve thought, and was not sure, himself, whether he meant the art or the devotion.

'We must go back,' they'd said, out on the cliffs. But that too was impossible, they could not retreat beyond the present or obliterate the past. What's done's done.

The preacher took his place, and the choir. Steve was moved, as always, by the singing, felt at home, in tune with the harmonies, and was enjoying the service until the sermon, which disturbed him. The carrying of crosses, the sins of our worldly life, and rising from the dead. The Chapel was full of flowers brought in for the Easter services. All the spring flowers, daffodils, crocus, narcissus. Steve studied the flowers and prayed silently that his sins might be forgiven, that he might rise from the dead past, up from the purgatory of memories in which he was wandering without direction. He prayed his own prayers, ignoring the preacher, whose voice ceased to penetrate when the sermon became mere amplification of that which had already been said, like a lesson to dunces. Driving the point home.

Steve's second prayer was simple. 'Lead us not into temptation. Lead us not into temptation. Not into temptation.' Accepting that the form of temptation was known, its definition to God unnecessary.

After Chapel they stood around outside, talking to people. The same people who had been at the pool in the morning, the same people that they saw every day in the shops, on the street, but mellowed by the service they spoke of other topics—enquiries after the sick, absent ones, those who were away. Men to men, women to women, masculine topics and feminine topics, with the young standing a little apart, shyly.

That was the way it was, with everybody in their best suits, their new spring outfits. All best-changed.

They were all pleased to see Steve and Mary together at the Chapel, after so long, and were anxious to talk to him, here, that he should feel one of them, that he belonged, though the talk was of other things, other things than the service and Chapel. From all but Silas Rouncefield, who adjusted his small black beret, and stooped his tall frame slightly in Steve's direction and said about the singing and the sermon, 'Glad to hear 'ee singin', boy. G-lad to hear 'ee. We need more basses. N-ever have enough basses these days,' attributing the imbalance in the harmony to lack of tonal qualities rather than the preponderance of women in the congregation, the more rapid dwindling of men. 'We don't have the basses we b'longed to have. The sarmin was too long,' he confided to Steve, with a voice alternately high and low, depending whether he spoke openly or in confidence; but equally loud.

'What do a want to go on s'long for?' his voice dying away in a resonant bass, and the tenor pitching in that the preacher might hear him. 'If we had a bit more singin', we sh'd have a few more people here.' And again, in deep confidence to Steve, 'I can tell 'ee *that*,' in a voice so deep as to be almost beyond audible frequency. Silas could sing bass or tenor, depending where he was needed.

James was there, and his wife. Tommy Blue. John Trevorrow and they. Mary's family. All the Penberthys. Pretty well everybody. You expect a good turn-out at Easter.

Freddie stayed with Martha, with the women, and they were introduced by the preacher to the strangers who had sat in the family pew. They were a family, father, mother, and one daughter. They looked like really nice people, and Steve hoped that he would not have to meet them. Martha called them over with one of her self-conscious gestures, screwing up her mouth. They stood there a bit longer, by the great door of the Chapel, Martha asking the questions—' How long are you staying? Where from?'—blocking the road, having to squeeze into the doorway when cars came by, Steve greeting the passers-by, those he knew, with brief smiles.

They all went for a walk, down as far as the quay, though the evening had turned chilly, as they will after a sunny day in spring, and there was a bit of a breeze come up from the south-east. They spoke about the weather, looking at the thin cloud gathering colour in the reddening western sky, and Freddie inevitably started on about the storms of winter, the dangers of the tides, the inshore reefs, all that stuff. Now and then bringing Steve into the conversation, 'Isn't that right, Steven?' 'Steven will tell you,' 'You ask Steven.' Using good English. Using Steve to confirm his stories but also acknowledging, admitting, to him that he really didn't know what the hell he was talking about. Wanting to tell the yarns, but admitting to Steve and himself that he was always ashore, that he had never experienced the dangers and the risks.

To Steve the conversation was boring. You couldn't tell a proper yarn to these people. A good yarn was worth the telling, worth hearing, over and again, but it had to be told proper. And these people from up-country just didn't appreciate the telling of a good yarn. A good yarn was about the people in it, you had to know them, and all these were getting was a string of embellished facts.

He knew the way the stories would be told, if he wasn't there, if Freddie had these people to himself—the embellishments, the gestures. Still, Freddie was only trying to belong. To be part of it. Part of the atmosphere, the guts of the place, but he was, through necessity, out of it, one who belonged, like me, only because of the shared experiences of our common past.

Try telling a good yarn to up-country people and they'll just as likely say they've heard it before.

Back up by the pub they met a few locals going in for an early drink—Tim, John Ashton, and a few more. Some visitors were already standing outside with glasses in their hands. Tim passed him a sympathetic look which Steve found extremely annoying. Why shouldn't he go to Chapel and a stroll with his wife. Nobody ever saw Tim's wife, unless it was to support him, lend an air of respectability at some official function where Tim would be out to make a good impression. And a good few pounds from any deals he saw in the making.

John Ashton said, 'See you later, Steve,' with a smirk all over his handsome features. 'Much later by the look of it.' The latter was an aside to Tim as they entered the narrow pub door together, but with John slightly behind, that Tim might reach the bar first and order the round. How could he believe that one as shrewd as Tim could be unaware of his moves?

'Always in the dam pubs,' Martha said to Mary, quietly, while Freddie was talking to the family from away.

'They're never out,' Mary said. 'Two damn rogues got together. Make 'ee say such words.'

They carried on up through Fore Street, looking in the shops with the people from away, comparing the prices here with the prices up-country, agreeing that everything was dearer here. The strangers came with them back to Martha's and Freddie's, where they sat in the thick-carpeted lounge. Freddie opened a door to display an impressive array of drinks, and Martha thought that all the hard work of looking after bleddy lodgers was worth it when you could invite people back and not feel ashamed of your home and furniture, and Steve stared moodily at the carpet, thinking of Cleo drinking wine with Tony and me.

'Wudn't Sarah Stevens in Chapel?' he said suddenly. 'I didn't see her.'

Chapter Twelve

After a hot bath and a large meal, for I was ravenous from the unaccustomed exercise of walking back from Zennor, I called in for a quick one and a bottle to take to Cleo's. The usual faces were there; Uncle Joe sitting at one of the long tables was talking to a middle-aged couple from the Midlands who sat with their daughter, and another local who I knew by sight. Tim and John Ashton were at the bar talking to Cleo's friend, Barbara. 'What's all this?' Tim was saying. 'You're looking bleddy 'ansome. What's going on? All dressed up.'

He was right. She was looking 'bleddy 'ansome'. Her auburn hair had been drawn back into a loose cluster by a simple ribbon of black velvet. She wore just a trace of make-up, and a plain blue dress emphasized the colour of her candid eyes. Across her shoulder was a shawl of white lace. Tim took her by the arm. He fingered the lace across her shoulder. 'What do you call this?' he said. 'A stole, is that it? Must have cost a fortune.'

'It's Cleo's table-cloth,' she said, and somebody cried 'Shut up,' as our laughter died away. 'Bleddy hartises!'

I sat at the table, for my feet had supported me long enough for one day and were protesting their fatigue. The couple from the Midlands sat in silence opposite; their rather pretty daughter glanced occasionally at our group but turned away whenever any of us caught her eye. John Ashton had managed to get himself between Tim and Barbara, so Tim came and sat with me. I was not fooled into believing that he wished for my exclusive company. It was the girl he was after, and when she turned once more from fiddling with her glass she briefly returned Tim's smile before averting her eyes.

'Proverbs,' I muttered into my beer, 'Chapter six, Verse twenty-five.'

'Eh?' Tim said.

' "Lust not after her beauty in thine heart, neither let her take thee with her eyelids." Proverbs, six, twenty-five.'

'My life!' he grinned. He turned slightly, and with his back to anyone likely to overhear, with that broad, infectious smile spreading innocently over his face, he said, from somewhere deep at the back of this throat as he held the thin stem of his pipe back over his shoulder, 'Actually, I fancy Barbara tonight.'

I smiled in the knowledge that this great confidence would have been revealed to any one of us.

'Actually,' he said again, 'I've fancied her for some time. In fact, between you and me, I think she's f-hucking g-horgeous and I'd like to screw the ass off her.'

He smiled even more widely and leaned back to observe my reaction, those great eyes wide open. 'My wife is away,' he confided 'and I have the keys of three of my flats in my pocket. *Harbour View*, perhaps? The lights reflected on the water? Possibly a little Chopin? A touch of the sweet white wine, hmmm? What do you think?'

'You're out of luck.'

'I'm never out of luck. You know me well enough.'

'John Ashton.'

'That tuss!'

I laughed aloud at his use of this Cornish obscenity. He was delightfully one of us, despite his English M.A. He turned his attention to the couple and their daughter. 'I hear you are looking for a house,' he said.

While I talked to the wife and daughter, who's name was Fay (she said), Tim told the man what type of house they required, where, how much they should pay, the advantages of a spare bedroom in a holiday town, where to get a mortgage should they need one, and arranged to see them at his office on the following morning. The contract was as good as signed. And they would get their money's worth, for if they didn't buy Tim's house somebody else would; Tim never bought a house unless it was eminently resaleable.

'You don't know anything about boats, do you?' asked the wife.

'Boats?' said Tim, his mind immediately recalling the several craft in the harbour which might be for sale.

'Friends of ours has a boat in the harbour. Needs someone to look after it. Apparently damn thing nearly sunk a while back.'

'Oh, yes. I heard about it.'

'Needs an eye keeping on it. He'll pay. You know what I mean. Retainer, like. To keep an eye on it.'

'Yes,' said Tim expansively, 'leave it to me. I'll fix that up. No trouble. Yes, I'll fix that up for you tomorrow.'

'He's not short of a bob. You know.'

'Just to keep an eye on it,' added the wife. 'We don't want to trouble you.'

'It's as good as done,' Tim smiled, getting bored with the subject, and turning at last to Fay with his smile broadening visibly. 'Just leave it to me, eh?' She returned his smile, though she had not been listening to their conversation, and Tim turned again to the parents and said, 'Tell you what! Why don't you come to a party? As my guests.' He looked at me. 'What do you say?' I returned an equally bland smile, thinking what a cheek he had to invite anyone to a party to which he himself was virtually a gatecrasher. But that was Tim. He might exasperate you, but you never took offence. Some people call it charm.

'Very kind of you,' said the wife, 'but we're for an early night. Fay has her own key, and we'll not be waiting up for no night-birds.'

'Fay will be coming then?' he said, not attempting to hide his delight.

'Your friend has asked her to go and meet a few folk.'

You have to give him credit for self-control—he didn't flicker a bleddy eyelid.

'Delightful!' he said.

The pub wasn't crowded, and most of those present were locals or resident 'foreigners' all more or less known to each other. It is a good time of year. Down there.

'No sign of Steve,' I remarked a little later when the parents were gone.

'Saw him as we came in,' John said. 'Been to Chapel, in his best suit.' He leaned back against the wall, disgruntled at sitting, preferring to stand, when his height showed to advantage, but having to sit if he wished to be next to Barbara, who had joined us at the table. 'His best suit,' he said again, contemptuously, with a superior laugh. 'No idea how to dress.' And turning to Fay, the one from Birmingham, 'You mustn't think we're all peasants down here, you know.'

I looked around the table. Apart from himself, we locals were all dressed quite simply. He looked out of place, so I said nothing. Steve needed no defending. I wondered where he was, and decided to go to Cleo's. Someone had placed a fresh drink in front of Fay so I suggested she follow along later with Tim.

They arrived soon after me, and even John had brought something to drink, though more to impress Barbara than for his own consumption. He never got drunk. There were a few there who were uninvited, like Tim and John, and Uncle Joe, but nobody who was an out-and-out gatecrasher, for which Cleo and Tony were grateful.

Uncle Joe went to all the parties in those days, talking to everybody, thoroughly enjoying himself, although only the locals understood him, so broad was his accent, and he brought his own welcome in the form of an infectious laugh and total lack of what is called sophistication. The concept of social, or fiscal, class had never occurred to him. Some parties are contrived, with the guests chosen for their variety and diversification of interests. There is little of that down here. How can there be?

The only new face to me was Wally, the young solicitor from up-country, with his slender frame in an immaculate pin-striped suit, his black hair sleeked back with something from a jar. Finally reconciled since coming here, he told me, to the fact that nobody gave a damn about how you earned your living, that he could drink in the saloon bar and not the lounge, that he could have so much in common with illiterate Uncle Joe and the penniless John Ashton. Still a little bewildered by it, Wally recalled that up-country these things would be frowned upon by what he called 'the profession', still not realizing that he was accepted only because he was himself—what he was, with no pretence. There was the difference. Being from up-country he could pretend, if he wished, which none of us could do.

He was talking about the hotel contract to Tim, whose short plump form contrasted sharply with his own slim elegance, but Tim left him to speak to Uncle Joe, to ask Joe about the boat, the stranger's boat. He didn't forget things like that, even when he was a little tipsy, although he could quite well have introduced Joe and the man in the pub, and let them sort it out, but that was not Tim. He had to be the fixer, the 'agent', as he called it, even for a little thing like bailing out a boat. There would be something in it for him. Not much, but something. 'My reciprocal', he called it. It was the principle of the thing . . .

'Only needs a quick check now and then,' he was telling Joe. 'Maybe let the plug out, eh?' and, as if there should be some doubt in Joe's mind, 'I'll see you're all right,' implying by the tone of his voice that Uncle Joe was receiving a favour, that Tim, the Universal Benefactor, had selected him for the honour of the responsible but trifling job of tending the stranger's boat. 'Maybe just a quick look at the moorings and things, eh? Give the engine a twirl, and that sort of thing,' and, beginning to feel out of his depth, 'You can always give me a shout if you have any problems. We can sort them out. Mind, I don't see that there should be any problems. Maybe a little more slack or something. Hmmm? On the moorings.'

Joe took a long swig from his glass and looked into it with amazement, pondering the contents. Tim liked to live his part, but he forgot, every time, that it was the whizz kids, the smart guys, the wheeler-dealers who were so easy to fool. It was when dealing with the likes of Uncle Joe and Steve that he let himself down. Joe knew damn well that Tim didn't know a bowsprit from a halyard, and he knew that Tim knew too. He also knew that Tim, for reasons best known to himself, had to pretend to know every bleddy thing. How Tim would ever cope with life if he couldn't read or write Joe didn't like to think.

'I'll keep my eye on her for 'ee,' he said, looking questioningly into his half-pint glass from which he had just drained the last of the liquid, the like of which he had never tasted before. 'What the hell was that?'

Tim laughed and sniffed the glass. Then he looked to where he had hidden a bottle on the way in, behind some canvases Cleo had piled in a corner by the door. It was gone! He sniffed again. 'Actually' (he said 'Aictully', drawing it out), 'aictully, Joe, that was a rather splendid and rare old St Emilion.' It was the bottle he had hoped to share with whoever he shared the night with. He reached for Joe's hand and drew the glass once more to his nose. 'Splendid and rare.' He smiled sweetly at Joe.

'Couldn't drink much of that,' said Joe, and made a move towards the kitchen, where there was a barrel of beer. 'Oh,' he said, half turning again to Tim, 'he idn' from London is 'e? The one with the boat?'

'No,' said Tim absently, still gazing at the glass in Joe's hand,' from up North. The Midlands. Somewhere up there.'

'Only I'm besting to go! To London,' Joe confided. 'To the Boat Show.' He smiled and scratched his head. 'I've never b'en b'fore. T'London.'

Tim's face brightened at the prospect of Joe, who could neither read nor write, fumbling around London. He considered the hilarious possibilities of a weekend with him in the city, but then remembered that Joe, while at sea, had travelled more, seen more cities, than he would ever do. Still, they could have some fun there.

'The Boat Show, eh, Joe? Wouldn't mind going myself.' Yes, why not? 'What about it? The two of us?'

The trip would go down as business expenses, to see a client, arrange some advertising, perhaps by road, give the Jaguar a spin. Joe could be his driver. 'Yes. We'll see about that.' A few days in London at that time of year, the quiet season, as you might say, would do a man a power of good. No chance of his wife going of course, not at that time of year, with the children at school. Yes, it would be something to look forward to. And if Joe was there to see and examine the stands there might be the possibility of an agency for some of the gear. Some of the expensive stuff, the echo-sounders and radar. Where the money was. 'Yes,' he said enthusiastically, 'we'll both go.' The salesman would think he was a dealer who had brought along an expert for his opinion of the equipment. 'You'll have to get a new hat,' he said.

'What's wrong with me bleddy 'at?'

There would be some laughs. Shimshai lived in London—knew his way around. Tim had stayed with him before. Yes, they could have some fun, the three of them.

'I'll fix it up,' he said. 'It's a long way off. But leave it to me.'

Uncle Joe was still half turned to the beer barrel, but he saw Tim's mind racing along, before the wind as you might say. 'It's a brear while yet,' he said, thinking that, although Tim was a good old sort, he didn't think much of having to tow him around the Boat Show, listening to him making a damn fool of himself. Too embarrassing. But then, it might be a good laugh, a good yarn to tell. He belched up the vapours of Tim's expensive wine and made a wry face. 'I'm on'y bestin'. Habn't made me mind up. We'll have a yarn about 'n . . .pembye. He made for the beer barrel, then came back to say emphatically, 'I didn't get where I am today without wearing a 'at.' It was lost on Tim, who never saw through such dry humour. How could a man so clever be so stupid? He used to walk into there, into the Fisherman's Lodge, when he was canvassing votes, smoking his pipe as if he went in every day. And he couldn't even be sure if they were having him on. Silas Rouncefield said to him once in his deep confiding bass, 'We reckon you'd be a good man to stand in the General Erection.' And Tim had gone out later saying, 'Hilarious. Bloody hilarious,' congratulating himself on his self-control. Back in the Lodge there were grins and twinkling eyes. But they would vote for him anyway. He was a good old sort. He was one of we.

I was too tired to dance and was thankful that Cleo's taste in music was similar to mine. There was not too much of the raucous stuff, and people could hear themselves speak. She seemed distracted, yet came over and spoke to me for some time, which compensated a little for the afternoon. Each time some new arrivals, whether invited or not, came to the door, she turned expectantly, hoping, yet not hoping, that it was Steve. I suspected that she was afraid I might ask what they had been doing, out there together.

As it happened the little cottage was not too crowded. Far more came than were invited, of course, but they were a congenial gathering and enjoyed themselves without wrecking the place. I found that my glass was never empty, what with this one and that one coming over for a chat and tipping something in it as soon as it was getting low. To my secret delight I saw Barbara in conversation with Uncle Joe, while John ambled from one woman to another, trying to chat them up. Tim was expounding to the girl, Fay, and I waited for his cheeks to split from all that smiling and grinning. All the other women knew John, and he was having little success. Joe was talking intently into Barbara's ear, his eyes sparkling, and she occasionally burst into a peal of earthy laughter. He was a genuine charmer, old Uncle Joe, and his honest humour delightful if you were not a prude, or a snob. 'Right on top of her bleddy 'ead.' I heard him say at one point, and smiled myself at the memory. Cleo had invited Maggie, but, of course, she declined. She wouldn't mix with that crowd. That arty crowd. Pity. I should like to see her drunk.

My amusement was short-lived. John Ashton came over. I could never fathom why he didn't realize how much I disliked him. I knew he disliked me.

'Hello, Shim,' he said, 'glad to see you are aloof from the drunkards.'

Now, if there is one thing that I detest it's being called 'Shim'. It is exasperating! I have a perfectly good Cornish name. If people don't like 'Shimshai' they can use that. Mind, I do think Shimshai is rather apt.

John had that supercilious look on his chacks, a sneering condescension. I don't know why he does it. We all know the silly bugger. 'Seems Steve is not allowed out,' he said gloatingly.

'How's your mother?' I said.

'Oh, she's fine, fine,' nodding his head in affirmation.

'And how's the job?'

'Job! Is that all you call it?'

He was a potter. Did I tell you? One of the few Cornish people to become directly involved in the world of Arts and Crafts. And he was a good craftsman, I have to grant him that. His long, elegant fingers were made for the work, but he had given it up to 'go into antiques'. He was working at home, doing up old furniture, 'restoring' he called it of course, for a firm in Truro.

'It's a craft,' he said, 'an art.'

'I thought pottery was more of a craft, an art if you insist, than what you are doing now, frigging around with secondhand furniture.'

He jumped on that like a flash. 'By God it is,' he said. 'And I would be doing it now if it weren't for that bastard.' He was talking about the man who taught him everything he knew about making pots. 'Ten years I gave that bastard, Shim. Ten bleddy years. For a pittance.'

I didn't want to spend my time at Cleo's party listening to John Ashton's self-pitying railing against everyone who had ever crossed his path. It is his yarn. Given half a chance he'll tell it to anybody. I had heard it before. 'Look around you . . .' he began. I did. 'Cleo needs a hand,' I said, and went into the kitchen where she was preparing plates of food.

Tony had bagged the armchair, which had been pushed over into the corner of the room, and later I sat beside him to rest my legs. I can't remember much else of the evening. Cleo gave up looking at the door. There seemed to be a continual stream of women coming to talk to Tony. They kissed him and sat on his knee and he kept muttering about 'a poor ould fella like me'. The crafty devil. The last time I saw Joe and Barbara they were hanging on to each other giggling helplessly. Tim went off with Fay, the bit of crumpet from Birmingham. In case she couldn't find the way, he said. When everyone else had left, Cleo came and sat with me on the floor at Tony's feet and we got quietly drunk, talking a load of philosophical nonsense, as people do at the tail-end of parties, before finally we fell asleep in a heap on the rug.

Chapter Thirteen

There was by tradition an unwritten law, no fishing, and, by implication, no boating at all, on a Sunday. Six days shalt thou labour . . .On a Sunday in those days all the craft in the crowded harbour lay afloat in tiers at their moorings, with the fresh paint and varnish of hulls and spars reflected in the still water, or lay, as they did now, at rest on the rippled sand. That is the way it was. They way it had always been. The Sabbath Day was still holy, apparently. Things are very different now. You can't tell Sundays from Mondays now. Who would have thought to see such changes?

By mid-May most of the boats were out. Brought from cellars and back-courts and car parks, or, in the case of larger craft, from the estuary across the bay where they had lain between the high tides of autumn and spring. High and dry, and safe from the storms of winter, stirred only occasionally by gentle estuarine ripples bearing turds from the sewers of Hayle.

From the front window Steve could see over the roofs of the close-packed houses of down'long and into the harbour.

Mary went again to check the dining-room, to ensure that she had forgotten nothing. That the table-cloths were clean, that there were no stains of washing water on the cutlery, that the cereals were out, and the salt and pepper. The first week was always the worst. Wasn't so bad when you were in the swing of it, into the routine.

They were not down yet, though she had heard them moving around upstairs and it was time, so she rang the gong. The gong had been old man Trewellard's, up to Talland Road. He brought it home from abroad.

It sounded very professional. Steve moved it out of the hallway in the winter, because every time he came home late from the Lodge or the pub he'd knock into the bleddy ugly great thing and wake up half the people in the terrace.

In the kitchen Mary began to fry the eggs and bacon and tomatoes, and cut bread for toast, so that everything would be freshly cooked when the people were ready. She didn't like things kept warm for people. People like things right.

Steve came in and felt the teapot, closing the door behind him for privacy, but Mary opened it that she might know when the people came down. The teapot was their own. A big brown much-chipped china pot with a blue lid from some other pot long since broken beyond repair and discarded. The people had their own blue-and-white pots to match the crockery, for people like things right.

'That's cold,' Mary said.

'It'll do.'

'Well, you'll have to wait for your breakfast.'

'Never mind about that. I'm in no hurry. I'll do my own d'reckly. I'll just have a cup of tay.' He poured himself some tea and sat at the table. 'Anything I can do?'

'Is that they, comin' down?' She peered round the door, furtively, as if she were in someone else's house. ''Es, my Lor'. They're down.' Rushing back to the cooker. 'I'm hardly ready yet.' Tapping an egg on the frying-pan. 'Now the yolk's broke,' she said. 'Can't serve that,' becoming nervous in her haste.

'There's plenty of time,' Steve said. 'Now, don't get in a tizzy.'

'*You* don't have to serve them.' Breaking another egg on the pan. 'I'm not taking no broken eggs in for people,' and as an afterthought, that there should be no waste, 'you can have that.'

'It'll do me. Nawthen wrong with that egg.'

'Oh, dammee,' she said near to tears and pulling out the grill, 'Now the dammee toast is burnt.'

'That's all right. Nawthen wrong with that toast.'

'*It's burnt!*'

Steve sipped his tea. 'Don't worry so,' he said, 'there's plenty of time. You can do more.'

'We ought to have a proper dammee toaster. I'm dammee fed up with trying to do everything to once on that ol' cooker. Fed up with it.'

He didn't answer, and remained silent, eating the broken-yolked egg and the slightly overdone toast all the while that Mary served the breakfasts. There was nothing he could do. Nowhere to go. So he sat there quietly trying to keep out of the way while Mary came in and out of the kitchen. He listened to her cheerful remarks to the guests—'Had a good night? Looks like being a fine day. Go easy in the sun'—and watched her face change from the mirthless landlady's smile to a frown of anxiety as she came in with the laden tray.

'I'll do the dishes,' he said, 'while you do the rooms.'

'I can't do no rooms till they're all gone out.'

'Well,' he said, trying to calm her, knowing that she could cope with the work in half the time if only she would relax, 'sit down and have a cup of tay . . . I don't s'pose you've had breakfast yet and you have plenty of time. There's only two rooms. I've made our bed.' Rising from his chair, 'I'll put the kettle on, and I'll have another cup myself.'

She sat at the table, with her chin in her hand, relieved that the guests had enjoyed their breakfast, that they had enough to eat, that there were no complaints. They had settled in and were happy, the occasional burst of laughter from the dining-room reassured her, and provided the weather stayed fine they would have a good week. Every year it was the same, the awful worry of the first few days. Especially Sundays, with the first proper meals after the guests' arrival following the journey down the day before when they were tired and irritable and upset by the slightest little thing. Mary needed the compliments of the first few guests to give her confidence to see her into the season. After that it was routine, tiring routine, but she enjoyed it—meeting people and giving them a good holiday. And making the money. She had no delusions about that. It was all for the money. Steve was too easy-going. Thought you could live on fresh air.

'What shall us do today?' he asked hopefully.

She was beginning to relax, but already seeking another task. 'I thought I'd move us into the back room, I'm going to Chapel this evenin'. Shain't have much more chance for the summer.'

'I thought we might go off somewhere.' He would refuse to move into the back room, as Mary knew full well. He had agreed to do it, to pile all their things in there, and sleep on bunks for June, July and August, the three peak months of the holiday season. He detested it, and would not move a day before or after the time. She was trying him on, trying to have her way, for there was little probability of filling the extra rooms at this time of year. So he ignored the suggestion. 'I thought we could go out the cliffs.' And to remind her, gently, that the years were going, 'We haven't been out there for years.'

'You were out there last week.'

'The two of us. Together. I meant the two of us.'

She wouldn't go. She would stay here, in the house, finding work, and then complain later that she never had a minute. 'You would enjoy it, once you were there.'

She rose from the table, terminating the discussion. 'I'm not able to walk all that way out there. I was up at half past six this morning.'

'And I was up at half past four yesterday morning to catch the tide, and never stopped till after half past nine at night!' He tried again. 'We can have the rest of the day off. Go somewhere else if you like, not out the cliffs if you don't want to. There's plenty of other places. Let's take the van and go off.'

'And when you're out, you never want to come home,' she said, filling the washing-up bowl, 'and I don't want to be late for Chapel.' She was not to be persuaded, and would be bad tempered all day if they did go off somewhere. He gave up.

'I told you I'd do they dishes,' he reminded her irritably, feeling already the guilt of taking the day off while knowing that Mary would be working here in the house.

'I might's well do them. I can't do anything else till the people are gone out. You can clear the table.'

He rose slowly and took the few things he had used for his breakfast to the sink. He wanted to put his arms around her, to ask her again to go out in the sun with him, but feared the rebuke. He stood beside her in silence. She had dark hair. Not black exactly, but very dark, now with a few streaks of grey. Her skin was smooth and clear and her face and arms slightly tanned from the odd hours when she had sat in a chair in the small front garden. She tanned well. He remembered how brown she was as a girl. Her brown legs and back in the modest one-piece she used for swimming, which used to hang loosely over her big round tits. She was wearing a light jumper, and they looked smaller now, but her waist was thicker and her legs beginning to lose their firmness although she was still quite trim. A long walk and a swim in the sea would do her good, he thought. She hasn't worn a cozzy since the girl was born, not even when she took the child to the beach when she was small. She was ashamed and embarrassed by a few stretch-marks and wore a light frock while sitting on the sand with Martha and the others, sometimes lifting it to her knees to paddle with the children in the sea. She, who had been such a good swimmer.

'You go,' she said without looking at him, 'you go on off, if you want to.'

'Well, I don't want to hang around here all day, doing nothing.'

'You go on. I'm doing dinner dinner-time.' Dinner-time is midday. 'You can have yours when you come home. I'll put'n on a saucepan if I've gone to Chapel.'

He felt that he was being thrown out as redundant. It would be like this all summer. Go off and keep out of the way. 'Yes,' he said, 'I think I will. I might as well. I'll take a flask and a bit of saffron,' attempting to make the decision his own . . . 'No point in hanging around here all day.'

Mary continued washing dishes in silence while Steve made two flasks of tea, cut and buttered some saffron cake and bread. He put them, together with a couple of apples, a towel and a book, in a canvas bag. 'I'll take the van,' he said as he laced up his boots. 'I'd better check the *Mermaid* over before I go off. Make sure everything is all right.' He wore his guarnsey, for there was still a bit of a breeze.

Mary submitted to a kiss as he left, glad to see the back of him, for she knew he wouldn't be happy while staying around the house, but would become more and more morose as the day drew on, finally going off to the pub or the Lodge. He was forever out. In the winter it was always the Lodge or the pub, and in the summer he used to go off, by himself. He always had, even before they were married. She worried privately that he wasn't quite right, not normal. To go off like that and be—to take his clothes off. It wasn't the sort of thing that normal people belong to do. She never mentioned it to him, the first time she had seen him tanned all over, as if she hadn't noticed, and neither did Steve. He had taken her out to his favourite place a few times, when they were courting, and after they were married, before the children were born, but she didn't like going. He would try to do it. Out there in the open, under the very sky. Where somebody might come along. As if they were school kids or, why, dammee animals. There was no sense in it.

Steve parked the van by the Fisherman's Co-op and went down along the lines of mooring ropes to check the *Mermaid*. He checked her every Sunday, the only day she was not in use, just to be sure. There was no need to climb aboard. He checked the moorings and the lockers. You never knew who was who, these days, so many strangers around that you didn't know who they were, nor what they were . . . not like it was. The breeze was dying and the day was getting hotter. It can be like that in May month; after all, it's only a few weeks to the longest day. He leaned over the gunnel, looking at the varnish shining and the brasswork glinting in the sun. She was a fine craft.

Two or three of the other chaps were down too. The part-timers, mostly, the ones who had jobs in the week and only went out on Saturdays. Saturdays and evenings when the tide was right. They were the ones whose hearts were on the sea, but who were forced to make a living ashore. There was no money in fishing. Not then.

She had her shoes off, carrying them in her hand, and her jeans were rolled up to just below the knees. She was wading through the pools already deepened by the rising tide. The man with her, a tall man, wearing navy corduroys, a pale blue sweater and white plimsolls, kept to the sandbank and dry ground, so they approached the *Mermaid* by diverging paths.

Steve saw them coming, and was trapped.

They had not spoken since that day. They had not met. Though Steve had seen her, once in Fore Street when he had gone down Court Cocking to avoid her, and once she had walked past the Lodge when he had been leaning on the railing with the chaps. They had smiled at each other, shyly, and Steve felt sure the men would see the red flush which swept over his cheeks. They were all too engrossed in looking at her, however furtively, and did not notice. 'A fine craft.' 'A fine craft.'

Now, there was no chance of avoiding her, of walking away from them. He would have to stop and talk. He expected her to wave, or sing out, when still a brear way off, instead of which she looked up at him only once, and kept her head down, watching her feet in the water until she and the man came together at the *Mermaid's* side. The port side, facing him.

'Good morning, Steve,' she said.

'Good morning,' a pause before 'Cleo'. Hesitant in using her name.

'This is Kevin Robinson.'

'How d'you do.' The were too far away to shake hands.

'Seems I'm in your debt,' Robinson said. 'I want to thank you.'

Steve looked at him directly for the first time, taking his eyes from Cleo to see the fairish brown hair, tanned face and eyes which were neither brown nor green, but both, and tired. Robinson had slight pouches under his eyes like a man who persistently doesn't get enough sleep.

'What for?' Steve asked him.

'Seems you saved my boat.'

'Oh!' Steve said, laughing. 'You're the stranger.' He left the starboard side to come round under the bow moorings to take the stranger's hand. 'We thought you'd forgotten all about her.'

'No. I just couldn't get down before. Joe told me all about you. Said she's have been a goner if you hadn't tightened the moorings.'

'She nearly went. We were only just in time. James and me. Couldn't have done it on my own.'

'Well, I want you to know how grateful I am. We made a poor job of the moorings, I'm afraid. I had to be in Liverpool the next day to join my ship. I've been away ever since.'

And they stayed chatting together, about one thing and another, moorings and tides, things like that, till the tide came to their feet and they strolled up to the slip and sat on a timber baulk.

'I'll soon be down for the summer,' the stranger said, 'and I've got Joe to keep his eye on her for me now. I've given him my address so he can let me know if anything is wanted.'

'Joe's all right,' Steve told him. 'You can rely on Joe.'

Avoiding the blue eyes of Cleo. Talking directly to Kevin Robinson, or looking towards the boats floating off on the incoming tide, as he spoke, 'You're in the Navy, then?'

'Merchant Navy,' Robinson said. 'I'm skipper of a freighter, on the South American run at the moment. Refrigerated cargoes, mostly meat, and bananas. Getting tired of it.' Looking at Cleo, 'Time I got myself a shore job and settled down.'

'You're not married then?' Steve found himself asking, annoyed with himself for asking a question which had been invited for Cleo's benefit. Knowing, before asking, that the answer would be 'No'.

'Never had time,' said the other. 'Besides, there's not much opportunity of meeting the right girl in the middle of the Atlantic.'

Steve reckoned Robinson was about thirty-five. A good bit younger than himself, and he had obviously done well in his career to be in command of such a ship at his age. He was momentarily jealous, but made an effort to conceal it.

'Thought you sailors had a girl in every port,' he said jokingly, to which Robinson replied as if reminded of the great weight of his responsibilities. 'For the crew, possibly, but when you are on the bridge, the busiest times are in port. More and more paperwork on every trip it seems.' He sighed, then looked around the harbour, suddenly brightening up at the prospect of his forthcoming long leave. 'This would do me,' he said. 'Might even pack it all up, and come down here to live.'

'What would you do with yourself?' Cleo asked him. 'You would be bored stiff after a few months.'

'Do a bit of fishing. A bit of writing.'

Steve saw Cleo look at Robinson with that frank stare of hers, and saw Robinson avoid it, as most men did, before continuing, 'There's always plenty to do.'

The wind was dying, and the rising sun was warm on the timber where they sat. A slight vapour rose from the concrete and granite of the slip as the last moisture from the night's rain evaporated before the heat of the day. Time to make tracks to the cliffs and leave these two together, Steve thought, and decided to seek the opportunity to go before some other topic arose which would require discussion. It would be warm out there, the sea-pinks beginning to flower. Such days are rare.

'And talking of things to do,' Robinson said, looking at his watch, 'I've arranged to see Tim Penberthy this morning.' He rose and held out his hand to Steve, who took it while remaining seated. 'Nice to have met, at last. I'm sure we will be seeing a lot of each other in the future,' the latter with a slight nod to Cleo.

'Yes,' Steve said, taken aback by the other's abrupt departure.

124

'If you need anything, give me a shout.'

'Will do! Bye. Bye, Cleo.'

'Bye!' she said.

His plimsolls left damp footprints on the slipway, and Steve stared absently at them drying out, deciding whether to make some comment on Robinson—'Seems a nice chap', or something like that—to signify approval of her choice of company. He said nothing, however, not wishing to look at her, knowing that her gaze was upon him, until the silence became an embarrassment.

At last he said, 'A local wouldn't do that,' and she was beaten, having to ask, 'Do what?'

'Look at his watch,' said Steve, 'with the north face of the William Craze up there for all to see.'

'The what?'

'The William Craze! The town clock!' He nodded to the church tower on the other side of the harbour, and they were laughing together, because they were together, but needed to appear otherwise, that they were laughing at his remarks, and Steve saw some of the men on the Platt looking at them.

People were opening deck-chairs, spreading towels on the sand. Some were stripped off already, exposing to the sun their white city skin which would be red and blistered during their sleepless night tonight. The men outside the Lodge and up on the Platt began pacing out their strides, missing nothing that went on, in and around the harbour.

'He paid for it, I b'lieve.' Grinning at her and thinking what a delightful open laugh she had. Noticing that her teeth were not quite even, relieved to find some fault in her. Thinking that he should go off now, go off on his own as he intended, and leave her here.

'No painting today?' he asked. And she shook her head, looking at him.

'No painting.'

If he didn't go soon they would notice the time he was spending talking to her, and would be passing remarks among themselves. 'Go for'n, Ste'. Heh heh!' Pacing up and down.

'And you? Not working?'

'Yes,' he ought to tell her, 'doing a little job for somebody or other.' And go off. On his own.

'No,' he said. 'Not today.'

'I thought it was too fine to stay indoors,' she said.

'It's going to be a fine day, sure 'nough.'

She swung one leg over the baulk, and sat astride it, with her hands in front of her, tapping on the timber with two fingers, belying her apparently complete relaxation.

'Going to Chapel?' she said, and he thought for a moment that she was deriding him, realizing his mistake when he looked directly at her eyes. 'No,' he said, and they sat for some time, saying nothing. Steve picked up his bag.

'You're going to the cliffs.'

'How do you know?'

'Your boots. And your bag.'

'Oh! Yes.'

That little moron of a traffic warden would shove a ticket on his van if he didn't move her soon. He was from up-country. He had no idea. Steve could see him up by the lifeboat house, watching the cars coming from the market house. Already a few cars were turning into the car park behind the pub. The early ones, driven by enterprising men who left the hotels and guest-houses, laden down with airbeds and wind-breaks, before the wives and children were ready. Showing the same initiative which enabled them to compete successfully in their working lives. Later, the families would arrive on the beach to find an established territory guarded by the displaying male. After a few days they regarded a particular patch of sand as their own, resenting any intrusion by others, endeavouring to arrive a little earlier next morning should their favourite patch be occupied. They were like bull seals, and often as blubbery.

One or two more had come to the Lodge. Tommy Blue was there, peering through his glasses at the incoming tide, assessing the weather from habit. James. A few more, yarnin'. Quizzy Maggie settled herself on the long bench outside the Friendship Cellar that was. Out for a breath of air, and to see who was who, and what was what, before returning home to cook her lonely Sunday dinner and take an afternoon nap before Chapel. George leaned over the railings opposite the pub, his eyes a little bleary still from the smoke and drink of the night before. Spending a few moments in the sunshine, looking over the bodies before unlocking the door and entering the gloom of the empty pub to prepare for the lunch-time session. Shaking his head over the chances he had missed in the past and those he would not see in the future. Yet smiling at those he had taken. Shaking his head and smiling in the Sunday morning sun.

A few people were buying newspapers from the piles laid on the ground by Annabella's place. The shops didn't open on Sundays, though they do now.

'Come with me!' said Steve, meeting her gaze and feeling a slight flush across the temple as he spoke. 'Go home and put some boots on. I'll pick you up at Porthmeor in ten minutes.'

His van was there, in front of the Co-op. But she knew exactly what he meant.

'All right.' She swung her leg back over the timber and left him. He turned his back on her departure and looked at the harbour, seeing nothing. Then he hitched his bag across his shoulder and strolled up to the Lodge. Taking his time.

'I see,' said Tommy Blue, 'that he's here.'

"Es, he's here. He's a sea captain.'

'A say capn.'

'B'en away to sea.'

'Away to say!' Tommy and the others pondered on this. On how a man who was a seaman could make such a lash-up of a simple mooring. A man who was a say capn.

'It's all office work now,' Steve said, 'being a capn.'

'Well, 'es.'

"Es, I s'pose.'

Tommy Blue gave one short snort of derisive laughter, thereby expressing, for once, his opinion. 'He's a fine *looking* man,' he said, and shook in silent mirth, passing a forefinger under his spectacles to wipe away a tear.

Steve stayed chatting for a while to Tommy Blue, and James and they. Silas Rouncefield turned up. Come down for the papers.

'Had your breakfast, Silas?' asked Tommy Blue. A favourite morning greeting. Better than 'How are you?' Anyone can see damn well how people are, but you can't tell if they've had their breakfast.

'Hi'm like High George,' said Silas, and they all grinned in memory of one gone. 'Hi had'n *hours* ago.' Grinning more than ever at Silas's voice, which changed rapidly from falsetto to bass. Silas rarely laughed these days, but enjoyed the humour in the memory of High George, who had always had his meals hours before anyone else and described them in picturesque language which was a thrice-daily source of amusement to all.

'Where 'ee goin' 'en, Steve,' asked Silas Rouncefield, pitching his voice for the tenors, 'with your bag and boots?' Down with the basses for the observation, 'Bit early for blackberries.'

'Oh, just off for a bit of a round.'

"Es, well, Hi don't blame 'ee. Used to go off m'self. Years ago. Away from all this . . .' He looked to see who was in earshot, glancing rapidily over each shoulder, and reverberated deep into Steve's ear'. . . *Bloody racket!*' and leaned back, squinting at Steve from under the folds of his black tam.

Steve assumed that Silas was referring to the faint distorted crackling from a transistor on the beach below them, or, on the other hand, it could have been the traffic he meant. The cars passing the Lodge on the way to the down'long car parks.

"Es,' said Steve. 'I'm going off while I have the chance.' He left them and went to the van. The traffic warden was coming along the wharf. 'Stupid bugger!' Steve muttered under his breath as he turned the starter and nodded pleasantly to the unsmiling face under the black-and-yellow hat. Black and yellow, Steve mused, like wasps and hornets. Must be more than coincidence. They probably had a whole jaffle* of Civil Service psychologists to work that one out. Nature's warning colours. Black and yellow. And Cleo would be waiting. He hoped no one would see her getting into the van.

*Jaffle: Cornish dialect, bunch or cluster—used derogatively.

Chapter Fourteen

She was walking along the road above the beach, and Steve overtook her and stopped, opening the van door slightly. She slipped in beside him and he drove off without a word, changing into low gear to climb the steel hill up to Ayr and out of town, past the pool and the granite camel formed of clustered boulders on top of Rosewall Hill.

The road led on through Zennor, and past tiny fields encased in granite slabs where Guernsey cows with long-lashed eyes ignored them and the world. Between the clustered cottages and barns of ancient farms they went, while to the south the boulder-studded slopes rose to massive, wind-intagliated carns thrusting through the gorse and bracken. The scenery was magnificent, with the fresh greens of early summer just obscuring last year's rusty fronds and whitened grasses; new leaves on the willows in the valley, and stunted hawthorns flowering bravely, despite the gales of winter. To the north, on their right, fields on the flat and narrow coastal strip were bounded by the fall of the cliffs and the sea; with each shallow valley guiding water from the upland catchment to the clear streams falling to the rock-strewn coves below.

The coastal strip narrowed to rough moorland by Carn Galver and Bosigran. Steve turned into a lay-by thronged with picknickers. Picnics eating. Picnics looking at the scenery, at the cars; picnics not listening to transistor radios and the skylarks' song. Picnics asleep in stationary ninety-mile-an-hour, four-doors-open saloons. Open-mouthed, snoring picnics, dreaming of in-trays and production lines. Picnics enjoying the wild scenery from the safety of their cars, as if they were in wildest Africa or the Matto Grosso. Enjoying the wilderness and the remoteness of the unspoilt coastline. And saying that if they won the football pools, they would build a house here.

They left the van and Steve led the way through the gorse and heather to the cliff, using the path that the more venturesome of tourists used to reach an outcrop of rock which overlooked the sea. And from here on, there was no path, for this was the last outpost of civilization in a road-bound society, and the cars were already two hundred yards away. From here on, no tourist went, and few Cornishmen had been.

The sea below, far below the path, was green and the cliffs to the west were black. Dry lime-green mosses which had flourished in the acid wet of winter crunched underfoot like coloured snow. Grey-green lichen on the stones, bright green of new grass and bracken, dark wind-parched green of heather clustered in the face of the salted boulders. Blue, sky blue, sky and stars of vernal squill. Some late primroses, pink campion, and in the damp patches, white clusters of sea campion starred the cliffs and tumbled down beside the stream, falling in a shower of sparkles to the sea. Bluebells—bluebells in prolific drifts, bluebells unavoidably trampled underfoot like crushed amethysts as he led the way down, down—down to the sea.

Down through narrow clefts in towering spires of rock, carved by the centuries into Pharaonic statues, and down into deep gullies where the sun never shone and ferns were unfolding for the summer. The rocks towered above them, dwarfing them, and the surf breaking below was echoed from some cavern in the cliff. Cries of sea-birds, wild weird cries, reverberating from the crags as, reaching the base of the spires, they skirted the edge of a zawn* where the sea entered a narrow, steep-sided fissure in the rock. The high towers behind shaded them, and she shivered, despite the exertion of the descent. They peered over at the clustered sea-birds nesting on the ledges below.

The long steep climb and the rocks behind isolated them from the world. No one came here. On other cliffs the arduous climb was made by anglers who fished for bass and pollock on the sandy bottom between the submerged rocks, but here the granite rose in jagged reefs offshore, and dark, hard stalks of oarweed would foul too many hooks.

'Nobody ever comes here,' he said, 'except me. Spent hours out here, and I always have it to myself.' He dumped the packs upon the ground and sat beside them, unlacing his boots. 'Like it?'

She did not answer, but sat beside him in the sea-pinks, hugging her knees, head on one side, looking along the coast and at the motion of the waves swirling over the half submerged rocks.

'You're very quiet,' he added eventually.

'Is there really a road up there?' she asked, 'and towns and factories and all those people? It is so beautiful here, serene. It is,

*Zawn: inlet in a cliff

130

Steve. Look at the colours in the sea, every hue from that pale lime green in the sandy shallows to dark brooding purple over the rocks. And how white the surf around the cliffs. I should have brought my paints. I could paint here. The mood of it—I would try to capture the purity and—it's completely natural and good. No trace of the ugly work of man.'

Steve laughed. 'You wouldn't have said that if you had come out here a hundred years ago. Over there, look. Beneath the brow of the headland. Old tin-mine workings. You can still see the foundations of the old buildings and the lines of the track leading down to them. See? All overgrown and obscured, but still there for all that. It would have been all ugly scars and rubble in those days. Just imagine the slog they must have had in bringing the stuff up from down there. And all with mules and ponies. But they're all gone now, poor devils, rotted in Pendeen churchyard, bleddy hundreds of them, coughed up their lungs for a few bob a week while the owners made bleddy fortunes—still, they're all rotted too; and nature soon creeps in to hide the filth and muck. Down at Bottallack it's lovely now, the wild flowers have covered the spoil-tips, and the mine buildings are quite romantic in a way . . . at least they built with granite. 'Ansome stuff for building. What are you laughing at?'

'You are funny!'

Suddenly, there was a dark shape hurtling down towards them from the cliff behind.

'Look!' cried Steve. 'A peregrine. A peregrine falcon.'

He saw the great yellow eyes as the peregrine looked down on them before flying rapidly around the cliff and out of sight. 'A peregrine,' he said, 'I haven't seen one of those for years. What a sight!'

'You seem to know all the birds,' she said.

'Oh, not really. I only know a few.' He felt a little self-conscious at his sudden display of enthusiasm, and by way of explanation added, 'I like birds.'

'You are funny,' she said again.

Steve made a face at her and continued unlacing his boots. Hardly worth putting them on for half an hour's walk, but shoes were no good for scrambling down the cliffs. Cleo was only wearing ordinary shoes, she must have got gorse in them, the prickles always get into shoes. She was taking them off, yes, there they were, sticking afast her socks. She picked them out. 'I've got prickles in my shoes,' she said, pulling the socks off; at least she had a thick pair of socks on. He'd suggested she wear boots or something.

'Why didn't you wear boots?'

'These are all I have.' Only one pair of shoes, but she didn't mind. Jesus, see Mary with only one pair of shoes, he'd never hear the bleddy

131

last of it. How can I go to Chapel with these ould things and all that stuff, and a new hat every bleddy now and then, every time somebody else had one. Hats are for keeping your bleddy head dry, that's what he ought to tell her; hats are for keeping your bleddy head dry. Cleo never wore hats, least he'd never seen her in a hat. 'Have you got a hat?'

'A hat? No. Whatever makes you ask?'

'Oh, I just wondered.' Only one pair of shoes, no hat. Wonder how many clothes she does have; not very many, but she always looks right, she always looks comfortable in her clothes, as if she didn't know they were there. Mind, she had a good figure. Trouble with Mary, you could spend a bleddy fortune on clothes and she still wouldn't look right. Conscious of everything she wore, down to the last trimmings. Expecting the clothes to do something for her instead of bringing the clothes to life. And now her figure was going. Said it was the children: 'You try having children'—she always said 'children' instead of 'cheldern' when she was telling him off—'you try having children, see how you like it.' How the hell can I have kids, I've done just about everything else a woman's supposed to do, everything from changing nappies to washing dishes and running arrants. You can't please 'em no-how. In any case a woman ought to look right with no clothes on. Used to be too shy, or ashamed, or something. Why? 'And they were both naked, the man and his wife, and they were not ashamed.' She had a good figure then, in the beginning. Now, she expected him to do everything. It all had to come from him. Why? Because of the few stretch marks? I don't mind them. Come to think of it I never have seen a woman with no clothes on in daylight, not in daylight. And Mary never saw me. Always made those remarks, 'Look at that g'eat thing. Put 'n away, for pity's sake,' when he wanted her to . . oh, God. Why? He sighed, 'Ahh dear,' as he put his boots in a hollow among the rocks.

'What are you thinking about?'

'Genesis, Chapter two, Verse twenty-five. But you didn't answer me. Do you like it?'

'Yes, I like it.' There was a trace of innuendo in her voice, as if she were still laughing at him. But she turned again to the sea. 'It's indescribable,' she said. 'I had no idea there were still places like this. I can see why you spend so much time out here. It's so peaceful. But what do you do? Just sit?'

'Just sit,' he said, half turning to her. 'This is my phrontistery.'

Just sit and let his mind wander through the tangled paths of daydreams. And sleep in the sun, with the music of the waves lapping the eternal rocks, and the breezes dancing with the bracken fronds. Daydreaming, sleep-dreaming. Just sit and look at it.

Worship it. This is my religion. My God. There is no god but Good. And this is Good. And even better with someone to share it with. Mary would never come here. She would never get down the cliff. It is hot. The sun is burning through my guarnsey. There's my boots and socks off. Soon we will both be naked.

'Whatever is a phrontistery?'

'A thinking place. From the Greek.' He smiled apologetically. 'I came across it in the dictionary when I was looking up "Phrygian".'

'And why were you looking up "Phrygian"?'

'I thought it was a naughty word. To do with sex. I was only young.' What a laugh she had. So open—free. She seemed to enjoy her laughter as much as whatever she might be laughing at.

'Oh, Steve. Isn't this lovely? Look at the sea. See how clear it is, how green there over the sand. You can see right to the bottom. Can we swim? Is it safe?'

They would swim together. She wanted that, as he did.

'It's safe just here. No currents, as long as you keep in from the headland, and as long as it's not rough. I swim here.'

'It's not rough now?'

'Oh, no. It's O.K. today. Fine. Just right. Perfect.'

'Are you sure no one comes here?'

He shook his head. 'I've been here hundreds of times, and I've never seen anyone else down here.' Her jumper rucked up. He could see her belly-button. And she didn't have one—just a slight horizontal slit with some very fine silvery down, glinting in the sun above the leather of her belt. She wore nothing under the jumper, as usual.

Steve took off his guarnsey. Then his shirt. He was tanned brown from his previous days in the sun. Not a deep tan, but a light, even brown. He leaned on his elbow looking at her. A brief ghost of mischief touched her face. She looked along the line of cliffs, more than a mile away, where there was no footpath, and back above their heads where the towering rocks hid them from the world. She sat up, and caught hold of the bottom of her pullover with both hands. 'Why not?' she said, and with a smooth movement pulled it over her head. They were as he expected. Beautiful, small, firm. He wanted to kiss them, there and then. She showed them to him by reaching behind her to lay the pullover on the grass. She undid the buckle of her belt, lay back on the pullover and wriggled out of her jeans, lifting her haunches off the ground to show him the tight mound in the pale blue lace. She smirked at him, for he could not take his eyes from her. 'It's only like a bikini,' she said.

'It's against the law, you know,' he said, admiring both her body and her impudence. 'The Council have made a bye-law—nudity is indecent.'

She turned from laying her jeans in the form of a bed and mouthed a soundless obscenity 'F—the law,' and laughed, lying on her belly to feel the warm sunshine on her back.

He lay on his front. He couldn't let her see it. They went to sleep, and the sun rose higher with never a cloud in the sky, while the inflowing tide lapped gently the sizzling barnacles encrusted on the rocks. The breeze died, too lazy to stir the bracken or ripple the surface of the sparkling sea. When he awoke, with a fine perspiration in the creases of his arms, she was sitting up, looking at him, completely naked. Her breasts were white against the brown of her legs and stomach, and her hair hung over them in a golden haze. She was like a dream, an apparition of beauty, and Steve knew then they would lie so many times together. That it was as natural for them to be unclothed in the sun as it was for the sun to rise in the sky.

She rolled over to him, kissed him on the shoulder. 'A swim,' she said, and ran to the sea. He was up in time to see the splash as she pierced the surface from a running dive, he kicked off his denims and was after her—diving in beside her as she surfaced. Later, when he tried to remember this moment, tried to picture her face, with the wet hair streaming behind her, the visions would not materialize. The details—of the salt water on her face; the wavering lines of her long legs swaying languorously beneath the surface; the ripples over her breasts as she swam upon her back; the white, wet teeth, as laughing aloud she splashed water in his face; her white bum and the dark, mysterious triangle; images which he thought he could never forget became lost among the remembrances of the sensations they aroused in him. The whole of his reaction was, he recalled, somehow negative, in the sense that this was one of the few truly natural and spontaneous actions of his life. They came from the sea shivering, for although the water was inviting in its clarity and sparkle, there was no stretch of sun-baked sand here to warm it as there was on the beaches in the bay.

In the thrift-lined hollow they towelled off the salty drops and rubbed themselves warm in the sunshine. Cleo dropped to her knees. 'Dry my back,' she said. So Steve took the towel and rubbed it over her shoulders and back, brown except for the narrow strap-marks of her bikini top, warming her and himself with the rubbing, and feeling the embarrassment of his rising erection swaying so close to her spine and the white buttocks resting on her bare brown heels. He heard a pipit singing, high among the boulders of the cliff, or circling overhead, but kept looking at her body, her shoulders, and fine-textured skin. He rubbed her hair, the long flaxen hair catching the sunlight in the salt water, bending her neck forward while she submitted entirely to his manipulations and he dispensed with the towel and rubbed her with his hands. Palms over her shoulder-blades, then over her shoulders, her neck, thumbs down the spine while his fingers traced the outline of her ribs. She closed her eyes and made little sounds of pleasure. 'That's nice,' she said.

He kissed the nape of her neck, burying his face in the cool hair, keeping himself away from her, that she should not know of his excitement. 'I want,' he murmured into her hair, 'to say something about how lovely you are. I'm not much good at that kind of thing,' moving his hands from the brown waist down to the white round-ness of her buttocks where he held them, sitting on his haunches, knees apart, felling the hard heads of sea-pinks among his toes and the pulses beating throughout his body. Her breathing was deep and even, intense but relaxed, he could hear it over the swell of the sea, rising and falling smoothly over the jagged rocks. She brought her hands around and placed them on his knees, looking all the while at the sea sparkling in the sun. 'Are you excited?' she said.

'Yes.'

Listening to her breathing, trying to control his own, 'Are you?' And before she could answer, he came forward, slipping his hands beneath her breasts, cupping them in the palms of his hands and feeling the beat of her heart and the hard nipples while he pressed himself into her spine.

'God,' she said, 'it's running out of me.' And he came back from her and passed his hand beneath her, between her heels, leaving a clear thread of viscous liquid catching the sunlight between her back and himself.

He had never known such lust as rose in him then. He wished to throw her to the bed of pinks and thrust his erection right up inside her till she cried with the pain of it, but as the juices ran on to his hand and he caressed her gently, firmly, smearing her in her own sweet secretions, she began to laugh, quietly, and said, 'Oh, Steve, I don't think I've ever felt so randy.'

And Steve laughed. Laughed at the absurdity which had been in his mind. And at the other absurdity—that he might be embarrassed if she saw the erection standing over his naked balls—if she looked at him.

So he lay back on the thrift, the lust dispelled by love, and she turned and kneeled over him, with her breasts hanging. She drew them twice across him, trailing his glittering liquid from her nipples, and then kissed his chest and stomach before running her parted lips up the length of him and tasting briefly with her tongue the tang of the salty water.

Steve drew her up to him, kissed her on the lips and they lay on their sides as he slipped into her and Cleo felt the convulsive waves of

135

orgasm surge through her body as Steve rolled them over and thrust up through her opening legs with three great pumping throbs which followed one another with increasing intensity after intervals when they embraced each other's salty bodies in utter relaxation and oblivion.

The song of the rock pipit, trilling and vibrant, rising and falling over the surf-sounds and the caressing breeze which stirred the pastel heads of sea-pinks all about them, was like a song of joy in their mingling minds. Slowly their breathing subsided and as their eyes opened and met, Steve said, 'I have never . . .' whispering, as if they were surrounded by a thousand ears, 'never . . .'

Cleo placed two fingers on his lips, and with a slow shake of the head blew him an ephemeral kiss through a wistful mouth. He kissed her fingers, knowing her mind. 'No,' he said, and laid his head upon her breast. 'No. Of course.'

The pipit came to ground on spread and shivering wings, trilling the final phrases of its song with high head and pouting breast, its whole being and purpose concentrated into the deliverance of the ecstatic sound.

That which had been . . . that which was to come . . was irrelevant. They lay in each other's arms while she thought what a lovely man he was. She loved the sensuality of his muscles and the admiration of his eyes. Soon she wanted him again, but he was replete, dreamy, satisfied. She ran her hands over his brown body. 'It's not fair,' she said, as she combed her fingers through his pubic hair and removed a strand of lichen which had become entangled there.

'What's not fair?'

'You are all brown. And I have these two horrible white rings around me.'

'Well, they are not very wide, are they?' He smiled as she drew away and settled herself on a towel. 'Come out here again. They'll soon be as tanned as the rest of you.'

'I would like that. If you would.'

He lay close beside her. Picked a sea-pink, and with it traced the curve of her breast and nipples, tickling her. 'I know a better place than this. A secret place.' He cupped his hand around her. 'You'd better cover up, or turn over, they are getting pink.'

'It must be truly beautiful, if it is better than this.'

'It is magic.'

'Why didn't you take me there today?'

'I wasn't sure . . . It's a pool, left by the high tide. A pool of spirits—piskeys.' To his surprise, she didn't laugh at him. 'They like me, I can tell. You might smile, but some places on these cliffs are evil. You feel uncomfortable there, vulnerable. There are some places where I could never swim . . . It's just a way of explaining things.' He was about to dismiss the subject of spirits. All that nonsense about piskeys and buccas.* But her blue eyes were so sincere. 'Do you think they would like me?' she said.

'I'll take you there next week. I'm sure they'll like you. They'll love you.'

The sun was in her hair, and he drew it forward to shade her breasts, draping it over them like a flaxen curtain. He lay with his arms around her, with her hair and breasts against his chest. 'They'll love you,' he murmured. 'And I love you.'

She clutched him in a spasm of emotion, burying her face in his neck. 'Oh God, Steve,' he heard her sobbing. 'What are we doing? What are we doing?'

*Piskeys and buccas: spirits of countryside and mines in Cornwall.

Chapter Fifteen

Through the long hot summer they met, making their way separately, secretly, to the gateway in the lane, restraining their emotions beneath the casual greetings, embracing only with their eyes. He would sling her rucksack over his shoulder and after climbing the gate they would make their way across the fields, conscious of a tension between them, talking little and of trivialities, fearful lest they be seen. Then as they climbed a stile, or paused at a gate where Cleo spoke softly to the horses which pressed their soft muzzles through the bars, their hands might touch, their eyes meet and smile, and the hurried pace of walking slacken to a loitering enjoyment of the living day. Through the fields, then by way of the old miners' road, overgrown with blackthorn and chattering with magpies, they came hand in hand to the cliff. As the mood took them they would descend the long grassy slopes and scattered boulders to the sea, sometimes slowly, picking their way, talking, or with an impulsive rush they might jump and run, slide, tumble and roll to the bottom in a breathless tangle of laughter and kisses.

Hidden there in the shelter of the rocks, lying on a ledge above the green pool, he reading and she drawing or writing poetry, or both gazing absently at the gobies slithering through the weed, they found sanctuary from the mad world of reason and contrition.

They were sensitive to each other's temperament, and did not force their way into each other's minds without invitation, but recognized the mutual need for solitude of contemplation within the sphere of the other's presence.

Their bodies became an even brown, and they delighted in the sensuality of good health and sunlight, swimming in the pool together, or one watching from the rock ledges while the other lazed through the unrippled surface, then dried by the warm air they might lie close, seeing through half-closed eyes the vague contours of their outlines, glittering with salt. Their eyes would explore and the hands delicately trace the moulding of their bodies. Cleo would sit beside him as he stretched langourously, and run the palm of her hand along the complete length, with her fingers reading the Braille of muscles under the taut skin. They enjoyed their bodies as they enjoyed the sun and the sea and the clean cool air. Steve might lie with his head cushioned across her thighs, her hair tickling the back of his neck, till she heaved him off because he was stealing the sun. From the first days, when they would find some hidden niche between the rocks lest there should happen to be a venturesome walker or an angler in the area, they became more confident of the solitude, less furtive in slipping into the pool, and roamed the rocks with a natural composure and tranquility.

'Do you remember,' she said, dreamily, one day after a long silence when they had been watching the seaweed swaying sensuously in the gentle swell of the rising tide, 'the first time you made love?'

'I remember,' he said, 'everything,' and went on, watching the slow swirl of the seaweed, back and forth, to and fro. 'Life is all memories. I was thinking about it the other day. Until I met you, I had somehow stopped living. Nothing was happening. All my experiences were over, and I found myself daydreaming the past, over and over. And none of it was very important, no single instance or incident, yet out of it all—all together—emerges our lives.'

'Wasn't the first time important to you?'

'There wasn't a first time.'

Cleo said nothing to this. She was getting to know him almost as well as I do. He would explain in his own time, when he had analysed this, or some other, thought which had suddenly occurred to him as a revelation. He leant back against the rock, aware of the warm sunshine on his abdomen and groin. 'Life,' he said, 'is *now*.'

Then, after a long silence, when she assumed the thought had left his mind or that he had fallen asleep, and she was thinking of another shore, he said quite suddenly, 'She's still here.' Opening his eyes, 'I see her nearly every day.'

'You don't mean Mary, do you?' she asked, guessing.

'That was the time I think of as the first. There was an eclipse of the moon. A total eclipse.'

'It sounds very romantic. Dramatic, in fact.'

'It was a dammee disaster,' and, as if her earlier remark had just penetrated the jostling memories, 'No, not Mary.' He had told no one, never mentioned it. 'I could think of nothing else for days,' he said, 'and I didn't know what a disaster it was. She must have laughed at me for years,' with that wry smile, the brow raised over the closed eye, 'and I was concerned for *her*. Girls got pregnant in those days.'

'They do now.'

'Not girls like her! She was using something. Shoved it up her as soon as we sat on the grass. I didn't know. Can you believe it?' Pursing the lips, speaking with the facial expressions, even with his eyes shut. 'It was the moon. A big red moon and a total eclipse. There really was. I remember thinking that the moon had hidden its face in shame. That's why I always think of it as the first time, but it wasn't really. A little further with this one, a little further with that one—I tell you, there wasn't a first time. Until this summer.'

'You must have been very young.'

'I was very immature. I was your original Virgin Soldier. Fear of the pox is a great moralizer. During my time in the services she had grown from a schoolgirl to a buxom wench with honest animal lusts that I knew nothing about. She was damn lucky I didn't marry her.' He laughed to himself, the embarrassment of those nervous fumbling hours with Iris Pollard gone at last, after all these years, because of Cleo. 'And so was I,' he muttered, about to doze off again.

'I didn't know you were in the services.'

'I do have some secrets.' He said it as a joke.

'Did you kill anyone?'

Steve sat up, totally in the present, scrutinizing her face, as if seeing her for the first time, and intensely aware of the difference in their ages . . . not the years, the ages. Of those who had known war, however remotely, and those who had not.

'How old are you?' Suddenly feeling that she was, in spite of maturing him, so young and innocent. He was angry with her, yet puzzled that anyone could be so mature in some ways, so innocent in others.

'You don't ask that of a lady,' she said, pouting. But he scrutinized her face so persistently that she turned away.

'If I had killed somebody,' he insisted, 'some poor bastard who, like me, was conscripted into some army to fight battles he knew nothing about, would that have made me more complete, more masculine? The Total Male?'

He was demanding an answer, that she might see the enormity of her question, but she was silent, watching the seaweed swaying in the tide.

'That is a question you don't ask of anybody,' he told her, speaking as master to novice. 'It's immoral!'

He lay back again, while she sat on her haunches, half turned towards him in the classical pose of a mermaid. 'I'm sorry,' she murmured. 'I didn't think what I was saying,' and rubbed the palm of her hand along his thigh, to make contact, to be together again.

'We've all killed people,' Steve said, 'even if only by paying taxes to buy the guns. The man who pulls the trigger, or presses the button, or shoves the bayonet in, is just the last one in the sequence. The one who is supposed to be affected by it—to feel some kind of elation and spend the rest of his life in remorse.'

They were silent for some time, until Steve said, exaggerating his accent, 'Still, we don't have to go on about such things. Do us?' He laughed. 'I tell 'ee one thing. I wouldn't be lying here with no clothes on if I hadn't been in the forces. Now, would I, you? As I said. Now, look! It's as I said. All the little things. All the little nawthens. They are your life. Little nawthens.'

'I don't see the connection,' said Cleo, trying to follow his train of thought.

'I rejected their morality!' He placed his hands under his head and wriggled into a more comfortable position, as if dismissing the subject.

'St . . . eve!' she said, in mock impatience. And he opened one eye and grinned at her.

'One day we had been on a route march, temperature in the nineties or even more, I don't know.'

'Were you abroad?'

'Yes. Now don't interrupt. All hot and sweaty with carrying our kit and radios and batteries, and God knows what else, when we came to this beautiful beach, in a bay, with lovely clear water. It was green, I remember—like this. We were not allowed to go in, even in our army airtex underpants, in case we offended the locals. And we'd just spent two weeks on an exercise learning how to kill the lot of them.' He laughed aloud, and said, 'It was indecent. Swimming in underpants!' He laughed to himself again. 'We were all in the services—Tim, John, Shimshai, even Freddie. Hardly ever mention it now. Only to younger people. It all seems a bit childish, now, looking back on it. All the stupid bullshit and boozing at weekends, yet I wouldn't have missed it. Did me good, in a way.'

'But you were too young to be in the war, surely? There wasn't any fighting.'

'There is always fighting! We were lucky, our lot. Malaya was just finishing, Korea hadn't started. We all came back. We've had it good, our lot. My race. One or two of the younger ones were killed in Korea, and what was that all for? Can you remember? Lots of the older ones were killed in the war. People I can hardly remember. My father was killed in the war, and that killed my mother, but she took a long time to die. I hardly remember my father. So there you are. You have to have your own morality, when you think about it. I never

thought about it much. Never thought about why we are as we are.'
He reached over and cupped his hand around the bronzed curve of
her behind. 'It's all your doing, all this questioning and analysing.
Never heard tell of no such thing.'

Cleo smiled at him, telling him with her eyes that she didn't believe
that. Steve did not argue. She expected him to ask her, and she
wanted to tell him, about the first time, but he didn't ask her. He
never did ask her, so she never told him, though she told me, much
later. She told me more than she told anybody, even Steve.

Chapter Sixteen

Kevin Robinson's meeting with Tim, that day when he met Steve down in the harbour, was fruitful for them both. Tim made a commission, his 'reciprocal', as he called it, and Kevin bought a cottage downalong with an unaltered cellar on the ground floor. There are not many left like that! Most of the cellars have been converted to kitchens and bathrooms and there is nowhere to keep any gear. Such are the changes—from a man's world to a woman's world. There was no money in fishing, but moving the living accommodation down one storey provided two bedrooms to let. Kevin was to live alone, and the cellar was for his gear—an arrangement possible only for those who made their money away.

The deal went through very smoothly and quickly. Kevin had the cash, and the only other potential purchasers were a young local couple who were trying to raise a mortgage, and the building society were not too happy about lending money on an unmodernized dwelling, so he was lucky. His stay, early in May month, was short, and he wanted to complete the purchase in time for his long holiday, beginning a month later. Tim had been known to turn a blind eye to the inflated incomes on some mortgage applications by young locals, but one couldn't do that kind of thing too often, and a quick, uncomplicated cash deal was not to be missed.

'Leave everything to me,' he said. 'No snags here at all.' Absently checking on ceilings and walls for signs of damp and cracks, which he wouldn't recognize if he saw them—what's the bloody surveyor paid for, anyway?—and muttering away as if to himself, 'Eminently resaleable, this. Eminently resaleable,' glancing through the bedroom window to check on the sea view, which there wasn't. 'I'll maybe even get the odd hundred off the asking price. No snags here at all.' Puffing at his pipe and making a mental note to see Wally about a quick completion, and drop a broad hint to wha's-is-name in the

Guildhall about the searches, get them off their asses for a minute or two. No snags at all, provided the Commodore here had the ready cash he claimed to have. 'The seller is after another place that has been priced a little on the low side,' he said, grinning in conspiracy. 'They'll want to move. No problems.' And then, 'Let's pop along'—he used expressions like that—'Let's pop along to the office now,' he suggested, looking at his watch. 'Just a matter of a couple of signatures and the cheque for the deposit and the deal is as good as done. We can maybe come back for a drink at lunch-time, eh?'

'On a Sunday? You don't mind?'

'When you have to move . . . eh?'

'Right!'

Tim grinned wildly, clutching the stem of his pipe in clenched teeth. 'You're pretty astute!' he said, lapsing into the patter which he secretly referred to as 'The After Sales Service', when he endeavoured to convince his clients that the manipulations had been of their own devising, making them feel like tycoons, for whom he was only the local agent. Kevin Robinson was not above this flattery, which surprised me somewhat, after what I'd heard about him. We never met.

'Well,' he said, 'I've been around long enough to know a bargain when I see one,' comparing our prices with those of the industrial and stockbroker belts in England. And that was that. Deal done.

He returned in June, expecting to surprise everyone . . . Cleo, Steve, Uncle Joe, but even though Tim had kept his word and mentioned the deal to no one, everyone knew he was coming, of course. He bought the house from Ephraim Pengelly, whose wife is Millicent Polglaze, that was, Martha's sister. Milly Yap Trap! She told Ephraim's business to everyone in the Rows, in confidence. Ephraim belonged to go to the Lodge.

The house (cottage, you would call it) was in the same row as Cleo's, but at the other end. The bottom end, though he thought it was at the top end, and, like others at that end, it had a flight of granite steps outside which led up to the front door. The loft door was on the street level. Lofts were never on the top floors, above the living-rooms, as this would entail humping all the gear up on blocks and tackle or something. Some lofts were over cellars, but cellars were never below ground. It's a sensible arrangement. Any fool can see that.

Like many who came here, Kevin Robinson thought the locals clannish, for he met very few except on the superficial level of nodded greetings when passing in the street, forgetting that they were all frantically trying to make twelve months' living in four. Forgetting, too, that they all had friends enough, more or less, and no need of more, whereas he was alone with time on his hands and practically friendless in this complex community. He enjoyed the first few weeks of his long holiday, putting to sea whenever the weather was fine and the tides were right, working his boat, doing the repairs or a bit of painting whenever they were not. Uncle Joe went out with him at first, to make sure he knew where the offshore rocks were, and to show him the marks when they were covered. Gowna, Browthen, Mester Carracks, Maen Derrens, The Bezzack, in case he went that far, and down to the Western Carrack and Carrack an Edhyn, teaching him the language too, though neither knew it. He showed him the North-West Tide and Godrevy Sound. He showed him Joey's Rock, but he didn't tell the yarn. He showed him how to make a fitty knot and a proper mooring. Kevin knew about engines and kept the fifteen horsepower Lister in perfect running order. But, 'He abm got a compass!' Joe told James.

'He abm?'

'Abm got a compass!' Tommy Blue told Silas Rouncefield.

'You ought to have a compass,' Steve told him. 'Sometimes the fog comes in thick as a bag.'

'I'll get one,' he said.

They went fishing for mackerel and pollack off the Stones on those days when there was no ground swell and, even though the fish were too scarce for the chaps to make a living, caught half a stone or so every day, more fish than Kevin knew what to do with.

The locals were all working during the week, and there was no boating on Sundays, not then, so when Joe tired of going out—it was, after all, work to him—Kevin found he was very much alone. Steve would see him out of the bay, listlessly dangling his line overboard, sitting in the stern with his feet up on the thwarts, and they would raise their hands to each other in passing, the passengers on Steve's boat looking at him with envy, longing for such a life.

When there were mackerel in the bay, Steve had a few hours on them before beginning with the passengers, even though this made for a long day and James disapproved, muttering about the people having to sit on fishy seats and having to wash everything down before the passengers came aboard for the ten-thirty trip. This was another of those silent perennial disputes between them, one that Steve tolerated in silence, for while James was understandably sick to death of fishing for nothing, Steve would do nothing else if there was a living to be made from it. Far better than this degrading showmanship which was running trips, and another reason for keeping to the *Mermaid*, though she was essentially a fishing-boat, rather than go in for a proper passenger launch, like 'Snags' and they. The only consolation about tripping was that he was still making his living, though a bare enough living, from the sea. In Cornwall the hoteliers made the money, the big money. Them and the proprietors of cafés, discos, gift-shops and 'Amusements'. Steve longed for the return of the fish.

Sometimes, when the weather was bad, a ground swell or strong winds, or there was an early tide and the boats lay at their moorings, Steve might have time for a quick pint in the pub.

The pub was invariably crowded in the summer, with people drinking outside and shoulder-to-shoulder at the bar. The skittle board was packed away for the season, for there was no room to swing the ball, and the faces on the walls, the portraits of locals, looked down searching for themselves among the host of unfamiliar features. George would pull a pint and pass it over the heads of the customers at the bar, calling Steve 'Sir' as if he didn't know him, and Steve would look for a familiar face, retiring to the far corner for a bit of breathing space.

Kevin Robinson had taken to coming in early in the evening, after he came ashore and before the crowds arrived. He looked much fitter, and had lost that tired look around the eyes. He looked younger.

One day in July, Steve wandered into the pub early too, and found Cleo and Kevin Robinson sitting together at one of the long tables in the public bar. They were sitting opposite each other, deeply engrossed in conversation, and didn't turn at the sound of the latch to see who had entered. If you take notice, you will see that the locals always glance at the door whenever the latch clicks, even though the conversation continues or the hands of euchre are dealt without pause. Steve turned to the bar with his back to them, and George greeted him with 'Usual?' and Steve nodded. 'Poor weather!' George said, though the evening sunshine was still strong on the faces of the old women sitting on the seats along the quay. It was the ground swell.

Whenever he saw her like this, suddenly, unexpectedly, there was that quickening of the pulse, the immediate turmoil in his mind, a sense of confusion, and a vague ache somewhere under his ribs. He gave George a handful of coins, unable to count, to concentrate, knowing that his face was flushed and sensing that their conversation had been of more than trivialities.

'You can't buy the dammee pub,' George said, shoving most of the coins back at him.

'Eh? Oh! Eh, I want some fags, too,' covering his confusion. He kept his back to them, envious of Kevin Robinson, who could sit openly with Cleo in the public bar of the pub.

Cleo saw him. 'There's Steve,' she said.

'Steve!' Kevin said. 'Come over here, and sit down with us.'

He went over, smiling at Kevin, nodding to Cleo. 'Hello,' he said, and sat next to her because Kevin was on the inside bench against the wall, and because he could not look at her, or she at him, without betraying everything.

'Not working?' she said, half turning to him.

'Bad weather.' He spoke to Kevin.

'But it's been a lovely day!'

'Lovely day ashore,' Steve muttered between sips of his beer. 'Brear ol' tumble outside,' and then remembering to explain, 'Ground swell! Can't get anywhere near the rocks. The seals won't be ashore anyway, not in this. They'll be washed off.'

'She wouldn't believe *me*,' Kevin complained ruefully.

'Oh, but I did,' she protested. 'I just wanted confirmation from an expert.'

'I *do* have a master's ticket.' They laughed, and Steve relaxed. He was with Kevin Robinson, talking to Kevin Robinson. When the chaps came in, he would be with Kevin Robinson, the stranger, who was with that party who bought High George's house.

At the other table four men played euchre, watched by two others, all locals, getting a few games in before the place became too crowded. One nodded his head towards Steve, and shrugged, the others looked briefly at Steve's back and wondered what the hell was up with him, why he didn't speak. They were dressed in smocks and jumpers and had brown, grimy hands and smelled slightly of diesel and stale fish-scales, and were playing euchre in the bar where their fathers and grandfathers had played euchre while smelling slightly of diesel and stale fish-scales too. The new landlord disapproved but so far had said nothing to them, considering that they might even be an attraction, adding a little local colour and atmosphere to the place. As long as they stayed in the public bar! He had dropped a few hints to George about discouraging them, and George had smiled blandly at him, not mentioning that one was his cousin, another his brother. The new landlord was from away, didn't know who was who, nor what was what. He didn't serve men with long hair either, but had no objection to skirts up to, and above, the crotch.

The card-players' voices erupted into shouts of frustration and glee after some particularly crafty play, and George shouted above their cries, 'Not so much noise, if you don't mind, please,' grinning all over his chacks. Assuming that the landlord must know who they were by now. What a place!

More people came in. Tourists who stared around the walls at the portraits before going to the bar, asking their women what they would have and the women thinking about it, looking over the bottles and optics as if choosing a dress, while George waited politely with his hands spread on the bar, smiling at them and dying to say, to be rich enough to say, 'For Christ's sake, make your bleddy minds up, caint 'ee?'

Kevin rose to buy a round of drinks for the three of them as some newcomers sat on the bench next to Steve. He made room for them, moving closer to Cleo. She looked at him but didn't speak. They neither of them spoke until Kevin returned, but pressed secretly against each other, thigh to thigh, drawing patterns of spilled beer across the table with their fingers, until Kevin resumed the conversation with some comment about his house.

The bar filled and became noisy. The three found it difficult to continue a conversation, leaning over the table to catch each other's words, and Kevin, who was a non-smoker, screwed up his eyes against the smoke. He suggested that they leave. 'Come and see my cottage,' he said, 'and have some coffee.' So they went down there, along the harbour, through the tourists in the yellow, mellow light of the summer evening, talking trivialities, the two men and one girl.

Kevin was pleased with his cottage. He had furnished it well, if sparsely, with comfortable chairs in the front room and the necessary tools in the kitchen, which had been completely modernized with units and a stainless-steel sink. He showed them through, and Cleo compared it with her own, commenting on the small doors and narrow stairs. Steve knew the place and had renewed the sash-cords for Ephraim before he put it on the market.

'Who did the work for you?' Steve asked, by way of making conversation. 'They've done a good job.'

'Mr Tuttle. Do you know him?'

'Oh, yes. Terry. I know him.'

Everybody knew him. He was one of us. Everybody knew the plumber who went about the town compressed beneath the weight of an overloaded tool-bag slung over his shoulder, held by two hands on the handle of a hammer, with his stout bandy legs bowed to breaking-point under the pressure of his lifelong burden.

Plumbers, generally, are a miserable bleddy crowd, tending to the morose, but he could be seen smiling to himself and to his reflection in the shop windows and the tall mirror that hung on the wall of Peark's that was. Sometimes, perhaps, he smiled at the absurdity of his own image, shuffling along, led by his elbow, through the crowded streets of summer. Or, perhaps, he smiled at the images of the people, for, being a plumber, he knew them at their worst. But his broadest smile was for his private joke.

There were times when, staggering along the cobbled streets, beneath his loaded frail, with his hands pulling on the hammer handle as it to strangle himself or twist the torso from his hips, the smile became so embarrassingly broad that he would raise his eyebrows in a many-furrowed frown and attempt to hide it. The result was a bemused, almost bewildered look of apology for his joke—which he had never told. It was of a plumber who opened the door of a lavatory to find someone sitting there. When he thought of it, his one-sentence-joke, the smile became impossible to control and he would turn off into an empty side street, say Academy Steps or Custom House Lane, there to lean against the wall in helpless mirth until composure returned.

'Sorry to disturb you, sir.'

One day, the situation would arise and he could tell it, or say it, with a proper English voice. It was too good a joke to tell before. '. . . to disturb you!' It was killing. Really.

'Joe has given up the sea again, then?' Steve said, when they were in the front room. Kevin brought three cups of coffee from the kitchen. Cups, Steve noted, not mugs.

'Yes, I've tried to sign a new crew,' Kevin said, looking at Cleo, 'but she seems to be a landlubber.'

'I told you. I'm working during the week. And boats don't go out on Sundays.'

'You have Saturdays, and evenings.'

'I'd love to come out. But I'm afraid I might be sick.' She was leaning back in the chair, her fingers bent lightly against her cheek. The room was getting dim in the fading light, and Kevin moved toward the switch. 'Leave it off,' she said.

It was high time for Steve to go upalong, home to Mary, but he was in anguish at the thought of leaving Cleo here alone with Robinson.

'If you get sick, we'll come straight back.'

'All right. One evening this week.' She smiled, that same elfin smile which taunted Steve whenever he thought of her.

'May I catch a fish?' she said.

Steve knew that the tides were all wrong for the evenings until Friday, but he said nothing, bitter that their meetings must be clandestine and furtive, sensing the first pangs of irrational jealousy, an emotion which he had previously considered beneath him, as primitive and unreasonable.

'I thought,' said Kevin, when they had been chatting for some time after the last light had faded, 'of giving a little dinner party. Would you come, Steve? And your wife? I'm asking Tim and his wife.' The implication was that Cleo would be there. 'Next month, before I go away.'

'When are you going?' Steve evaded the invitation.

'Oh, not until September.'

'For how long?'

'All winter.'

'But you will be back next summer?'

'I'm not sure,' he scratched the back of his neck in gesture of indecision. 'They've offered me promotion. A bigger ship. A new ship. It's a splendid opportunity, but I really am tired of the solitary life. On the other hand,' he mused, 'I can't stand too much idleness. The winters here must be very quiet.'

'They would be for you,' Steve said, 'but what about the house? Would you sell it, if you went back to sea?'

'I really don't know,' he turned his back briefly to Cleo. 'It's not important at the moment. I can easily let it in the season. Tim would look after that.'

Another step towards the desecration of the town, towards turning downalong into a granite holiday camp for the English (Lamentations 5: 2).

'Good idea!' said Steve. 'Better than money in the bank.'

It seemed that Cleo was in no hurry to leave. She began fingering through a magazine on the arm of her chair.

Steve rose and said he ought to be going. 'All right for you idle rich,' he said, 'but some of us have to be up in the morning.' To his immense relief Cleo rose also. 'We're not all idle rich,' she said, 'we working girls have to be up early too.'

Kevin was visibly disappointed at her departure. 'Shall I see you to your cottage?' he said, but she replied that it wouldn't be necessary as Steve was going that way, and in any case it was not very far, and this was not like the cities where it wasn't safe for a girl to walk alone, and at last they were in the street together, walking slowly in the dark between the lamplights, having too much to say for conversation. They reached her door and stopped. She had the key in her hand.

'Do you like him?' Steve could not prevent himself from asking it, in a subdued and apprehensive voice.

'Yes. He's nice.' And, seeing the look of sorrow on him, reached for his arm before remembering their situation. 'Oh, Steve!' she said.

'Shall I see you on Sunday?' He felt he dare not ask.

'Yes, on Sunday,' she said.

He gave her a wistful smile and left her, looking at Quizzy Maggie's windows to be sure she was not looking through the curtains. Even at this late hour.

Chapter Seventeen

At two hours' flood the sea flowed over the low sandbank between the twin quays which curved protectively, like finger and thumb, around the tiers of boats lying askew on their keels where the ebbing tide had left them in the early morning. The neap tide was a gentle, barely perceptible flow and, with no ground swell, brought the boats to rights and floated them with wavelets lapping the planks of the clinker-built punts and skiffs. The pleasure-boats had been shoved out early and now they lay at anchor outside the harbour, bows into the slight north-west breeze, anchor ropes dipping and rising, showering droplets of water into the green of the shallow sea.

Steve stood with one foot up on the harbour railings, elbow on knee, chin resting on the cupped palm of his hand. He was looking at the movement and colour of the boats, the sea, and the few early strollers on the wharf. On the harbour beach old men were dejectedly removing the green tarpaulin from the stack of deck-chairs and placing some of them in position along the wharf and beach in anticipation of the daily crowds. Four figures dragged sacks along the beach, leaving four snail-trails in the sand, with many diversions where they turned from their advance to pick up yesterday's litter and last night's seaweed.

There was a cluster of skiffs at the quay steps, each made fast with a long painter curving up to a bollard at the top of the quay. The rising tide was stirring them and the painters tautened and slackened in unison as they stirred, while the morning sunlight glinted on their wet planks and reflections in the water.

Along the wharf, where the sun glowed warmly on the granite walls, shopkeepers polished their windows and hung postcards and beachballs around the doors. Refuse bins were being dragged from cafés, and scraped over the cobbles to the back alleys where later, in the heat of the day, tourists would hold their breath as they squeezed past the dustcarts jamming the way.

A pack of homosexual dogs, evicted from their various homes, raced joyously by, down the slipway and across the sand with tongues lolling from laughing faces and heads held high.

Aboard the *Mermaid's* skiff James sat in the stern, a faint blue haze drifting from his pipe. Steve cursed him for a lazy bastard, and turned his back to the scene, leaning with both elbows on the rail.

The day warmed as the sun rose and the tide flowed over the beach. People came down to the sea front; the early ones carrying newspapers, and breathing deep breaths of sea air as if to trap them, store them, take them home to be released in the winter of some smoky northern town; the later ones laden with gear, beach gear: towels, sunbeds, rubber dinghies, food, drink, cameras, lotions.

'Give her the lotion, boy. Give 'er the lotion.'

Steve touted for passengers, but half-heartedly, for he was pretty well booked up with a block booking from Freddie and Martha. A weekly arrangement which suited Steve even if James moaned a bit about people having a cheap trip, and it suited Freddie for occasionally he could put on a pair of jeans and go too. Get away from Martha for a while, play the local, the Jack-ashore, for the benefit of their guests, and he could tell stories in the evenings.

Steve thought of Cleo, wondered if she would work, or lie in the sunshine on a day like this. And he went down to the skiff, down along the wet sand to where James sat smoking his pipe in the skiff offshore, and the tourists were beginning to think about their day. The day would be fine, perhaps the heat would drive them on to the sea and all the trips would be full. But in the sunshine somewhere would be Cleo.

No need for me to go aboard. He could do all that by hisself. He saw James pointing to the quay. He hasn't got the damn fuel. Steve walked to the quay and up the steps, brought down the can of fuel, carrying it on his shoulder and already he was hot. James at last came ashore, wading through the shallow water, and took the fuel to the skiff, with his sea-boots rolled up. Once, he had taken off his shoes and rolled up his trousers, showing the stark white shins and blue veins of old age, and Steve had somehow felt embarrassed to see them. Then he took Steve to the skiff, carrying him pick-a-back—'piggy-back', we called it—and they both climbed aboard, where Steve shipped the oars and began the long row out the *Mermaid*.

And James said unto Steven, 'What's this I'd hear about you 'en, Ste?'

'What's that 'en, James?'

'Why—you knaw. Why—this what I do hear.'

'You hear all sorts in this bloody place.'

'About you. And this here woman.'

Steve rowed on steadily, his mind struck dumb. James's words were rejected, but returned, battering his consciousness. 'And this here woman. And this here woman.' Again and again, until their enormity finally registered and his arms became weak and he was aware of the hot flush up his cheek. He rowed on, grateful to James for telling him there, where there was no one else. There in the skiff, with just the two of them, where he could not escape.

So now they would all know. If one knew they would all know. The tongues would be wagging, confidentially over cups of tea, and heartily over pints of beer. Hints dropped and his sins related in counterfeit reluctance. Every past transgression recalled and divulged to the uninformed until eventually there would be no one who did not know. And when the tale was exhausted in its telling, there would come the embellishments.

Some among them would condemn him. Some would pity him. Very few would blame him, for the blame would fall on Cleo. That there woman. The woman from away.

'I don't know,' said James, 'how you come to mix with such people.'

'What people?'

'Why—' James searched the archives of his vocabulary for an appropriate epithet, 'why, these here—hartisis! All that crowd.'

'They're all right.'

James grunted and stared to the distance. The two of them were in the skiff, Steve rowing out to the *Mermaid* and James sitting facing him in the stern. There was no escape.

'They edn our sort, Steve. Not our sort.'

There was no wind, and the flowing tide advanced cautiously over the rippling sand beneath the keel, flowed over the dried sandbank, preceded by a salve of yellow foam with the bubbles from the holes of annelids and razorfish, reluctantly encircling the forts and castles of the children's morning. The sounds of summer reached them as a muted symphony. Cries of infants, and the screams of adolescents immersed and caressed in semi-nudity by the uninhibited sea. Cars' engines and distorted music. The sounds of summer and dry land muffled by distance and the immediate dip and splash of varnished oars in the grip of suntanned hands, and the thump of a Frenchman's diesel approaching from the north.

'They edn *our* sort. Understand?' Folding his arms and crossing his legs, screwing up into a tight little ball of condemnation. While Steve rowed rhythmically on, barely hearing him or the sounds of summer—only the gossip. Knowing that the storm had broken and unable to accept it, yet, like the flow of the tide it had been, from the beginning, inevitable.

They came alongside and climbed aboard, making the skiff afast with the painter, then James filled the fuel tanks while Steve wiped down the seats and decks. 'Bleddy gull-shit,' he said, and got no response. Another half hour before they could get alongside the steps, and it would be half an hour of hostile silence. The rest of the season would be worked in silence too if Steve should let it. James was naturally untalkative but the difference between natural reticence and deliberate non-communication was that of companionship and animosity. A season of it would be unbearable.

'I thought,' said James at last, 'that you had sense enough to know better.'

'You did.'

'Y-ess. I ded.' A pause. "Ess, I thought that.'

Steve was on the point of saying something facetious like 'Well, you thought wrong' or 'You never can tell', and starting a quarrel to clear the air, but after glancing at the older man's face he realized that there was no condemnation. James meant what he said, no more.

The sense to foresee, and avoid, the consequence of loving Cleo. The sense of responsibility to those who would suffer as a result. But he'd had the sense to foresee these things without the strength, or whatever it took, to resist it.

James looked at him. Though Steve avoided his eyes and watched the antics of the distant children, or the mast of the approaching Frenchman and the steady turbulence of the twin crests curling from under her bow, he knew the expression on James's face without the need of seeing it. At last he turned to him.

'Now!' said James when their eyes had spoken, 'I'll say n' more.'

'No.'

'We'd better have the anchor up.'

'Aye.'

'Start up the engin' while I cast off the tezzack.'*

They came alongside the quay on a gentle swell of the flowing tide, and Steve helped the passengers aboard before climbing the steps. With the extra weight the keel was hard on the bottom, and James, after casting off, was waiting for another inflow. With the engine slow astern a surge of eddies swirled beneath the bilges.

'Ee, what's oop?' said a woman.

'Are we stoock?' said a man.

'Are we sinkin'?'

James raised his eyes under the peak of his old cloth cap and turned

---

*Tezzack: a short line tied to an anchor rope.

his lips in despair at the degradation of it all before Steve, with a slight nod of sympathy, turned away up the quay.

The situation, his relationship to the community, was so different when he came ashore than it was before he left the quay with James only half an hour before. The scandal was going the rounds then as it was now, and no one's opinion of him had changed in that brief period. But, whereas prior to James's reference to 'that there woman' he had persuaded himself that the affair was a secret and himself, as possessor of that secret, in some way superior, he was now placed, by a revealing phrase, outside the secrecy of gossip. And with the knowledge of exposure came the question of how much they knew, how long it had been known and by how many, and the realization that within a very short time Mary would find out, if indeed she did not know already.

Walking up the quay and along the wharf, through all the thronging people, past Salubrious Place and Mount Pleasant, cleaned of their historic filth and cat-shit, past the quaint and charming streets and houses which in another age had been condemned as slums and festering pestilence. Listening to the accents of a score of counties and a dozen major towns, all harsh to his Western ears. Wishing they had never come, pondering on the westward drift. Nodding to the other boatmen who closed in on the path of his trajectory to tout the passers-by with extra vigour and enthusiasm, lest by negligence they allowed a fare to slip from their grasp and be taken by a rival. Fighting among themselves, competing for survival like rats on a shrinking island, helpless against the waves of migration which would eventually drown them in uniformity, swamped by the global surge of people trailing west like water on the surface of a spinning top.

Seeing the people on the harbour sand, lying in full sun with their backs against the inclined granite wall, mildly contemptuous of the inherent prudery in bikinis and trunks disguised as daring, of the wearing of clothes for sunbathing. Smelling the viscous scent of lotions dispelled from languid thighs and bellies in the warm rising air. A fussing woman in a flowered frock, kneeling before a teenage girl with spindly legs and straggly hair, screening the girl with a towel while she changed, helping with straps. Who wants to look at your damned prissy daughter, Mrs Flowerfrock? Anybody would think she was the Queen of bleddy Sheba. Hating them all. The girl turned, and with an expression of simple joy, looked up at Steve. His eyes were held for a second while the mother arranged the costume to cover as much as possible of the spastic body, and the father, sitting fully clothed in a deck-chair, gazed at the distant sea. Steve smiled at her and looked away. Looked right away, seeing nothing. No one wanted to look at Mrs Flowerfrock's daughter, and the Flowerfrock family wouldn't be gossiping about the petty affairs of some obscure fisherman. Past the pub, feeling the insignificance of individuals in all the seething mass of humanity. The loves and tragedies of individuals were nothing beyond the anguish in the separate hearts. Each must suffer the joys and sorrows alone, for no one could feel the agony of another's pain.

Steve considered the crowds around him. 'Would you like,' he asked an appropriate pair of peeling women who did not answer, 'a trip to Seal Island?' And added as they avoided him, 'Only five bob.' And on up through the thickening, sickening, crowds to his pitch by the lifeboat house.

The harbour was divided among them as in the past when the crews had, for the counting of fish, a section of wharf or quay allocated to each buyer. But now there were no certain divisions, only the unwritten but strictly defined rules of custom and precedent. It was 'not done', though it was done, to tout on somebody else's patch. Some said the lifeboat house was best, for you caught them as they first came to the harbour. Some said the slip was best, gave them a chance to make up their minds—to see the sea and the weather. Some saw that they didn't know what the hell to do with themselves and would only go for a trip when they were on the quay and saw others climbing aboard the boats, and they were right too. The trouble was that by the time people reached the quay they were sick and tired of being asked to go to Seal Island. 'For the hundredth bloody time I've been asked to go to Seal Island this morning. I'm sick and bloody tired of it. All along this bloody harbour,' one of them said to old Jimmy Tyke that time.

'Well,' said Jimmy, '*Do* you want to go to Seal Island?'

There was a chance the man could have had a heart attack. He drew in a great breath of exasperation, but the crow's-feet of mirth trod briefly in the corners of Jimmy's eyes and the man said, '*Yes*, damn you. I do want to go to Seal Island. And my wife, and my kids. But don't you dare ask me again tomorrow.'

And even then Jimmy didn't laugh. He didn't laugh till after, up in the Lodge when he told the yarn.

That was old Jimmy Tyke. Another one dead and gone.

'Seal Island Trip,' Steve said mechanically, 'leaving right away.'

He went that evening to Cleo's house, he went early while the sun was still over Clodgy and the reddening sky promised another day of sun tomorrow, for there was no reason for secrecy now. Mary would soon know—might know already.

He went down along the harbour, chatting to this one and that one, checking the lie of the moorings as he went. Checking the swell, the skiff, the tiers. Stopped for a while on the Platt. Yarning. Leaning on the railings while the chaps walked up and down, up and down. Twelve paces. Twelve paces.

'Look at them old men—walking up and down.'

'Why are they walking up and down? Up and down.'

The strolling evening crowds, ambling by, looking for somewhere to go, something to see, smelled of scent and aftershave, sun-tan lotion and talcum. The day had been fine. There were many red and peeling ones. Some of them smelled of stale sweat.

He wondered how long it would go on, this aimless holidaying, this wasting of lives, before people realized the brevity of their days and became as miserly with their time as they were with their money, ekeing it out, for it was so precious. So precious . . .

Cleo was at home but the door was locked—she was a stranger still—so he must knock and wait until she let him in. They didn't speak for a while, and they didn't kiss. They never did, not when they met. Each time it was a fresh encounter, a new exploration. Nothing in their relationship was as indifferent as a casual kiss.

'Coffee?' she said eventually, and he nodded, watching her coming and going, in and out of the kitchen. Steve watched her, openly absorbing her presence while she occasionally gave him one of her shy smiles.

Cleo sat at his feet, as she so often did, and rested her head against his knee, holding her cup in both hands. He felt, beneath her hair, the fine neck and small, almost lobeless ears. She felt so delicate, yet so strong.

'Cleo,' he said at last. 'Oh, Cleo.' And again, with a deep sigh, 'Oh, my lovely Cleo.'

She was silent for a while, slowly sipping her drink, hearing in his voice something which told her all, staring at a canvas on the wooden easel, but eventually said, with that aura of tranquility with which she faced the inevitable looming tragedies of her life, 'Mary knows?'

'Yes. I don't know. I expect so. Today or tomorrow, it's all the same—the same as it's always been. *They* know.' They were sure to know.

'People, you mean. Other people. The gossips. The malicious tongues of this narrow-minded God-fearing town.' He felt her trembling with anger, with despair. 'I hate them,' she said, with a sudden irrational bitterness in her sorrow.

'They're not the way you see them.' He turned her head and looked down into her eyes, holding her gaze. 'They're not malicious! The gossip—it won't be malicious. From a few perhaps. Not many.'

No! that's not the way it would be. Though the result would be the same. 'Compassionate gossip,' he said. 'A new concept for you. Compassionate gossip.'

Steve Trevorrow has got a bit of spare, a bit on the side. What about his wife? What about Mary? Poor Mary. Poor Steve—can't blame him s'pose. For a bit on the side! She's a fine craft, can't blame him. Wonder what he'll do. Mary will know—she's sure to know. What will she do?

'What will we do?' asked Cleo. And little tears came. Little tears which barely moistened her eyes. They were the tears for the tears to come, for she knew what they would do. They both knew what they would do. In the end. But she rejected it. Refused to accept it. Clung to a futile hope that there could be some way in which their love could last. Desperately searching for a love from Steve which was consuming enough for him to abandon everything for her. To give himself, totally, to her. They could go away—live somewhere else, have a new beginning, a new life together. It could be done. Here at last was the test, the trial by emotional ordeal.

'Will she be reasonable about it?' she asked, trying frantically to maintain her composure, trying, in despair, to force him to stay with her, but knowing the folly, the uselessness of it. 'Will she divorce you?' Looking at him unblinkingly, demanding his decision.

He looked away at first. Looked out of the window at the pattern of granite stones in the wall of the house opposite. Tommy Blue strolled by, passing the time of day with Quizzy Maggie. They thought that no one heard them, for they were alone in the street, and there was a certain familiarity, a certain softening of Maggie's normally strident tones. They were the same race, the same age. They had gone to school together. 'Hello, Margaret.' 'Hello, Thomas.'

Turning back to Cleo, Steve said, 'She d'love me. Mary d' love me, too.' And there escaped from Cleo a great choking sob, and Steve fell to his knees and held her, as one holds a child, murmuring as he stroked her hair. 'Oh, my cheeld. My flute, my flute and arrow.'*

Had he been strong enough, had he not loved her so much, had she only the will to abandon this hopeless passion, they would have suffered so much less. But they continued meeting, continued loving, continued revealing themselves to each other, like two spring flowers unfolding from the buds of winter past. With each meeting the tension grew, as the uncertain future loomed ever before them, though outwardly they became more carefree, less furtive, for there was little reason for secrecy now that everybody was aware. Now that Mary was aware. Now that, like everybody else, Mary knew.

*Flute and arrow: from the Cornish *flogh caradow*, 'my beloved child'.

158

She knew before he left the house if he was to meet Cleo. No matter how casual his lies, about going for a drink or down to the Lodge, she always knew and, while saying nothing, implored him with her eyes to stay, or busied herself in the kitchen, ignoring him. At times she lost control and belayed him with streams of abuse, so that his departure was in a temper of defiance, and he would go to Cleo's house, openly to Cleo's house, for peace and consolation.

They had hushed and bitter rows over trivial disputes in the kitchen when he tried to help her on those days when the tides were early. Mary spent ages talking in the dining-room, while he was impatient to finish the work and go to Cleo's cottage, her studio. He dare not go in and clear the tables himself, and declare his eagerness to go out, but would wait at the sink, boiling with impatience, listening to the conversation vibrating in from the hall, where Mary would be standing with a tray of dirty crockery; 'clome', we used to call it but the word has died out.

She would talk and talk, holding the tray, with one guest half-way up the stairs, engaging in chat which Steve had heard a million times before. The weather, where they'd been, what they'd seen . . . all that stuff.

Steve found himself hating her, and his obligations to her, and would groan in despair; for in so many many ways she deserved his love, for all the past.

For weeks she didn't mention Cleo, though her suffering was intense. Until, one day, in fury and despair, she cried, 'Oh, go on. Get out! Go to your fancy woman.' And there it was. In the open at last.

Steve said nothing, looking at her. She backed away from him, reaching behind her for support from the table, unable to believe her own voice, and afraid that he would lose his temper and strike her, or go through the door for ever. She sat heavily in a chair, still holding the table with one hand, breathing deeply, as if from a great exertion, then crushed her fist against her mouth to control the welling tears. Waiting for his reaction. 'What fancy woman?' said Steve, demanding confirmation that she did, in fact, know all, and using this inane question, neither confession nor denial, to obtain it.

'That bleddy artis',' she spat. 'The bleddy slut!' And her sorrow was suppressible no longer. She turned and lay her head upon her folded arms across the table and sobbed, pathetically, 'Make me say such words.'

The people were going out. He heard them laughing in the hallway by the board with all the pinned-up brochures of attractions in the county—fake tin-mines, model villages, museums of this and that, miniature railways, zoos. One of Mary's attempts to provide the facilities of a proper hotel. There was also a list of church and chapel services, and a little card advertising trips of the *Mermaid*. He closed the door, lest they hear her sobbing. Helpless to console her, he loved her. He loved them both.

He approached her at last and sat in a chair next to hers. If she had but turned to him, put her arms about him, or implored him, with some expression of endearment, to put his arms about her. If she had only softened the façade which she had built around her emotions and let him see her as she was. But no! The years of inhibition and suppression had too powerful a hold on her emotions to be broken with one submissive gesture. She felt, when her sorrow subsided, only hate and humiliation, that he should see her so. A thing of weakness and defeat.

Steve placed his arms about her shoulder, but she shrugged him off, violently rejecting his overture. 'Mary,' he said, but she rose and went to the sink, dry-eyed, and the moment of reconciliation was lost.

Chapter Eighteen

My next involvement with the . . . 'the yarn', I would say, had I not become so far removed from all that which meant so much to me, from all that which made me . . . was in September. Each year I went and wore the blue robes with which my country has honoured me, for services to Cornish literature, and the journey had become the spiritual renewal of my Celtic origins. No Englishman can comprehend the connotations and emotional pride of such an honour, indeed, not a few have been known to laugh and make foolish attempts to deride the ceremonies. However, the Celts have always been more cultured than the Anglo-Saxons. I said 'cultured', not 'educated'.

We go and stand by the ancient megaliths, using the language, remembering the dead, honouring the learned ones, in a simple ceremony, sincere and poignant, which brings us all together, the dead and the living. Oh, yes. They are all there, the Ancient Ones, there is no doubt of it.

That year I had the extra reason for going, to see Cleo again. She wrote me the occasional letter from which I gathered the extent of her involvement with Steve, though she said nothing explicit. I asked her whether or not she would like to see the ceremony as it was being held so close that year, up there on the moors. She had never heard of it, though this didn't surprise me, but came to watch. I saw her, standing slightly apart from the small crowd of onlookers, as I took my place in the Great Circle. She chose not to look at me directly, for which I was grateful as I should have ignored her, and in so doing she at least demonstrated her sympathy with the emotions we feel on these annual pilgrimages to the holy places of our ancestors. She has a Celtic mind.

On that day the sky was lowering dark, with breaks of blue through which the sun sent rays of light to strike the distant hills. Carn

Galver, Trendrine, Trink, Trencom! The last flowers of heather and gorse above the turning bracken and yellow grasses of the bogs were lit, and lit again, as the sunlight passed eastwards through the grey shades of autumn. There were a few drops of rain, just a few large drops which left dark streaks on the blue robes, but they passed, and then, when all were gathered at the Great Sword, the brilliant light came upon us in our turn, and the green turf, the rusty bracken, the grey lichen on the stones, and the blue sea of robes, all illuminated . . .

All she said was, 'It must be very important to you, to come all this way every year for such a short ceremony,' and gave me to understand, by her apologetic smile, that this was not what she meant at all.

We drove back that evening by a roundabout route, over the moors and along the coast road, that I might show her the colours and changing moods of the autumn scenery. The dark skies on those showery days emphasize the brooding nature of the wild landscape. As we stretched our legs in a short walk, after parking the car on the roadside above Zennor, two ravens flew low over the stone walls, commenting to each other in their deep, guttural voices. *Prruk craaaack, pruk pruk*, remarkably musical despite the deep pitch.

'There go,' I said, 'two pruking great ravens,' and her laugh was music to me after seeing her so forlorn over the past few days.

'You wouldn't use that expression in one of your precious lectures,' she said, making fun of my dry, academic life-style, as she called it.

'Oh, no,' I agreed. 'One is obligated to use the archaic "sepulchral croak" as in, for instance, "As we walked over the dark brooding moors we heard the sepulchral croak of two funeral-garbed ravens". How's that sound?'

She knit her brows in counterfeited concentration. 'It has a familiar ring,' she mused. 'I think I must have read the book. How does it continue?'

We stopped, as I went on improvising, ' "And the handsome young squire . . shook his black tousled locks . . . and broke into a canter . . . his dark brooding eyes . . . flashing us a haughty glance . . . as he descended the rugged track . . . past the eerie old tin mine . . . to the dark brooding house on the sea-dashed cliffs." Have you read it?'

'Many times.'

'And under many titles,' I said.

'But how would you describe it? There is a brooding atmosphere, in the sense of waiting, incubating, that I try to capture in my paintings. The landscape seems restless, seems full of suppressed energy, as if it hasn't fully developed. Yet it all looks so old and timeless.' She suddenly took hold of my arm, linking hers in mine, and made us

162

walk on, saying, 'Let's call at the village pub for something to warm us up,' obviously disturbed by something in our conversation, and I suspected it concerned Steve.

'Do you love him?' I asked, the first time I had openly referred to their relationship, and she pressed her cheek against the shoulder of my coat. A gesture of affection, yet effectively hiding her face from me.

'Yes.'

We had reached the car, and I was searching through my pockets for the keys, before she looked at me.

'I had the same conversation with Steve,' she said. 'Yet it wasn't the same conversation at all, but the feelings, the emotions it evoked were the same. Exactly the same!'

She looked directly at me. There was nothing I could say.

'You are so alike, you two. It's uncanny. Despite being so superficially different in your looks, your speech, your physique . . .' I felt a little peeved at this. Steve was always fitter and more muscular than me, but only because of his more physical life-style, as I called it. '. . . education,' she went on, 'career, you are like two spectres of the same character.'

I grinned at her. 'Then, why don't you love me?' I said. And she put her tongue out at me. She put her tongue out!

In the village pub, where I expected to walk in on to slate flag-stones, there was a deep fitted carpet, from wall to wall. 'Good Lord,' I whispered too loudly as we entered, 'A carpet! It must have cost a fortune. It's terrible!'

She silenced me with a brutal elbow in my ribs, and I wheezed my order to the landlord. 'T'hwo halfs of B'hitter.' His accent was the South Midlands, Leamington or somewhere. I took the drinks over to the far end, to the table by the big fireplace. 'He's a bloody stranger,' I said. 'Has no idea.'

'Not so loud! From the way you talk, you and Steve, nearly everyone in the damned county is a bloody stranger.'

'They are,' I said, still wheezing a bit, 'they are.'

'You should complain. You're never here!'

'That,' I told her, leaning across the table for emphasis, and to keep my remarks from the few other people in the bar, 'is the problem. When you are always here the changes go unnoticed, but when your visits are occasional and brief, they hit you in the guts. There is something different every time I come home. Another house, another shop, changed, with new owners from up country.' Here I tried to be clever again, 'Lamentations, Chapter five, Verse two,' I said. But Cleo would have none of this. She merely looked at me, demanding the quote.

' "Our inheritance has been turned over to strangers, our homes to aliens." ' Because of her look I said it defensively, humbly.

'I'm a stranger.' That frank stare again.

'Not you,' I said. 'You don't count.'

'You may not think so, but others do. I expect that all the damn strangers "don't count" to somebody.'

'I know, I know. But you wait. We are almost gone. The Welsh, the Scots next. The Irish. Then the English. Then you'll hear some screams. And to add insult, they'll call themselves British.' I was still leaning over the low table, but some tourists at the next began taking interest in our conversation. 'They will refer to the "British identity" being swamped in European uniformity. It is inevitable, perhaps desirable, for then there will be no strangers, but a little sad, don't you think?'

'The sooner the better,' she said, as if tiring of the subject, her melancholy returning. I had never known her so temperamental. The full extent of her emotional involvement with Steve had not yet struck me. Her moods were of course the indirect result of the impossible situation she was in. The predicament of hopeless love.

When we left the pub the sky was dark and the wind had risen, bringing showers which dampened the road and hastened the night. By the time we reached her cottage it was quite dark, and our coats were wet from the short walk from the car park in the rain. We were alone. Kevin Robinson had gone away and Steve was at Martha's and Freddie's with Mary. Cleo prepared something to eat, I forget what, and we sat talking in the dark, over the unwashed plates, for hours. She could discuss these things with me, openly, and unashamedly, as if her emotions were an essential part of her, to be accepted with her friendship. Cleo was not a secretive person, unlike Steve, from whom I gathered the extent of his involvement only after several years, and much prompting.

Of Steve himself I could say but one thing to Cleo, and this long after she had told me the extent and depth, the intensity, of her love. I could only say, 'He will never leave her, Cleo.'

I told her about Mary, something Steve could never do, and she told me of Kevin Robinson. He had proposed to her. Proposed to her! Cleo was not the kind of woman one proposed to, for God's sake, she was the kind you love.

She finished her job at the end of September, and there was no Indian summer that year. The westerlies were almost continuous during October, with but brief spells of sunshine between the successive depressions swirling in from the Atlantic. The leaves were wrenched from the trees while the green sap was in them still, and the bracken on the hillsides was flattened to the ground by the buffeting winds and lay compressed to the boulders in a dark damp shroud. Like many city-dwellers, Cleo enjoyed the winds, and often went up to the headland to see the great rollers roaring in and shattering themselves into columns of dazzling spray against the weary rocks. She might take the low path, bordering the turf and the furthest extent of the sea's clutching grasp, just to feel the full strength of the wind and spray, tasting the salt in the droplets running from her eyes and into the corners of her mouth. At times she felt an impulse to open her coat and spread it like wings and hang over the path like the gulls. The winds were exhilarating. At night, with the fire lit in the cast-iron grate, the muted roar of the winds over the roofs clanking the wires on the aerials, she curled up in her armchair and enjoyed the counter-sensation of safety and comfort in the cosy warmth of High George's cottage.

To the fishermen there was no danger in these winds. They didn't go out, and that was all there was to it. The boats were safe enough in the estuary, or on their moorings in the harbour.

The season finished early, for the latecomers are usually itinerants who stay only if the sun shines. They can be seen, desperately trying to prolong the summer, lying on the beaches fully clothed, or wrapped in rugs and blankets, staring at the sea.

The shopkeepers, and the proprietors of guest-houses and cafés, 'hoteliers' and 'restaurateurs' they call themselves (you have to laugh), were secretly relieved at such an abrupt finish, for they were exhausted after many days and long hours of tedious drudgery. They could lay off the staff, put up the shutters and write indignant letters to the press about the lack of advertising and 'promotion' by the Local Authority, who took the rates for a year out of a three-month season with no attempt to provide amenities which would attract people in spring and autumn. It had been a good year. Short and sharp. And the fine weather had done more for next year's bookings than a million spent on advertising.

Steve laid up the *Mermaid* at the beginning of October, when it became too late for hope of a fine spell, and a few jobs came in. He tried a bit of fishing but the winds were too strong. He should have laid up at the end of September, on the high tides, but thought it worth trying for the mackerel. 'You never know,' he said, 'they might come back.'

'And pigs might fly,' said James.

But Steve had tried, as always, putting out in the nor'wes'lies when the winds began to die, cursing the weather, which didn't give a man a chance. Rounding the headland into the wind, watched by clusters of birdwatchers checking on the migrant auks and petrels, a lone fair-haired girl, and the men on the Platt.

'Gone mad,' they said, and told him so, like James, who stayed ashore.

'Pile of silliness,' he said, 'bein' beaten to death out there and not payin' for the fuel. The fish is gone. Gone, my lad. And that's that.'

Now, at that time, there seemed no chance of the mackerel ever coming back, no chance at all. And now look at them. Whoever would have thought it?

Silas Rouncefield picked no blackberries that year, for the summer was too dry, and the damp autumn brought mildew and those horrible little flies which cluster on the insipid, watery fruit. 'Nawthen's like it was,' he said.

For a while Steve found himself with time to spare, and he strolled downalong in the mornings to have a yarn in the Lodge. Everybody knew by now, but nobody said anything. James never mentioned it, not after that day in the skiff, but Steve knew, was continually conscious, of the gossip among them all. His thoughts were incessantly of Cleo, but despite his leisure time he saw her only once or twice a week. He could not bear being away from her, yet, when with her, was distraught at the distress he was causing her . . . and Mary. At times he hated himself for his weakness, and could not comprehend what either of them saw in him, why they wanted him.

Then John Ashton mentioned it . . . he would! 'I loved that girl,' he said. 'I loved that girl more, Steve, than I have ever loved any woman in my life. See how she treated me. And now you. Women are not to be trusted, Steve. I hate the bleddy lot of them.' Steve regarded him with indifference.

Sarah Stevens confronted him too. It was early one morning when he had just come ashore from shoving the *Mermaid* out on the ebbing tide. He saw her from the bottom end of Fore Street, by the Chapel. Steve reckoned, later, that she had seen him from her window and come out to intercept him in the street when there was no one else about.

He groaned to himself when he saw her. She was pretending to look in Dicky Dudgel's shop window . . . fishing tackle and stuff like that, skin-diving gear and watches that are waterproof to 200 fathoms.

She watched him approach. He suddenly felt weary and old. His beard felt thick, untidy, and his eyes listless. He prepared himself for her castigation and, with a resigned gesture, raised the peak of his cap to clear his eyebrows.There was a smile in preparation on her face but he evaded it until the last moment, averting his eyes until he could postpone the contact no longer.

She told him, with her hard-pursed lips and cold eyes, that she knew how he suffered. Her smile was terrible. There was no pity. There was bitterness, there was remorse, there was gloating revenge that he should suffer one fraction of what she had suffered, and there was utter self-control, the culmination of years of emotional self-denial. 'Good morning, Steven,' she said.

He hurried away from her after a quavering 'Mornin' Sarah' and entered Virgin Street in a daze, burying his eyes in his hands, muttering 'Oh, God, what else?'

The harbour gradually emptied of its fleet. The winds and ground swell had sunk a few moored punts, and the rest had been taken up. Uncle Joe had put Kevin Robinson's boat up in the estuary on the September tides. She was safe.

Cleo was relieved to finish her job. The pottery had done well, and she could have stayed on but she had saved enough to pay the winter bills and now she painted. Tony came to see her now and then, and she often went along to his studio for coffee and a chat. He invariably made his usual rude remarks about being disturbed but always cheered her up and gave her encouragement. She saw a melancholy beauty in the almost empty harbour with its few remaining boats, the forsaken moorings and half-buried chains in the wet and unmarked sand. She spent hours walking alone, or standing looking at the clouds over the bay, the damp streets, lamplight in drizzle, and painted also the memories of summer. So soon. Was it all, so soon, already memories?

The quickest way to forget a man, or a woman, is to get another. She tried to convince herself that she was infatuated with Steve, that she had been in love with love—the idea of love. That the brown bodies and the taste of salt under the caressing sun had induced a romantic image which she was too emotional and immature to resist. That perhaps she and Steve had been using each other as emotional catalysts in order to develop aspects of their respective personalities which had hitherto lain dormant and unexplored.

When Kevin came, he pursued her. Brought little gifts. Expensive little gifts which at first thrilled her, and then embarrassed her, and she had to be sharp with him, that he should buy no more. However, she enjoyed his company for he was a good man, kind and thoughtful, and she often went with him to dinner of an evening after work, when she was grateful not to have to cook and wash up after a tiring day. He took her to Truro to hear the Bournemouth Symphonietta and Steve saw them driving up Tregenna Hill. She felt guilty. But why? Why should she?

Before the boats were laid up, Kevin took her fishing, and they would see Steve, and wave, and Steve would wave back. He grew to hate Kevin Robinson . . . no, not Kevin, but what he represented, the rival who could provide Cleo with all that he could not. He was feeling now what Cleo had felt for Mary. Whenever Steve was not there, Kevin was. She grew used to his company and felt at a loose end when he was not there after the shop had closed. She was using him, and did not pretend otherwise. Once he came to her cottage and found her in tears. He wanted to marry her, wanted to possess her as his wife, and would have given the earth if those tears could only have been for him.

'I don't love you, Kevin,' she told him, time and again. 'It would be cruel to marry you.'

'You could learn to love me,' he said, and she knew she never could, not after a remark like that. Not the way she loved Steve.

His pursuit of her was verbal and logical. He offered her security, a home, time and money to paint whenever she wished. He was genuinely interested in art, and saw that her talent was real and unique. He offered her travel—this after she had used his long absences at sea as a reason for not marrying him. 'You can come with me,' he said. 'As captain, I can take my wife.' He saw a flicker of interest. 'America, South America, Australia, Africa, we can see the world together.'

'You have already seen it.'

'With you, I could see it through new eyes.' It was remarks like that which put her off.

'I think,' he said one day after he had asked her yet again to marry him, for the summer was coming to a close and he would soon be leaving—time was running out, 'that you should at least go away for a while,' and she realized that, marriage or not, he was concerned for her happiness. 'You will destroy yourself,' he said, 'if you are not careful.' Not once did he mention Steve in these discussions.

And then he had made arrangements for an exhibition of her paintings in a gallery in Birmingham. 'Forget London,' he said, 'until you are better known. In Birmingham your pictures will sell. I know.' She was panic-stricken, and said she couldn't do it, and demanded to know what right he had to arrange her life. Here was another reality she didn't want to face. She was furious, yet thrilled at the prospect, and while refusing to agree, pressed for more information on the gallery, the prices, how many pictures, what about the frames, and most important, how could he arrange a one-man show in that gallery when many strugglers were submitting canvas after canvas and getting them rejected. And hers unseen. 'It's who you know,' he said.

She had exploded into fury, and excitement, again. 'I want my paintings to stand on their own merit,' she told him, 'not have them exhibited simply because I know someone who has influence.'

'Don't get so excited,' he tried to calm her. 'They haven't accepted them yet.'

'Well then.'

He explained that he was to take them up with him, they wanted twenty, and if the gallery thought they were unsuitable, there was an end to it. There were other artists submitting work all the time.

'Oh,' she said, deflated, 'that's different.'

'Just get twenty finished pictures by December, for the show in January. They'll be accepted. I know.'

Then they had gone through her work, sorting them out, putting the best in a line around the walls, the others in a stack against the door. She picked the one of Maen a Mor and placed it in the stack. 'That's one of your best,' he said. 'You should include it.' But she refused.

'Sixteen,' she said when they had sorted the canvases, 'I can do four more when I finish working in the shop,' and she had thrown her arms around him in one of her spontaneous outbursts of emotion.

'I must tell Tony,' she exclaimed. 'He'll be furious.'

'No reason for him to be furious.' He held her close to him, after her arms left his neck, and prevented her from drawing away. She kissed him on the cheek, thereby forestalling a more intimate embrace. 'Why not?' she asked.

'Tony is due for fame. I have even bought two of his paintings. As an investment, but don't tell him so.'

'What do you mean?'

He refused to elaborate, however, and she had not the guile to see his reasoning. He was shrewd enough! The day Tony died his paintings would be valuable. He was one of those artists, and there are not many, whose art transcends that of their contemporaries who made a fortune in their lifetimes and were soon forgotten. The most fashionable art is that which is supposed to be ahead of fashion, exploratory. Hmm.

Kevin would be leaving at the end of the month, and he planned to take these sixteen pictures with him, and then Cleo would take the other four when they were done. She would get away for a few days in November, and Kevin would see her in January at the exhibition. It was all arranged before he left.

Cleo mentioned nothing of this to Steve. She painted her four pictures, and more, and asked him which he liked. Of course he chose the memories of summer, seeing in them the emotions they had shared, somehow interwoven with the texture of rock and lichen, and it had been her intention to surprise him with the announcement of the one-man show when, and if, it was presented. At the back of her mind was a vague plan to get him away too for a while, perhaps by deceiving Mary into believing he was at the Boat Show in January. She could not accept this deceit as being of her own devising, and continually thrust it away to the recesses of her mind, but there it was, and emerged as a plan for a complete week of Steve's time all to herself. She had never had him to herself. Never. Not one night had he slept with her, not one hour had they been together without the spectre of his other life waiting to drag him away. When they made love now, here in the cottage, there was always the terrible necessity of staying awake afterwards; they could not sink into that sublime oblivion of sleep in bliss after the ecstasy and exhaustion of minds and bodies. There was always the awful moment, which they both dreaded, when he would murmur with his eyes still closed and his lips buried in the soft down of her neck, 'I must go.' That moment when, had it been with any other, she would have felt used and discarded. Many times she said it, 'You must go,' to spare him the need of making the dreaded decision that the time had come again to part.

The worst moment was when the front door closed behind him and she lay there, listening to his footsteps receding into the distance of the still, dark night, with the sensuous smell of his body yet lingering in her bed. Then she would resolve that there could be no more of this torture, try unsuccessfully to sleep and forget him, but sob into her pillow after those minutes had passed when he would have walked through the streets, entered another house and climbed into another bed. They said, both of them, that there was no need of physical love, that they were content with each other's company, so on some evenings when Steve came to her they sat and talked, and he kissed her as he left. Then she went to her lonely bed in despair that he would be with Mary, while she lay alone, and the next time he came they would fall upon each other hungrily, that they might devour each other and be as one forever.

Steve knew that she was seeing Kevin Robinson, and was racked with an illogical jealousy which intensified with the hopelessness of their predicament. 'Take him,' he told her. 'Marry him! He will make you happy,' and she felt his arms crushing her as he groaned, 'My love. My love. I can't bear to think of him touching you.'

'But you sleep with Mary.'

'Oh, don't,' he said, 'please don't.'

Chapter Nineteen

November brought cold east winds which cut in from the bay and drove the men from the Platt. They went inside and sat around the stove. 'It's a lazy wind,' they reminded each other. 'Rather go through than around 'ee.'

There was nothing to see outside, no boats, no fish, no bodies embalmed in oil, so they sat inside and told the yarns. 'We was up to the North Sea one time . . .' 'When we was over to Ireland . . .' 'Last of all Mathy looked agin me . . .' They were good yarns, and deserved good telling . . . 'For the ear trieth words as the mouth tasteth meat.' The Book of Job, thirty-four, three.

'. . .''Where's the car park?'' he said. And High George looked agin 'im and 'e said, ''Car park?'' 'e said, with his false teeth clamped together like a vice and not movin'. You knaw the way 'e was. Talkin' from the back of his throat somewhere. ''Car park? You d' steam ahead for a fathom or two, car' y'r mizzen afor'ard, come about, starboard your helm, tack up over the hill, and you'll make a perfect landfall.'' ' It was Tommy Blue's yarn, he told it the best. 'Dead and gone,' he said, in due respect, when the chuckles died away.

Steve was down to Back Road West, renewing the sash-cords and rotten door-jambs for Joel Baragwaneth, who had gone in for engineering and moved away. That east wind comes through here like a knife.

'Cowld job there, Ste'.'

''Es. But better'n so much ol' wet.'

He had the same conversation twenty times that day, and each time it was different. Some said, 'I say, bit nippy, working there,' to which the reply was, 'Perhaps. But I prefer this to incessant rain.' Some said, 'Cain't 'ee find somewhere warmer than this?' to which he said, 'At least it's dry.'

Uncle Joe came along. 'I've had a letter,' he said.

'A letter!'

''Es.'

'Who from?'

He passed it over. 'I abm got me glasses,' he said. Uncle Joe had perfect sight.

The letter was from Kevin Robinson. Steve read it through, and then read it aloud for Joe. It thanked Joe for his help during the summer, enclosed a cheque (which Joe had cashed—perhaps he could not read or write but he was not daft,) and said he was sorry, but he would not be going to the Boat Show after all as he had business in Birmingham at that time. 'Be writing after Christmas, K. Robinson.' He handed the letter back, and Joe put it away in an inner pocket. He didn't get many letters.

'Going to the Boat Show 'en, Joe?'

'Got a mind to.'

'Who with?'

'By myself. Tim said he was going. Two or three others said they might be going. Cain't make their bleddy minds up. You goin', are 'ee?'

'No, I don't reckon to.'

Joe nodded, and strolled off, it was too cold to hang about.

'See 'ee 'gain,' he said, and came back to say, 'Do 'ee good to go to London.'

''Es, do me good.'

Steve said nothing of this to Cleo, though from time to time he saw letters in Robinson's handwriting in her cottage, and she had not yet told him of the forthcoming exhibition of her pictures. The gallery had agreed to hold the show on the strength of the sixteen which Kevin had shown them. They were enthusiastic, and had suggested prices beyond her expectations.

Cleo didn't give a damn about the neighbours now. Maggie didn't speak; she made a point of not speaking. She would come to the front door just so that she wouldn't speak. To make sure that Cleo knew that she wasn't speaking. After what she was doing to Mary. Steve always spoke to Maggie, always made sure she knew when he went to Cleo's house. Once, he even knocked on both doors at once, and that kept her in, she wouldn't answer the door when he knocked on it. For Steve didn't give a damn either, and his tongue was a match for Maggie's. Steve didn't give a damn for Maggie, or anyone else . . . except Cleo and Mary.

When the east wind died of exhaustion and the winter sun warmed the granite walls, Maggie brought a chair outside to sit and see who was who and what was what. Sit with her old tabby cat curled up contentedly asleep on her lap, while the sun shone into her diminutive hallway. The passage! She was sitting there the day Steve told Cleo.

Cleo was still a stranger in that she kept her door locked. 'Good afternoon, Maggie,' he said, forcing her to acknowledge him. She looked at him with distaste, but Steve didn't give a damn and kept gazing at her while she avoided his eyes and looked up the street, absently stroking the cat.

The door opened behind him, and he turned and entered. There was a look in his eyes which told her, before he uttered a word, and she closed the door quietly, waiting for him to speak. The sun entered the window on a slant, sneaking a bright rhombus into the room and on to the wooden floor and her bare brown feet.

'Cleo,' he said, and pleaded with her for help, in this awful thing he had to say. She was silent.

'Cleo, I can't see you any more.' She merely looked at him, although he thought he detected a slight, involuntary shake of her head.

'It's got to stop,' he said in desperation. And slumped into her chair. 'I can't leave her. I can't walk out on her. I can't do it.'

She was standing before him, with her head bent, looking at her hands, which were clasped in front of her.

'It's a good time,' he said, 'now that you have . . . Kevin.' He was going to say 'Robinson'.

She nodded, and said 'Yes', though it was barely audible.

'You won't be alone.'

'No.'

He looked away from her, pulling nervously at his beard with finger and thumb. So, here it was, she thought. He had made up his mind at last. Mary would keep him, as there had never been any doubt. There was nothing to be done, and she felt a great void enter her, as if her heart had died, but there was nothing to be done. How she loved him, and he was gone! Strange, she felt no tears, no urge to cry, she was beyond tears, and she looked at him, as for the last time.

Suddenly he came from the chair and held her like a man demented, saying, 'You're lovely. You're beautiful. My love, my love,' and she took him to the floor. 'Steve, my beautiful man. Hold me. Hold me.'

Neither of them gave a damn for anybody or anything, except each other. Steve stayed with her until very late that night, for neither of them could bear the parting, and should Mary say one word, he would tell her things she would never forget. But the decision had been made. It must end, though this wretched, exquisite melancholy of parting was in itself an emotion so tender as to be unbearable.

At last, he left her, and walked dejectedly through the deserted

T.S.E.—L

streets and down along the quay before taking a turn for home. Mary was sitting by the remains of the fire. She never went to sleep until he came home. This was one of the tactics in the battles against him, and if he was very late, as now, she came down and sat by the dying fire, so that he was met with a figure of misery to claw at his conscience and spoil the night.

He came and sat opposite her, with his hands on the arms of the chair, and looked at her so long and hard that a fear came into her heart that he was going to murder her. She could neither rise nor stay. She felt a little twitching muscle in her cheek as his look searched into her.

'Go to bed!' he told her, in a voice so weary yet so determined that she knew he had beaten her. He had beaten her by losing some of his love for her, and she was numbed by this revelation. She sensed that the affair was over, and that she was not to lose him, but from this time he would be his own man, and she had no hold on him. No real hold at all.

She went to their bed in fear that she had killed him, while he sat and stared long into the ashes.

It was all to himself. There was no one to talk to. Even Shimshai had gone away again, and James would allow no mention of it, either by way of explanation or excuse. Not that crowd. Hartisis. Damn strangers.

Steve tried to push her from his mind, to pretend that she had never existed. He went to Martha's and Freddie's with Mary, and listened to their accounts of holidays abroad for the umpteenth time. — Mundane, emotionless experiences, of continental plumbing, or some new wine or other. He found himself working at weekends, in order that time should not allow him the opportunity to remember. He did not see her for three weeks, even though he went several times to the pub, and walked purposely along the streets between her house and the shops, unable to resist the possibility that they might meet in the road. He found himself becoming utterly disconsolate, and finally he could resist no longer. Life without her was impossible, and on the Friday he went to her cottage and knocked again on her door.

'She's gone!' Maggie said.

Steve felt as if the silly old cow had punched him in the guts.

'She's gone off. Gone off in a taxi,' and her face said, quite plainly, She's gone off and you didn't know.

'What taxi?' he said, as if he didn't believe her and, being Maggie, she told him. He went to see Sam, asked him where she had gone. 'Birmingham,' Sam said. 'Took the train to Birmingham.'

'Thanks, Sam.'

'That's all right, boy. How 'ee keepin', these days?'

'Oh, all right. And you? How's Iris?'

'Comin' on. You know she lost a cheeld.'

'I heard so.'

Cleo had told no one. Left no message. He called to see Tony, who said only, as if Steve was unaware of it, 'She's a sensitive girl,' in the softest brogue. 'Oh, she is that.'

He saw Tim, and asked if her cottage was for sale, and Tim was no more able to cope with this tragedy than he was with the tragedies in his own life, and he patted Steve on the back, saying, 'She'll be back, boy. She'll be back,' visibly distressed to see what love could do to a man like Steve.

After a few days she returned. Everything was arranged for the show. They considered her last four paintings to be her best and were delighted with them. Cleo sensed, for the first time, the underlying commercialism of art, but simply could not be bothered about any of it. Kevin had made all the arrangements and she was happy to let him take charge of the whole business. He was gratified at her dependence on him and took her submissive attitude to be a sign of acceptance of his role in her future life.

One evening when they were dining in a restaurant where the soft lights and the music of Mantovani were supposed to be conducive to that kind of thing, he asked for the first time about Steve.

'It's over,' she said. And to her relief he showed no sign of pleasure or self-satisfaction, but reached across to her hand and said only, 'Did it hurt?'

'Uh-huh,' with a little nod and smile which persuaded him that he could do no other but love and protect this beautiful, vulnerable girl for the rest of her life.

'In January?' he said, 'Shall I come down and fetch you?'

'Let me think about it?'

She allowed him to kiss her, but would not stay with him, so he fetched her every day from her hotel and on the last morning took her to the station and put her on the train. He arranged everything and she was glad to lean on him. He was a good man.

At her cottage door, as she placed the key in the lock, she forgot herself and said, 'Hello, Maggie.'

And Maggie said, 'How do, my dear,' for something forlorn in the voice had aroused the tenderness long dormant in Maggie's nature. A little later she knocked on Cleo's door. 'Your milk,' she said. 'I kep'n in the fridge,' and returned to her own lonely cottage muttering, 'Poor cheeld. Poor cheeld.'

This was as near as Cleo ever became to being one of them, and this after she had decided to move away, to sell High George's cottage and go. What else? How else?

She went to see Tim. 'No problem,' he said, 'no problem.' To sell her lovely little home where she had known such happiness, such ecstasy and agony. 'No problem.'

She was remarkably calm now that the decision had been made, and drew relentlessly on the emotions of the past months to further her art. That at last should not be squandered. She collected all the fragments of prose and poetry she had written about them and their emotions, read through and through them, viciously forcing herself to endure the agonies again, and painted until she fell into deep slumbers of fatigue.

She went out only for her shopping, or to see Tony, who had the tact never to mention Steve, though it was obvious that he was continually in her thoughts. She was sitting one morning reading through these papers when that familiar knock came upon the door. She was paralysed with fear and longing, and when she finally opened the door he was turning away, to go on up the street to the Lodge. He waited until she said, 'Come in,' and he stood in her front room, in his jeans and blue guarnsey, with his hands in the pockets of his reefer jacket, and the cap pulled low over his eyes.

'I just . . . called in . . . to see how you are.'

'I'm fine . . . thanks.'

'What are you doing?' His eyes fell upon the papers.

'Oh, just looking through some old papers. Nothing important.'

Silence. Some children chanting in the street . . . *Olika polika re pasolika. Olika Polika. Nell!*

'How's Mary?'

'Fine.' His fists were clasping, unclasping, in his pockets.

'Oh, Steve!' she gasped at last. 'Why did you come? Why? *Why?*'

'I thought I should go mad,' he said.

The void in her dead heart was suddenly filled again, and there was a great surge of love towards this man. 'It's over, Steve. Finished.'

'You went away! I didn't know what had happened to you. I was afraid you might . . .' He passed his hand over his eyes.

She went to the rug by the hearth and gathered up the papers. 'Here,' she said, 'read these,' holding the sheaf towards him. 'I was going to burn them.' It was the only way. 'It's over, Steve!'

Useless, it was useless! They fell against one another and fought hopelessly against the bitter, silent tears, clinging to each other as if to life itself. Cleo felt that blend of despair and passion which obliterates the past, the future, conscience, everything! Her tears dried and she became filled with the warm glow of lust, and she began to fight him savagely, for all he had done to her, for all the pain they had brought upon each other. They fought viciously, like writhing cats, called each other all the bitches and bastards they could think of, until they lay naked and bathed in sweat before the fire, their lips and mouths drawing ravenously upon the very last dregs of emotion, lust and love.

For a while, they fell asleep, like children, and awoke, still dreamy and dazed, when the embers died. They were cold, and helped each other to dress, searching about the shattered room for their respective clothes. Giggling a little now and then, and stopping to kiss. 'You bastard,' she said. 'You bitch.'

She put his hat awry upon his head and they kissed again before Steve turned from her, his eyes still closed, the moisture of her lips and her hands in his begging him to stay, though she whispered 'Please go now.' So he unlatched the door and went out without looking back. He knew she was crying. Outside, he leaned for a moment against the wall before turning down the street towards the harbour. He didn't really know where he was going. He ached in all his fibres, for the emotion of parting had exhausted him, left him weak, tired, and empty. The wind had backed to the south'ard, and a fine drizzle glossed the granite cobbles, condensed on windows, and dripped from the sills to the gutters where already a trickle gathered speed and dripped into the iron drains. He remembered the papers in his pocket, and paused, but continued down the street, turning up his collar as much to avoid the passers-by as to keep off the wet. To return now was more than he could stand, and Cleo might assume that he had come back to her, and there could be no more of that, for there was hurt enough in this.

He turned down through Quay Street and along the Wharf. He passed the Lodge, where they were all inside, out of the rain, and he saw the row of faces peering through the small panes of the window, but he made no acknowledgement of the nods, turning his head as though into the wind and rain. James was standing there in the lee, sheltering from the rain, and called to Steve as he passed.

'Ste'!'

'James! A'right?'

'No! Now no. He edn alright.'

Oh God, Steve thought. Not now. He stepped in the shelter of the Lodge and shook the raindrops from his collar. 'What's up?'

'Wha's up? Wha's up? Where've 'ee be'n? Tha's wha's *up*.'

Back there, Cleo was crying. And he would never see her again. This time she would go and never come back. For his sake.

'Well?' he said irritably. 'What is up?'

'The glass. Tha's wha's up. But he edn up at all. He'd down! And still falling. The wind backin' here to the south'ard and we sh'll have a blow here dreckly and a boat down Lelant that we habn't looked at for a month. That's what's *up*.'

'She's all right, James. It's only an eighteen-foot tide, and the forecast is moderate south-west.' He barely heard what James was telling him. 'It's only a small front passing through,' he said wearily.

'Front! Hmm. Front! And what about the ground sea?' He walked to the end of the wall and back. 'You ot to be down there, Steve, You understand?'

''Es, well now, I'm not down there. I'm here. And now I'm going. See 'ee again.'

He turned up his coat and stepped off the Platt. To hell with the moorings. To hell with the boat, the harbour . . . to hell with everything! He quickened his stride, ignored the people who passed the time of day, and made off, with his head down, through the streets and up the path to the cliff. Forgetting everything but Cleo. Remembering everything of Cleo. His mind was full of her and it was over.

He remembered the things she had said, and fragments of her writing. Disjointed recollections flooded his brain like a swirling tide-race, with lines of her poems flying like spume in an autumn gale.

He walked on and on. A gust of wind took his cap off and he let it go, not faltering in his stride as it fell in the mud behind him. He walked on, with the rain on his back, drenching his hair, sticking it down on his head, and he knew that the balding patch would be showing through, and the grey streaks leading the trickles down over his temples and under the collar of his coat. But he knew now that there could be no fighting against his forty years; soon they would be sixty. Then an obscure, smelly death at the end of it. But he didn't care. Perhaps his virility would soon decline and his balls shrivel up, thus freeing him of his desires, and the accompanying desolation and anguish. Perhaps only then would he be granted some semblance of contentment.

He wiped the dripping raindrops from his face, pushed back the strands of hair from over his forehead, and smelled, even through the wet, the perfume of her sweet body lingering on his hand. She would haunt him thus until the end of his life . . . until the end of his life her eyes would smile in the darkness of his restless sleep, and the murmur of the sea would breathe her whispered words over, and again, whenever he sat quietly by the shore or heard the surf at midnight. He would see her hair in the cornfields, and its sparkle in the lazy tides of June. The soft mists of autumn would brush his cheeks with the dews of her lovely body.

The sea below the cliffs, sheltered from the south-west wind, was flat and grey, and soon merged into the indefinite horizon of the rain-soaked distance. Herring-gulls, alarmed at his approach, left their ledges to hang over his head, calling with shrill cries which drew others to them, till the sky above the cliff was full of their wings and yelping calls.

The path narrowed, became no more than a track, though a highway for foxes and shuffling badgers about their noctural meanderings, and the dripping stems of gorse prickled his shins and shed their load of water onto his trousers as he passed. His shoes squelched in hidden puddles under the bracken fronds. Through the shoulders of his jacket wetness sought the woollen fibres of his guarnsey, and spread across his back.

There was some shelter under the lee of Maen a Mor, the great pinnacle of lichen-covered granite. The papers in his pocket were the only tangible part of her to be discarded, and he would do it here, there could be no keepsakes. No mementoes. He would do it here where their two beings had reached uncontrollably for each other in that dream's beginning which must now end.

'Who are we mortals,' she had mused that day on the cliff, 'who feel so deeply happy for a moment in life? Surely this is a day that will be embedded deep in me. For my life is alive, and I shall sing like the birds above . . . and be sad, softly, like these waves lapping gently below.' All those phrases with which she had revealed herself, and embarrassed him. And her scribblings, as she called them: 'I have been flooded with tenderness towards a man who to me is worthy of more . . .' He recalled her struggle for expression. 'He is a mountain and does not know,' she had said. More of the poetry, like the lines and metres lost, came surging through his brain, the thoughts implied, and her feelings for him. Her impressions of his character which she showed him unashamedly. 'He erupts like a wave bursting between rocks and receding to the depths of the sea.' He had never heard his 'moods' described like that before.

He remembered the last line of her very first poem to him: 'And a glorious peace has settled'. God! Didn't she know the torment that peace was costing him? 'Holy Jesus!' he said aloud. There's no fool like an old fool. And no wounds hurt like old scars opened. Was all this no more than a reliving of a past? A past which itself had been no more than mere nebulous dreams of a future which had never materialized? Was life no more than dreams and memories, turning upon themselves in circles of uncertainty?

Whatever it was, here was one part that was finished. He had ended it. There was only this one last act to perform, yet even now he felt again that surge of emotion in his heart and guts, the welling longing for her presence and the touch of her small, sensitive hands.

He took the papers from his pocket and tore at the envelopes, savagely ripping them open, and removed the sheets of white paper, spreading them in his hands, where the rain fell on the bold black script and ran in streaks to the corners. He read them all, once through, then tore them into shreds, released them from his palm, and watched them snatched away in the wind; some sticking momentarily to the wet heather, others swirling far over the sea, turning and spiralling until lost to sight in the grey distance. Everything was here. All her emotions towards him poured out in her articulate, beautiful prose, or her strange, disturbing poetry. Why, he asked himself, had he never conquered the reluctance to express himself like this? Why had he been so introspective and inhibited? God knows, I feel, he thought.

At last there remained only 'Landscape with Nudes'—'Notes for a Landscape with Nudes', she had called it. And he remembered the hot flush of embarrassment he had felt as she read it to him, that day, beside this very sea.

And she had used this and her memories as what she called 'the soul of a painting'. Now he read it through again, read it a dozen times, while the drizzle fell on it, until the ink ran in black smudges from every line, and the words were obliterated into indecipherable streaks. He saw the image behind every word and comma, saw them both in it, and the sensuous hours they had spent together out there. Lying in the sun.

He knew every word, comma, full stop and turn of her hand by heart, there was no need to keep it. But he could not bring himself to tear it up. Eventually he kicked a stone from the turf, wrapped the paper round it, and, standing on the edge of the cliff, threw it as far into the distance as his strength could throw.

Through a long arc the white missile descended. He thought it would never reach the sea. A passing gull stalled, swooped once towards it, turned away. Take my memories to the black depths, you stone, take all this to which I have no right. It is over and I can forget her. As her words sink, so shall my yearnings. Down into the dark caverns of memory. The falling stone, through some optical illusion, appeared to be drawn back to the shore by some gravity of the cliffs, and he thought for a moment that it would strike the rocks below, but as it fell further he watched to see the splash as the last obliterating turbulence in this happiest, saddest, chapter of his life.

Then the paper, caught by some mischief in the wind, unfurled!

The stone splashed alone, and her lines settled flat on the surface, while her voice came to him in the murmur of the surf, her kisses in the rain. He leaned back against the rock, rain dripping off him, running off his hands. 'Go away,' he whispered. Then, staggering to the edge of the cliff once more, he raised his arms and face to the rain and the distant misty horizon. 'It's finished,' he shouted. 'Damn you! Go away. Go away.'

Far below, the white square drifted slowly to the ocean. The soft sighs of the waves rose past the dead heads of the clustered sea-pinks and up the sheer granite precipice . . . I love you, I love you, I love you.

Chapter Twenty

Come February, things are more or less back to normal. People are relaxed, refreshed after a long rest and, for the fortunate ones, a holiday abroad. Herring-gulls strut in pairs over the wet sand of the empty harbour, wailing in anticipation of the spring. The dogs, even those which were kept shut in for the summer, are out in packs again. They race around the harbour and the streets, uninhibited in their quest for bones and bitches in heat, though finding few of either. There are not many cats—not now.

Here and there one sees the desultory preparations for a new season of activity. Shutters taken down, a window repaired, empty cafés given an airing, but the frenetic preliminaries of March and April are not yet under way. It is still a bit early to start scraping and sanding and overhauling engines, but a good time to see to the moorings and the gear, making up new sets of feathers, things like that. The strangers in the shops, the ones who had thought to make a fortune after seeing the crowds spending money when they first came here on holiday, stand in the doorways of their premises and gaze forlornly at the empty streets, fighting the panic induced by approaching postmen with letters from their banks. Perhaps they could sell at a profit. Some properties change hands every year, it seems. High George's house that was is up for sale again. She has gone away—that there artis' woman. The one Steve was knockin' around with.

Some days in February are so warm that it is not necessary to light the fire in the stove, and the chaps can stand on the Platt, or walk up and down, yarnin'. They told the yarn about Tommy Blue for the first time, that year. About Tommy Blue and the say capn. 'He's a fine *lookin'* man,' Tommy said. Tommy Blue, dead and gone . . . 'For we are but of yesterday . . .'

The best one for telling the yarn about Tommy Blue and the say capn was Uncle Joe, because he could do Tommy's voice and look over make-out glasses with squinted eyes. Though Joe had perfect sight. 'He's a fine *lookin'* man,' with a quaver in his voice. Some of the old ones still told yarns about the likes of Man Friday and Spring-heeled Jack, but not many could remember them . . .' and our days on earth are but a shadow . . .'

Martha and Freddie had been to Crete. Martha was enthusiastic as ever about their holiday abroad, omitting to mention Freddie's preference for that beach where the girls were topless and almost bottomless too, and the fact that he had become so desperate that she could wheedle anything out of him for a couple of times doing that. Mary got on to Steve about a holiday abroad, but cautiously, reluctant to broach the subject in case he lost his temper, or worse.

'Wouldn't mind going to Spain,' he said, and she had written off, full of excitement, to so many travel agents that the house became littered with brochures and leaflets. The last thing he wanted was to go off with Martha and Freddie, but, for Mary's sake, agreed to it. They would work extra hard this summer and she would have the holiday of her life. She deserved it. Eight months to go and she could talk of nothing else. 'What shall we eat?' she said, and 'What shall us wear?' He smiled at her and pulled her to his knees, on the sofa, in the front room, surrounded by pictures of blue seas, golden beaches, palm trees and beautiful young brown bodies. 'Wear what you like,' he said, 'Eat what you like.' Nuzzling into her soft breast and driving the other image from his mind. 'Whatever you like.'

It was in February too that Uncle Joe had another letter. He brought it into the pub for Steve to read as he had forgotten his glasses. Kevin Robinson's boat had been sold. Someone was coming down to fetch her. '. . . and I have arranged with Tim for the sale of the house. I don't suppose I shall be down again. Thanks for everything. Kevin R.' Joe had cashed the cheque.

Steve didn't want to know anything about it. He only wished that they were happy and that he would never see her, ever again. He shoved the letter back to Joe, asking himself why a man as intelligent as Joe had never learned to read or write. 'How the Hell didn' you learn to read and write? You bleddy tuss!' But Joe only grinned at him. Until Steve grinned back. 'Tuss,' he said, glancing to see who had come through the door. 'Tell me about the Boat Show.'

In the end, a brear few went. And there was high jinks, by all accounts. Uncle Joe would only say, 'What a crant. What a bleddy crant,' shaking his head in disbelief. Grown men, here. You can't take them nowhere. He had something more to say . . .

'I saw she, up London.'

Steve thought he was going to faint. The colour drained from his face as he closed his eyes in an effort of self-control. 'I thought she was up Birmingham,' he said weakly, clearing his throat, 'with Robinson.'

'She's up London,' Joe said, lowering his voice to a thrown whisper after a quick glance around the bar, 'with Shimshai.'

'Shimshai?' Steve's features registered a brief smile of incredulity, like one told an obvious lie, as if he thought Joe was teasing him, but Joe was quite serious, and was regarding him expectantly. Steve's involuntary smile became a quick laugh of astonishment. 'Are you sure?'

'She seemed happy enough,' Joe said, and watched Steve intently for his reaction. They stared blankly at each other. Joe sucked his upper lip to stop himself from grinning and Steve gradually joined him in silent, shaking, tear-streaming laughter.

'Shimshai?'

Oh Shimshai, you pitiless scribe . . . For thou writest bitter things against me, and makest me to possess the iniquities of my youth . . .

You bleddy tuss, Shimshai.